THE LAST EMPEROR OF ROME

ROBERT STEVEN HABERMANN

The Last Emperor of Rome
All Rights Reserved.
Copyright © 2017 Robert Steven Habermann
v4.0

Cover Photo © 2017 Wikimedia. All rights reserved - used with permission.

Outskirts Press, Inc.
http://www.outskirtspress.com

ISBN: 978-1-4787-9001-3

Outskirts Press and the "OP" logo are trademarks belonging to Outskirts Press, Inc.

PRINTED IN THE UNITED STATES OF AMERICA

AUTHOR'S NOTE

The Last Emperor of Rome, a tale of love, betrayal, and turmoil, takes place during the final thirty-five years of the Western Roman Empire. It was a time of palace intrigue, assassinations, barbarian invasions, declining institutions, struggling political alliances, and a general breakdown of the Imperial system of government which had ruled much of Europe and North Africa for the previous five hundred years.

Before his entry onto the national stage, little is known about Emperor Julius Valerius Majorian, the major historical character in this novel. Therefore, I've invented much of the storyline, including his early life, his family, and his career in the Imperial Legions.

In those instances where the story is fanciful, I've tried to keep it well with the broad context of the history of the late Western Roman Empire. As Bernard Cornwell wrote in *The Historical Note* following the text of his novel entitled *The Last Kingdom*:

> I have feathered lavishly, as historical novelists must, yet as much of
> the novel as possible is based on real events.

I concur.

I wish to thank Betsy Ashton, Vernon Danielsen, Esther Johnson, John Koelsch, David Kunca, Karen Peters, Byron Petty, and all of the members of *The Valley Writers Chapter* of *The Virginia Writers Club* for their advice and counsel in bringing this book to completion. You're the best!

*The coin displayed on the front cover and known as the Solidus Majorina Arles, Comitatesian mint, was minted in approximately 460 AD during the reign of Emperor Majorian. The coin depicts the Emperor as being helmeted, diademed, draped, and cuirassed bust right, holding a spear in his right hand and a shield that is bearing a Christogram on his left shoulder.

TO ALL OF OUR HEROES;
THOSE WE REMEMBER
AND THOSE WHOM
WE'VE FORGOTTEN.

A LIST OF THE PRINCIPAL PLACE NAMES MENTIONED IN THE TEXT OF THE NOVEL WITH THEIR MODERN EQUIVALENTS.

Arausio – Orange, France.

Aurelianum – Orleans, France.

Belgica – a Roman province located in Belgium, Northern France, Luxembourg, and part of the Netherlands below the Rhine.

Britannia – England and Wales.

Caledonia – Scotland.

Carthage – near Tunis, Tunisia.

Carthago Nova – Cartagena, Spain.

Civitas Turonum – Tours, France.

Constantinople – Istanbul, Turkey.

Dacia – Romania.

Dalmatia – a narrow coastal region located on the eastern side of the Adriatic Sea north of Greece.

Dertona – Tortona, Italy.

Gaul – a Roman province encompassing much of France and Switzerland.

Germania – a Roman province which borders to the west on the Rhine River, to the south on the Danube River, to the north on the Baltic Sea, and to the east of the Vistula River.

Hispania – Spain and Portugal.

Lugdunum – Lyons, France.

Massalia – Marseille, France.

Mauretania – Morocco and Algeria.

Mediolanum – Milan, Italy.

Nemausus – Nimes, France.

The Catalaunian Plains – the actual location of the battle on the Catalaunian Plains remains unclear, but the current consensus is the mêlée took place in the vicinity of Châlons-en-Champagne (formerly called Châlons-sur-Marne).

Thrace – Greece

Treverorum – Trier, Germany.

LIST OF THE PRINCIPAL CHARACTERS

Note: The characters marked with an astcrisk are not historical figures. To avoid confusion, I've utilized the Gregorian calendar to number the years rather than the Roman system. The current method was devised in 525 AD and it replaced the dating calculation system developed by the Romans during the reign of Emperor Diocletian in 296 AD.

Attila – (August 15, 398 to May 29, 453) often referred to as Attila the Hun was the ruler of the Huns from 434 until his death in 453.

Childeric – (c. 440 to 482) was the King of the Salian Franks from 457 to 481.

Claudius Aegidius – (c. 424 to May, 464) was a Roman general from the Kingdom of Soissons in Northern Gaul.

Claudius Gaius Donnimus – Emperor Majorian's father.

*Cluny – a young male slave from Ethiopia.

*Elmina – a young female slave from Caledonia (present day Scotland).

Eparchius Avitus – (c. 395 to 456) was the Western Roman Emperor from July 9, 455 to October 17, 456.

Flavius Aëtius – (August 15, 398 to September 21, 454) was Master of Soldiers from 433 to 454 and perhaps, the most influential man in the Western Roman Empire during this timeframe.

Flavius Ricimer – (c. 418 to August 18, 472) was a Romanized Germanic general.

Flavius Stilicho – (c. 359 to August 22, 408) was the Master of Soldiers in the Roman army. Half Vandal, he was married to the niece of the Emperor Theodosius I.

Gaiseric – (c. 389 to January 25, 477) was the King of the Vandals from 428 until 477.

*Gaius Gallus Gallipolis – a Roman Senator.

Gunderic – (c. 413 to 473) was the King of the Burgundians from 437 to 473.

*Hector Ulysses Asthenias – Emperor Majorian's principal secretary.

Julius Valerius Majorian – (c. 420 to August 7, 461) was the Western Roman

Emperor from 457 to 461.

Leo – (c. 400 to November 10, 461) also known as Saint Leo the Great, was the Pope from 440 until 461.

Lucius Quentin Marcellinus – (c. 429 to 468) was a Roman general who commanded the region of Dalmatia.

*Maltychosis – a slave priest in the city of Rome.

Marcian – full name, Flavius Marcianus (c. May 392 to January 27, 457) was the Eastern Roman Emperor from 450 until 457.

*Octavia Isabella – the first wife of Emperor Majorian.

Petronius Maximus – (c. 396 to 31 May 455) was the Western Roman Emperor for two and a half months in 455.

*Placida – the sister of Emperor Majorian.

*Rudolpho Gustavus – a young officer from Belgica on Count Ricimer's general staff.

Theodoric I   (c. 400 to 451) was the King of the Visigoths from 418 until 451.

Theodoric II – (c. 429 to 466) was the son of Theodoric I and the King of the Visigoths from 453 until 466.

*Ursula – the second wife of Emperor Majorian.

Valentinian III – full name, Flavius Placidius Valentinianus (July 2, 419 to March 16, 455) was the Western Roman Emperor from 425 until 455.

PROLOGUE

From the tower of the church just beyond the prison walls, I hear the bells ringing, calling the faithful to Evening Prayer. The sun is setting on what will probably be my last full day on this earth. Yesterday I was the Emperor, and tonight I'm a condemned prisoner.

Having been duly appointed by the Senate and People of Rome and there-after crowned on December 28 in Anno Domino 456, I went by the titles, *Lord Emperor Julius Valerius Majorian Augustus, Pontifex Maximus, Dominus Noster, Princeps Senatus,* and *Nobilissimus Caesar,* among others. Stripped of the impe-rial purple robe and the diadem, I am chained in this prison cell by my former friend and trusted advisor, Count Flavius Ricimer. Unless things change, to-morrow I'll be executed.

At one time, Ricimer and I were brothers-in-arms when we joined in a quest to restore the borders of the once great Roman Empire. The fact we almost succeeded brings me some satisfaction. Our campaign was probably the last, and perhaps the best, hope to revitalize the Western Empire. I fear Rome will never have this chance again.

In almost total darkness, I hear the cries of agony from men who will likely share my fate. I cringe at their pleas for mercy. I do not join their voices, how-ever, because I know my condemnation is irrevocable. There will be neither mercy nor a stay of execution for me. Ricimer has crossed the Rubicon.

My senses soar as panic engulfs me, and I wonder how I can begin to face the challenges of tomorrow. Will I beg for my life like so many others before me? Do I still retain the moral courage of my convictions to face death on my terms? Honestly, I don't know.

And I wonder whether historians will be kind to me. Will they view my reign as a shining hour, or will it be as forgotten as the men who are held in this prison? I pray someone will tell my story. I want those who come after me to understand the hopes we held for Rome and to see how close we came to restoring the glory of the Empire.

With a profound sense of anger, I contemplate the treachery of Ricimer, a person whom I'd once regarded as no other man and who eventually betrayed me. In sadness, I also recall a once grand city and a once great empire – both of which are called Rome. These former strongholds of culture and power, once ruled by Augustus and Constantine, were graced by the footsteps of Cicero and Paul. In the throes of a spiraling death dance, they lie in ruins.

As recently as sixty years ago, the Empire stretched unbroken from the green mountains of Caledonia to the brown deserts of Babylon, and from the bountiful vineyards of Treverorum to the ancient pyramids at Giza. Emperor Theodosius ordered upon his death, however, that the Empire would be divided between his two sons into Eastern and Western halves. Shortly after Theodosius' passing in 395 AD, barbarian armies assaulted the Western Empire, and the city of Rome has twice been sacked.

In silence, I watch as three guards drag a prisoner from his cell to an uncertain fate. Just twelve hours ago, I was their commander. I wonder how they view me now. Do they feel pity, joy, or nothing at all? They nod, point, and whisper; I'm certain they know who I am or, rather, who I was.

A meal of bread and stew sits undisturbed at my feet. I have no need for nourishment; it will not serve me well. The captain of the guard told me a priest would visit me later this evening. It will be an unnecessary trip, however, as I've made my peace with God. I need neither absolution nor benediction.

Feeling abandoned, I shiver as I sit on the cold floor. My ankle chafes from the weight of the heavy iron chain. With my execution scheduled for the early morning, I know I'll not sleep much tonight. Rather, I'll reflect on those days from long ago, before my dreams of glory were ever dreamt, before the curse of betrayal was ever cast, and before Octavia ever made her fateful decision. My eyes weigh heavily, but my mind is sharp. I can almost envision the place where my long journey began; a place not two-hundred miles from where I languish tonight.

CHAPTER I

Nemausus, the Capitol of Narbonne Province, Gaul – late May 442 AD

With my eyes tightly shut and my senses alive, I recall the joy and anticipation of my first days after graduating as a commissioned officer from the Military Academy of Rome. I'd finally made it through a grueling four-year curriculum of academics, leadership training, and tactics. 'In the name of Rome,' I was declared ready to continue the long, proud tradition of her military graduates; to serve my Emperor and my Empire honorably; just as my father and grandfather had done so many years before me.

Those first days following my commissioning were heady days for me. A thousand thoughts filled my head. Where in this great empire would I be assigned? What battles would I fight? How would I die? I knew in my heart that I'd find glory, and I knew I would uphold the sacred trust which was placed upon me. My dreams were only eclipsed by my optimism; my boundaries were limited only by my imagination; and my goals were constrained only by my desire to accomplish them.

I remember closing the door to my room in the barracks for the final time as I walked down the hall to say my farewells to those other young officers who lived with me, rode with me, and marched with me during the previous four years. All of them were brothers; all of them were potential adversaries; and most of them, I'd never see again.

After piling my belongings into a trunk and dressing in my last crisp field uniform, I left the Eternal City – the place where I transitioned from a boy to a man – and set out for the port of Ostia where I boarded a ship for home. Following a two-day sail from Ostia to the city of Massalia in Southern Gaul, I rode a public coach on Via Domitia to the city of Nemausus and walked a few short blocks to my father's residence on Tiberius Street.

My father, Claudius Gaius Donnimus, was serving as the Minister of Finance for Master General Flavius Aëtius, who commanded the Legions in the Western Empire. I'd enjoy two weeks of vacation at my parents' home before reporting for my first assignment on General Aëtius' staff at Camp Aurelius in Northern Gaul.

Stopping in front of my parents' home, I noticed above the high wooden double door of my parents' home, the familiar mosaic of a menacing dog and the inscription "*Cave Canem.*" Smiling, I remembered our long-deceased dog, Brutus, who was well-known in our family as a lover and not a fighter. He might have licked a burglar to death if he displayed any notice to the burglar at all.

Grasping the big ring in the mouth of an ancient iron wolf's head, I banged twice on the sturdy oak door. Shortly, Josiah, my father's principal household slave, opened the door, and led me through the atrium and into my father's private sanctuary, the tablinium. I was happy to be home again.

My father immediately rose from his chair and walked over to me. "Jul, how wonderful to see you. My, how you've grown. You're a man now; you must be nearly six-feet tall."

"Yes, Father, and I've probably gained well over thirty pounds since I was home last."

We embraced for a long time. He looked up at my face and tugged gently at my whiskers. "I'm not sure I like your beard," he said, "but I guess many young men these days grow them."

I smiled and nodded. "Yes, it's the fashion in Rome." Subconsciously, I stroked the beard. "I think it looks good on me; a bit like Marcus Aurelius, don't you think?"

We both laughed. "How was your trip from Rome?"

I hadn't seen him in almost three years. He looked older and shorter. His hair, while still full, was almost entirely grey, and he was slightly bent over. His blue eyes were splashed with red; perhaps from too much reading in the inadequate lighting of his office. His grip, however, was still strong, and his smile was genuine.

"It was a long trip, but I enjoyed the crossing from Ostia," I said. "The sea was relatively calm, and you know how I love the salt air."

"You've always loved the sea."

"But the ride up from Massalia was bumpy and hot. I see the Governor hasn't repaired the Via Domitia. It seems much worse than when I first left for Rome."

My father smiled and said, "But he still claims he'll fix it someday. He's quite the politician, you know."

"Yes, I've heard. So, how are you doing, Father?"

Resplendent in his white tunic with purple border and a silver sash fitted snugly around his waist (indicative of his rank in the senatorial class), he smiled and replied, "General Aëtius keeps me active. It seems as though he's always on another campaign somewhere in the Empire. But soldiers want to be paid, and supplies need to be acquired. So, I stay busy."

I sat down on a chair in front of his desk. "Is he doing well?"

"Aëtius? Yes, in fact, I spoke to him last month. He's looking forward for you to join his staff. But I hope you can spend some time with your mother and me." With a sparkle in his eyes, he said, "And Octavia has been asking about you."

I smiled at the mention of her name. How I longed to see her again.

My father, sensing my eagerness to see Octavia, patted me on the shoulder. "You'll see her soon, son. But first, tell me about Rome. Has it recovered from Alaric and the Goths?"

I recalled that Alaric and his army sacked Rome in 410 AD; the first time the city had fallen to an enemy in over eight hundred years. "While much of the damage has been repaired, weeds are still growing in the Imperial Forum. Father, a lot of maintenance still needs to be done."

"I see."

"The Flavian Amphitheatre, while still holding games, is almost entirely covered in moss. Yes, Rome is still quite a mess in many places."

He frowned, "That's a shame. I guess the city isn't immortal after all. As a young man, I remember cheering *'Ave, Roma immortalis'* during the triumphant parades and while attending the chariot races in the Circus Maximus. I guess Rome's no more mortal than the men who built her. But, Jul, I still remember Rome as such a splendid place."

"Yes, I'm certain it was. I guess you know the Emperor recently rebuilt the Basilica Julia – but not to its former glory. There's still so much remaining to do, though."

"Well, these things take time, I guess; and with money being so tight these days, it may take a lot longer."

He slowly shook his head and sighed, "I heard that Rome's population is now less than half the size of its former self."

I touched his arm, "Yes, and it's getting smaller every year, Father. Had it not been for the Pope remaining in Rome, and I hear whispers he'll join the Emperor in either Constantinople or Ravenna, the city would all but disappear. The Academy is in good shape, though, and the Senate still operates with impunity."

Suddenly, I noticed a twinkle in his eyes. "So, they're still causing a lot of trouble, huh?"

"They're politicians, aren't they?"

"Yes, they are. Some things never change."

Looking around my father's sanctuary, I saw the memorabilia of a lifetime that he'd collected and proudly displayed in his office. A large bust of Augustus sat prominently on a corner of his desk, and the family crest adorned one wall. A warrior's spear from the Gallic War leaned against a wall in the corner.

Sitting prominently on his counter, I noticed several delicate mythological figures made from silver which had been mined near Corinth, a miniature Egyptian obelisk reputedly taken from a pharaoh's tomb near ancient Thebes, and a darkened elephant tusk, rumored to have come from Hannibal's invading army. I know he cherished these memories in his private retreat from the world outside.

A few moments later, Josiah entered the tablinium and announced refreshments were being served in the atrium. Smiling, my father winked at me and said, "Well, we better not keep the women waiting. Your mother is anxious to see you, Son."

He arose from his chair, and Josiah took the toga off of its stand, draped it over my father's left shoulder, wrapped it around his body, and hung it back over his left arm. Nodding to Josiah, we went to meet my mother and my sister, Placida, waiting for us in the atrium.

Enclosed by high-ceilinged porticos and adorned with several tropical plants and statues of ancient gods and goddesses, the atrium contained a large opening in the tiled ceiling to let in light and air. A bronze figure representing the god, Mercury, graced the center of the water fountain, and four couches surrounded it. As a child, I'd spent many days in this room, and when we entered it that afternoon, memories of a happy childhood filled my mind.

Mother and Placida rose and embraced me. Tears of joy tumbled down my mother's face as she squeezed her youngest son close to her heart. She'd been sick lately, and at one time her physician believed she wouldn't live to see this day. In the late afternoon light, she appeared pale and fragile. Holding on to her, I thanked the Lord Jesus that He hasn't yet taken her to heaven.

Over the years, I've been told I resemble my mother more than my father. I share her straight nose, full lips, pale complexion, and long and slender arms and legs. From my father, I received his tall stature, his blondish-brown straight hair, and his broad chest and neck, the legacy of our Dalmatian ancestors. I also inherited his love of literature and his commitment to public service.

I embraced my sister. Placida, then eighteen years old and the youngest child of Claudius Gaius and Faustina Amelia had grown into a lovely young woman. With long reddish-brown hair and soft green eyes, I still remember she wore a pale yellow stolae that day. A golden sash fitted the garment at her waist, and a string of Corsican pearls hung loosely around her neck. Only twenty months apart in age, we grew up as each other's best friend and confidant. Together, we learned about life in our little corner of the Roman world.

"Jul, how I've missed you." She kissed my cheek and held close to me for a long time. "So, what's it like as a commissioned officer; a Tribune, no less? I'm sure half of the eligible ladies in Rome were breaking down the Academy's doors to have a good look at you."

"I don't know about the ladies, but I'm honored to be assigned to Master General Aëtius' command. I'll report to his Legion in less than two weeks. But tell me about yourself. Are you still betrothed to Caspian?"

A smile stretched across her face. "Yes, and we're set to wed on August 21st at St. Cecilia's near the Porta Augusta. You remember the church; it occupies the site of the former Temple of Diana. I hope you'll attend."

"Unless I am off fighting some barbarian horde in Germania or North Africa, I wouldn't miss it for the world."

The following morning, I left my parents' home and walked up Tiberius Road to the Baths of Honorius to undergo my mandatory daily calisthenics – a regimen I looked forward to each day. The Academy taught us good health came from a combination of frequent bathing, daily massages, a temperate diet, and vigorous exercise, with the latter required of all Imperial officers when not serving in a field unit. I've followed this regimen throughout my life.

My hometown, Nemausus, had an interesting history. The city was named for the mythical son of Hercules. The surrounding area was established as a Roman colony in 28 BC, and by 442 AD, Nemausus was a prosperous city of approximately sixty thousand inhabitants.

Four centuries earlier, Emperor Augustus built a massive defensive wall (almost four miles long and reinforced with fourteen towers) around its boundaries, which the city quickly outgrew. An outdoor amphitheater dating from the time of Emperor Antoninus Pius stood at the city's center.

The public baths, although over fifty years old then, were still in a splendid condition that spring. Open grassy areas with several large shade trees, flower gardens, fountains, and benches were located all around the perimeter of the baths. People of all ages and classes strolled along the paths, and groups of children played games in the morning sunshine. Enjoying the setting, I walked up to main entrance, paid the attendant the sum of two quadrans, and entered the massive building.

The complex consisted of a large gymnasium on the right-hand side of the structure, and three large bathing areas on the left side. A large atrium, located in the center of the building, was filled with poets, politicians, and prostitutes, and each group provided a particular favor in exchange for a particular price.

My father once told me a story about the Roman custom of daily bathing which many barbarians found to be curious. When asked by a certain barbarian why a respectable senator chose to bathe once a day, the senator reportedly answered, 'Because I don't have the time to bathe twice a day.' The story still makes me smile.

Sadly the passion for bathing has diminished somewhat in recent years as Christianity has spread throughout the Empire. Public nudity is now being frowned upon by the Church, and many Christians have adopted the injunction of St. Jerome who preached that those believers who've been washed in the blood of Jesus Christ have no need ever to wash again.

My physician, however, thinks daily bathing helps contain the spread of disease. He noted that cities where wide-spread public bathing still prevails reported lessened incidences of widespread epidemics and plague. I've continued to bathe daily whenever I can.

Upon finishing my prescribed two-hour exercise regimen, I followed the usual practice of proceeding from the hot pool to the warm pool and ending in the cool bath. After I'd finished bathing, I located a barber who shaved off my beard with an obsidian blade. I suspected neither Master General Aëtius nor Octavia wanted a bearded officer standing at their sides. Upon leaving the baths, I began preparing for one of the most momentous evenings of my life.

Dressed in my formal military uniform and silver helmet, I left my father's residence after our evening meal. With the purpose of my visit weighing heavily on my mind, I walked the short distance to Octavia's home on Caligula Street.

Horace, their principal slave, met me at the door, and I was escorted to the tablinium to conclude the final negotiations with her father, Cassius Cyrus Josephus. He was a local merchant who imported grain and livestock from Egypt and the high plateau of Algeria. I'd known him almost all of my life. Octavia, his middle daughter, was the principal subject of our discussions.

Offering me his hand, he smiled and said, "You're a long way from the Academy, Tribune."

Feeling a little nervous, I replied, "Yes, I am, Sir. Yes, I am."

Cassius Cyrus Josephus was a red-faced, brown-eyed man who was about forty-five years old. After shaking hands, we embraced and began our delicate negotiations. Following the certification of her virginity, the amount and substance of her dowry, and the acceptance of his blessing for the marriage, I signed the matrimonial contract. The time had arrived for me to ask Octavia for her consent.

Entering the atrium, Octavia and her mother arose from their couches. Octavia ran to embrace me; we hadn't seen each other in nearly three years. While probably frowned upon by her parents, she held me close. "Oh, Julius, you look so good to me."

Somewhat embarrassed by her outward show of affection, I said, "And you to me. Oh, how I've longed for this day."

Separating from Octavia, I bowed my head toward her mother and said, "It's wonderful seeing you again, Madam."

Tears of joy ran down her face, and she also embraced me. Then, returning to Octavia, I felt a rush of emotions I'd rarely experienced in my life, even in the heat of battle. After getting down on my right knee, I took Octavia's hand in my right hand and asked, "Octavia, will you marry me?"

I presented her with a simple iron ring, the traditional symbol of betrothal from the early years of the Republic. I saw her nod in approval. She accepted the ring, and after placing it on her left hand, she whispered, "Yes, Julius, I'll marry you."

Rising, I took her into my arms, and I felt a sense of great joy. I'd waited for this moment for a long time, and looking into her eyes, I knew she felt the same way, too.

Then her parents applauded our match. Upon her father's signal, Horace brought in a bottle of their finest wine and four wine glasses. Her father led the traditional toast for a long life, many children, and abundant prosperity.

Exhaling, I experienced a peace of mind which I'd also rarely known before. My life was quickly falling into place. I knew who I was, what I wanted, and where I believed I was going in this world. I was marrying the only woman I'd ever loved, and it seemed nothing could interfere with the grandiose plans I'd made while studying at the Academy.

I was young, healthy, and comfortable in a Roman world that still seemed to be near the zenith of its greatness. My horizons seemed endless. Thus far, I thought I had made all of the right choices.

Octavia and I spent considerable time together during my remaining days in Nemausus that late spring, planning our wedding, cementing our bonds, and enjoying each other's company.

Upon arriving at her home early one afternoon, I found Octavia seated on a wooden bench in their garden surrounded by a columned portico. I still remember the details of that day so well. She was attired in a simple yellow tunic which hung to just below her knees, and her light brown hair was loosely tied and lay softly over her left shoulder. Her face was milky white as if she never ventured into the sunlight, and all along her forehead and temples, she displayed a multitude of tiny curls.

Her hazel eyes, outlined by almost undetectable eyebrows, held my complete attention, and with her small nose and soft full lips, she appeared as if in a vision to me. She wore sandals, tied up from her ankles to mid-calf, and she clasped her hands on her lap. A gentle breeze blew in the cedar trees which surrounded the columns, and the sound of the trickling water flowed gently from the fountain which relaxed me.

"I still remember the first time I ever saw you," she said.

"You do?"

"You were standing with your father on the steps of the Temple of Gaius Caesar during Saturnalia, and many people in town were celebrating the season. You were dressed like Mercury, and I dressed like Diana. Do you remember?"

I smiled and recalled that long before the Church began celebrating Christmas in December, Saturnalia was a weeklong national celebration held during the winter solstice. The festival consisted of public and family gatherings followed by private gift-giving, seasonal merriment, and a jovial atmosphere. Being a renewal of light and the coming of the New Year, Saturnalia concluded on December 25th – the Jubilee Day called the *Dies Natalis Solis Invicti*, the 'Birthday of the Unconquerable Sun.'

I also remembered that while the Church leaders actively discouraged the faithful from participating in this ancient pagan celebration, the Governor let the people have their fun. Yes, I could still recall the frivolity, joyful music, the banging drums, and the blazing torches, all aimed at fending off the evil spirits and for encouraging the return of the sun.

Many celebrants were dressed in bright costumes to emulate the ancient deities, and the festivities reflected the customs of a long lost age when gods and goddesses were supreme and ruled the world. Saturnalia was always a joyous season in Nemausus.

I kissed her gently on her forehead. "Yes, my love" I said. "I remember it well.

My father presented General Aëtius to the Governor as *Saturnalicius Princeps* — to misrule in a chaotic and absurd world that year. Do you remember?"

"Oh, yes."

"Our fathers knew each other," I said, "and I remember seeing a shy little girl of six or seven years who tried to hide behind her father's cloak."

"You were actually intimidating to me then. Funny how you don't frighten me anymore, my love."

I squeezed her hand and replied, "But you'll promise to obey me on our wedding day, won't you?"

"Of course, my prince, I'll promise to obey you, but you know vows are made to be broken."

She laughed and won my heart all over again.

Octavia knew of my love of poetry and often asked me to recite it for her. One afternoon in her garden, she asked, "Do you love me, Jul? If you do, let me hear a poem about your unending passion for me."

I paused for an instant. "Well, do you remember the poet, Lucretius? He once described Venus in the same way I see you, my love. He wrote:

> *Oh, Venus, this is where love derives its name;*
> *From which the first drop of her sweetness came*
> *And dripped into our hearts followed by a burning anxiety.*
> *For even if the object of my love is not there,*
> *The images remain*
> *And your sweet name rings and resounds in my ears.*

Do you like it?"

For a moment, I saw tears in her eyes. She held my hands tightly and kissed me ever so gently on my mouth.

On many afternoons, we'd take long walks around the town, hand-in-hand. Our chaperone followed us closely but usually far away enough so she couldn't overhear our conversations. I've been told fewer couples utilize the services of a chaperone now. Things were so different in those earlier days.

I was always mesmerized by whatever Octavia said to me, and by her wit and her laughter. Sometimes we'd shop in the markets near the Forum, or we'd walk slowly along the river. Those were simple, happy times which I'd often think about when I rested on my bed in a field tent in some distant military camp. It's funny how the little pleasures of life can be so compelling even after long periods of absence.

While these springtime days with Octavia were enjoyable, we both knew they couldn't last. Soon my period of leave was over, and I was on my way to join Aëtius' General Staff. Aside from coming home briefly the following August to attend Placida's wedding, I wouldn't see Octavia again for nearly another year. I still recall the profound sadness I experienced when kissing her one last time before leaving Nemausus to begin my military career.

CHAPTER II

Near Civitas Turonum, Gaul – June 442 AD

When I reported to Camp Aurelius, Master General Aëtius was temporarily in the lower Loire Valley mobilizing elements of the VII Legion for a military strike against the Bagaudae – a group of Alemanni insurgents who began migrating into Roman territory in small groups in 290 AD during the time of Emperor Diocletian.

After initially revolting against imperial authority in 334 AD, the Bagaudae were crushed by Emperor Constantius and later peacefully settled in Northern Gaul. Beginning in 420 AD, however, renegade bands of these warriors began attacking some of the smaller villages in the lower Loire Valley, and in 442, Emperor Valentinian III tasked Aëtius with the mission of quelling the menace.

Upon reporting, I was assigned to the Headquarters' Detachment as the Assistant Tactician. My immediate duties entailed advising Aëtius and his general staff about the new strategic theories which I learned at the Academy to combat insurgencies. My studies considered the newly developing military approaches regarding how best to utilize diminishing Roman power to defeat a growing barbarian menace.

Due to a combination of the all-too-frequent civil wars, barbarian invasions, and the incidence of a series of mysterious plagues arising from the Far East, the Legions had been decimated over the previous two centuries. Instead of raising armies solely from the populace of the Empire itself, the Emperors began using the practice of purchasing the services of mercenary forces (principally drawn from groups who were once hostile to Rome) to augment and enhance the depleted Legions.

While the practice of adding barbarian troops to the Imperial forces brought initial success in crushing local uprisings and invasions, soon the mercenary force commanders were learning the battlefield tactics and strategies of the once invincible Legions. Consequently, to stay ahead of the mercenaries (who might later confront Roman authority), Emperor Valerian established three regional military academies in 255 AD to develop new strategies to ensure the future of the massive Empire. I knew I had a tough job ahead of me.

It was during my initial assignment in Gaul when I met Count Flavius Ricimer, a man who would greatly impact my life. I learned his grandfather's name was Wallia, the King of Visigoths, who served honorably with Emperor Constantius in 416 AD during the Burgundian campaigns, and that his mother was a princess of a Suevi king. Being the third son of the King of Galicia (and thus, not in the line of succession to his father), Ricimer was raised, as was the custom at the time, in the Court of Emperor Valentinian III in Ravenna.

Following his fourteenth birthday, he entered into the military service of Rome, and he received a commission when he turned twenty-one in 439 AD. All in all, Count Ricimer was a well-connected soldier of noble barbarian stock who displayed unimpeachable allegiance to Rome. We became fast friends, and we eventually shared quarters in the Officer's Barracks at Camp Aurelius.

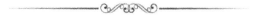

My first years in military service were tedious but also exhilarating. There were constant meetings, troop assessments, and often-unmet deadlines concerning matters of pay and supplies. Keeping the men occupied, however, was never a problem; training, drilling, and patrolling were standard components in their daily regimen.

Initially, service in the Legions was a difficult adjustment for me. Early on, I began experiencing a complex combination of anxiety, anticipation, exhaustion, pride, confusion, and dread. As time passed, however, I learned to be more comfortable with my role as an officer; but the anxiety became problematic at times for me.

In November, 442 AD, I was given my first field assignment as the commander of the First Cohort. Ricimer was already in command of the Second Cohort, and I learned a lot from him. In December, I directed my troops in my first hostile skirmish, which took place a short distance from Campo Augustus.

Then in January, I killed my first Bagaudae soldier as my troops attacked a heavily fortified compound near Septiminus. Although there'd be many more killings to follow, it was something I could never quite stomach. Troubling nightmares, resulting from these skirmishes, would often haunt me when I'd relive the savagery all over again in my dreams.

After acquiring more experience and combat training, I frequently bivouacked in remote field camps while on patrol with my troops, and for months without end, I found myself far away from the relative comforts of the Officers' quarters at Camp Aurelius.

Despite some minor retrenchments, the troops of the First Cohort fought courageously and successfully, as we pacified the Greater Loire Valley during the long cold winter of 442 AD. At the same time, Ricimer was commanding Aëtius' main contingent of forces in Hispania, and in March, the VII Legion routed the Vandals and other affiliated tribes on the snow covered hills west of Tarraconensis.

In early April, General Aëtius triumphantly returned to Camp Aurelius following a long winter of fierce fighting. The First Cohort served as the honor guard with Ricimer chosen to lead the victorious VII Legion back into camp.

On that day, I witnessed my first triumphant parade, and I was privileged to be a part of the pomp and circumstances surrounding the spectacle of a returning victorious legion. Marching in front of a cheering crowd of an estimated ten thousand citizens from the city of Civitas Turonum and the surrounding countryside, I counted over fifty wagonloads of booty and plunder of all descriptions, a large assemblage of slaves, and a sad-looking casern of chained prisoners as Count Ricimer and the Golden Eagle rode into Camp Aurelius.

Master General Aëtius, Governor Claudius Ventenius, and several members of the Senate beamed as they watched the festivities from the grand reviewing box. It had been a long time since the army of the Western Empire generated such an overwhelming military victory. All in all, it was a spectacular day for Rome!

Back in Camp Aurelius, Count Ricimer and I spent many of the remaining days that spring talking about our battles, our upbringings, and our hopes for the future. We were quickly bonding as brothers, and in June, I asked him to stand beside me as my chief witness for my upcoming marriage.

With long flowing blond hair, blue eyes, and a well-cropped beard, Ricimer looked like the archetypical German warrior. He was a little taller than me and quite handsome with the face of a god. He also retained a hearty laugh, a big heart, and ambition for glory. For many years to come, he was my closest friend.

Following a typical day in the garrison, we met one evening to share a bottle of Sicilian wine in the Officer's Quarters. There he told me about his life.

"Well, making a long story short, my father's name is Rechila, the King of Galicia. I'm the third oldest of four brothers. With my brothers, Gustave and Oronoco – the so-called heir and a spare – being in direct succession to the throne, they remained with my father in Galicia to learn the challenges of royal power. One of them will eventually succeed him on the throne. To avoid the possibility of a dynastic war, my younger brother, Olaf, and I were sent off to Rome at age 8."

"That sounds cruel to me."

He shrugged his shoulders and nodded, and told me that they were placed into the care and custody of Emperor Valentinian in the Court at Ravenna. Along with twenty-two other young men of barbarian nobility from the reaches of the Empire, they were taught what it meant to be a Roman subject. Still, there was a look of sadness in his eyes.

I asked, "What did you do in Ravenna?"

"We were schooled in the classics until we obtained our fourteenth birthday when we entered into military service and assigned to a legion located somewhere in the Western Empire." Then he said, "Olaf is stationed now in Leptis Magnus, I think."

He stopped a moment, took a sip of wine, and continued his story. "There's a great temptation for us to learn the secrets of Imperial tactics and warfare, and after that, turn on our masters for our personal glory."

"I recall an instructor mentioning it to me at the Academy."

"One of our colleagues was Attila. After serving two years with General Stilicho on the Danube frontier, he switched his allegiance and is fighting the Eastern Legions now in Dacia. Don't worry, my friend; I've no such desires. In my heart, I'm a Roman."

Ricimer stopped again and looked out the window; a cavalry unit just arrived in our garrison. He continued, "Like you, I was assigned to Aëtius' command, and I've been serving on his staff for the last three years. I haven't been home to Galicia since I entered military service."

I took a sip of wine and asked, "That's rough; do you miss your family?"

"As I said, in my heart, I'm a Roman, but I sorely miss my mother and my sisters. And I'd like to go back and see the mountains and rivers of my homeland. It's such an excellent place. I know you'd love it, too, if you saw it. I do see Olaf every couple of years or so. However, we're not close anymore."

"Maybe someday you'll show me your country?"

"Perhaps, but I know I can never return home in peace." Once again, sadness appeared on his face. "I'd be perceived as a direct threat to the throne. Now, I can only return as head of an army."

While barred from becoming a candidate for the Imperial Throne because of his Germanic origins, he also told me how he longed to unite the Germanic peoples occupying Gaul, Belgica, and Alemannia into a powerful political union which could one-day persuade the Senate to rethink its ascension policy.

I saw a gleam in his eyes as he said, "It's time for all citizens to be eligible to sit on the Imperial Throne. Rome needs to seek aspirants from all corners of the realm – and not just from Roman stock. The current practice of passing the throne from father to son is probably the worst kind of government."

I smiled. "Yeah, I agree. We've been plagued with incompetent sons of equally incompetent emperors. How often in the past two-hundred years have we been horrified by the sons of emperors who, after obtaining the throne, have turned out to be even more monstrous than their malevolent fathers?"

He nodded his head. "Yes, it has to stop! Just think of all we could accomplish if we were united as one people. And unless we are unified under one common rule, the Western Empire will collapse one day – and with it, the rest of the civilized world."

I agreed with him. "But as you well know, the Senate is very conservative. Aside from a couple of ethnic Romans who happened to have born outside of Italia, the Senate has been reluctant even to consider a non-Italian candidate. Perhaps, you will be the first foreign-born emperor. You'll certainly have my support."

"And you'll have my support, my brother. I know it'll happen, and together, we'll change the world one day. Yes, the whole damn civilized world."

Little did we know in less than twenty years, his prophecy would come true.

CHAPTER III

Nemausus – July 12, 443 AD

The Church of St. Perpetua, formerly the Temple of Gaius Caesar, stood tall against the background of a bright blue Gallic sky. Raised almost six-feet off the ground on a flat podium, the twelve Corinthian columns, standing over thirty feet high, framed the ancient façade. Built by Marcus Agrippa in 16 BC as a temple to honor Emperor Augustus' eldest son, it remained the jewel of the city for the succeeding five centuries.

Constructed of white marble with a broad portico which stretched for almost a third of the building's length, the building was consecrated as a Christian Church in 356 AD. Despite its age, it retained the character of a classic Greek-style edifice and continued as a focal point in the growing city of Nemausus.

It was our wedding day, and as the years have passed, I've relived this day over and over again in my mind. I can still recall almost every detail! Flowing red ribbons adorned the length of the six front columns of the church. Bouquets of white jasmine were placed on the twelve front steps and landing to usher the bridal party into the inner sanctuary.

Standing on the top step with my father, my brothers, and Ricimer, I still recall watching the procession (consisting of Octavia, her bridesmaids, her family, and many attendants carrying incense, flowering plants and ornaments) leave the staging house nearby and approach the church.

As the bridal party reached the bottom step of the ancient temple, four costumed trumpeters – outfitted as Legionaries – suddenly appeared between the columns and began playing the traditional wedding fanfare. Immediately after that, four children, dressed in simple white tunics with gold sashes, stepped forward and released snow-white doves into the air.

Then, as the trumpets went silent, the massive front doors of St. Perpetua opened, and the Archbishop, robed in golden vestments and carrying a silver scepter, stepped forward to meet the wedding party.

When Octavia reached the top step on the arm of her father, he kissed her softly on her cheek and placed her right hand in mine. Tears welled in his eyes as he said in a loud voice so all of our guests could hear, "Julius Valerius Majorian, I entrust to your care and protection, the life and well-being of my precious daughter, Octavia Isabella. May you both live a long life in peace and prosperity to see the faces of your children's children's children."

Dressed in the traditional bridal way, Octavia wore a red embroidered *tunica recta,* which was tied at the waist. Her veil was oblong and almost transparent, and it covered her from her head to her hips. She also wore the traditional amaracus wreath, an ancient symbol of innocence and virginity. As the trumpeters began playing the entry march, she placed her left hand on my right arm, and we started to walk into the sanctuary.

My sister, Placida, served as Octavia's matron of honor, and she followed us on the arm of Count Ricimer. She wore a full-length shawl of midnight-blue silk over a simple white linen stola, and a string of pearls fell around her neck.

Stopping at the massive brass doors, which provided access to the sanctuary, the Archbishop presented the first blessing. He said, "Just as Christ loves His Church, may you learn to love each other; in the name of the Father, the Son, and the Holy Spirit."

The sanctuary consisted of a single, surprisingly small and windowless interior room. Just above a small plain altar, a colorful fresco of Christ with several of the Apostles was affixed to the back wall. Once the doors were closed, the chamber displayed the appearance of late evening despite the fact it was midday. Candles and flowers filled the sanctuary with light, shadow, and scent.

With only our immediate families, the wedding attendants, and the clergy present inside the sanctuary, the ceremony was relatively short. We exchanged the traditional Roman vows, which had been updated to reflect the recent dominance of Christianity. Once the Archbishop gave his final blessing, the massive bronze doors opened, and the trumpeters played the jubilant marriage flourishes.

My heart was filled with joy. Hand-in-hand, we exited the church and descended the church steps. Then the procession, known as the *dedcutio in domun marti,* moved slowly and joyously from the plaza to our new home, which was located only three short blocks away from the church.

After I carried Octavia over the threshold, her mother brought in the *spina alba* – a wooden torch lit from the hearth of Octavia's former home – and started a fire in our fireplace. In the traditional way, young girls gently tossed walnuts at Octavia, symbolizing a blessing for fertility. It was a happy occasion, and the festivities lasted late into the evening.

Once the last guest departed our home, I took Octavia's hand and led her into our bedchamber. While kissing her softly, I untied the string from her *tunica recta* and gently removed the amaracus wreath from her head. I said, "I've never loved you more than I do now." Octavia smiled, encircled her arms around my neck, and kissed me deeply on my mouth.

There are times we remember all of our lives; they are indelibly fixed in our minds. I can still remember each and every detail of the next few moments we shared together. I said words of love to her which I'd never spoken to anyone else, and I heard those sweet words I'd longed to hear from her since the day I left the Academy. Timing my movements to her signs and sounds, we moved together in unison as one entity, and we consumed each other.

Later watching the shadows dancing on the ceiling in the evening's stillness, I held her close to me. Although her eyes were partially open, she was almost sound asleep. As I ran my fingers through her long hair, we laid beside each other in the dimness of the hot and steamy night. Feeling a profound sense of joy and contentment, sleep finally took us the rest of the way to morning.

Awaking in the sunlit room with her sleeping silently and cuddling close beside me, I gently took her arms from around me and got out of bed. Looking out onto the street, I saw a beautiful morning waiting for us outside the window. A few moments later, I returned to bed and embraced her.

As I kissed her softly, her eyes began to open, and I saw the most satisfied look on her face one could ever imagine. I whispered, "Good morning, Darling." As she kissed me, the passion of the previous night returned and consumed us once again.

After a blissful week with my young bride, I reported back to my military unitnear Civitas Turonum. Sadly, I saw Octavia only three or four times a year during my first seven years of service to Rome. These years, however, were some of the most satisfying yet loneliest times of my life.

Although we were often apart, Octavia and I frequently sent letters to each other. In 14 BC, Emperor Augustus created the *cursus publicus* to transport messages, officials, and tax revenues between the provinces and the Capitol. The system was later expanded to accommodate civilian and private letters, messages, and small packages.

A series of forts and stations were established along the major road systems connecting the regions of the Empire. These relay points provided horses to dispatch riders, often soldiers, for the movement of mail, supplies and other materials. While the transport time between Nemausus and wherever I was stationed in the Western Empire often took weeks and even months, most news reached its destination eventually.

Dear Husband,

Thank you for your long letter. I've already read it ten or more times. I was so glad to learn you returned safely from the campaign in Atrebatum and your troops only sustained minimal casualties. Will you remain in garrison for a while now? I hope so. With all the bad news coming into Nemausus lately, I worry about you so much.

I've some good news and some bad news. Your mother slipped and fell last week when she was walking in her garden. Josiah found her. She broke her right hip and her left wrist. Because your father is growing older, we decided to move your mother to Felix's home so your brother and Irena can better nurse her. I am so worried about your mother. Her complexion is ashen, and her strength is almost gone. I hate to trouble you with this terrible news, but we need to plan for her loss.

The good news is Minerva is walking now and happily chasing little Julius around the house. They seem to love each other very much. Minerva looks more like you every day, and I hug her as much as I dare. Julius has his first tutor, a Greek slave named Demos, who also taught your brother's children. He seems quite competent, and young Julius seems to like him.

Have you heard when you are coming home again? I know I ask you this question in almost every letter but, Jul, I miss you so much. Every night before going to bed, the children and I pray for your safe return. They miss their father, too.

We've had frigid weather for the last week or two, and I am counting the days until spring arrives. Just a few moments ago, the sun finally came out. Maybe the worst of winter is over. Is it still cold there?

The post leaves for Civitas Turonum in a few hours, so I need to close. Please tell Ricimer hello from us. I pray for his safety, too

Remember we love you.

Your affectionate Octavia

Initially, I planned to remain in the army for only four years, and enter the political arena. However, it seemed like the entire Western Empire was constantly in turmoil. Under the command of Master General Aëtius, we defeated a much larger Frankish army at Tourmacumin in 445 AD, and we crushed another invading Frankish military force near Atrebatum in Belgica Secunda the flowing spring.

But whenever Imperial defenses were perceived as being particularly vulnerable, hostile barbarian forces would flood into the Western Empire. If these raids were successful, more attacks would occur. If the incursions went unpunished, the possibility existed for a full-scale invasion. So, we had to remain vigilant and repel each barbarian attack as quickly and as forcibly as possible.

Although Aëtius retained tactical control over the general military operations in the Western Empire, Ricimer and I soon commanded the VI and VII Legions respectively. We delivered decisive victories for Rome on the battlefields near Vicus Helena and Trentalum in 447 AD; thus, pacifying the upper western frontier for another four years or so.

Yet, despite the fact we'd spent so much time apart, by the spring of 451, Octavia and I had four healthy children.

CHAPTER IV

The city of Rome served as the Capitol of the Republic, and after that, the Empire, for over a thousand years before Emperor Constantine moved the seat of government to Constantinople in 330 AD.

When the Empire was later divided by Emperor Theodosius in 396, the Capitol of the Western Empire was placed in Ravenna, a city of approximately sixty-thousand people – counting slaves and foreigners – situated on the Adriatic Sea. The selection of the site was made partly for defensive purposes. Ravenna was surrounded by swamps and marshes whereas Rome was considered vulnerable to attack.

In late May, 451, Ricimer and I were called before the Court in Ravenna to discuss a dire military situation facing the Western Empire. Earlier in the spring, the Huns, led by Attila, crossed the Rhine River and destroyed the cities of Divodurum and Mediomaticum. Ricimer had already been briefed by Aëtius and his general staff by the time we met late one afternoon outside my hotel.

As we began walking west toward the palace, I asked, "So what's the purpose of this meeting?"

Ricimer replied, "The Emperor is worried about Attila. As we speak, the Huns are wreaking havoc in Upper Belgica. We need to drive them back across the Rhine."

"Yes, I've heard some rumors, but I don't know many of the specifics. Why did Attila leave the Eastern Empire? I heard his army was essentially invincible."

"Well, for the previous two years, the Huns had been terrorizing Thrace and Macedonia – burning villages and slaughtering the peasants. Then they began their siege of Constantinople. Equipped with new military weapons, such as battering rams and rolling siege towers, the Huns were ready for the probability of a prolonged blockade of the Eastern Capitol."

"Then what happened?"

Ricimer tugged at his beard and briefly looked off in the distance as a small barge was floating down the canal. He looked worried. "Apparently, Marcian offered the Huns a sweet deal to end their blockade of Constantinople and leave the Eastern Empire; you know, perhaps as much as ten tons of gold."

"Did you say ten 'tons' of gold?"

Ricimer smiled. "Yes, because Marcian's troops couldn't defeat Attila on the battlefield, and because the Emperor didn't want to risk a prolonged siege, he eventually decided to buy them off. I hear Attila also wants future payments from the Eastern government for several more years to come."

"So, now he's attacking us?"

"Yes, the Huns moved westward, and once they arrived on the Rhine, Attila joined forces with the Franks and several other tribes. I've been told they plan to invade in Northern Gaul come summer. They're already ransacking Belgica and Germania."

I asked, "How do we know about Attila's plans?"

"Well, we have spies in their camps. Now, Valentinian wants the Huns contained or better yet, destroyed. Aëtius needs us to help him quickly come up with a battle plan."

The news was most troubling to me. Attila was a formable adversary and wouldn't be contained with mere promises. Furthermore, Valentinian didn't have ten tons of gold in the treasury to buy him off. We'd have to defeat Attila on the battlefield.

As Ricimer and I walked through the city, I began to notice the nuevo-classical architecture of the new sprawling Capitol. It had been a couple of years since I last visited the city. Unlike Rome, which is suffused in elegant decay, Ravenna was sparkling fresh and new. The oldest of the Imperial palaces was erected less than fifty years ago, and new buildings were being constructed almost everywhere we looked. I was delighted in the Capitol's vivacity and raw newness.

Dust was scattered everywhere, and the streets were bustling with workers and construction equipment. With each passing year, it seemed the city changed its form and appearance, as the old Greek-revival structures were being torn down and replaced with more modernly designed palaces, churches, marketplaces, and amphitheaters. Unlike Rome, Ravenna seemed vital and alive to me.

Ricimer mentioned the Emperor hoped in the near future, Ravenna would surpass Rome in power and prestige; so the glory 'that was Rome' would to one day become Ravenna's legacy. From what I observed that afternoon, Valentinian was certainly well on his way to accomplishing the goal. Maybe the Emperor could even convince the Pope to move the official headquarters of the Church to Ravenna.

As we continued to stroll along the bustling streets of Ravenna in the late afternoon, Ricimer looked over his shoulder and watched an attractive young woman carrying a water jar walk passed us. "My, what I could do with just five minutes with that woman," he said. "Oh yes, just five minutes, my friend. You know, she wouldn't be able to walk comfortably for the next three days."

After watching her stroll away from us and eventually turn down a cross-street, he exhaled noisily. Turning back to face me, he said, "Let's find a tabernaria. I think there's one down Hadrian Way on the left. I could use a glass of beer right now."

Beer, often referred to as 'cervisia,' was considered by higher society as a vulgar choice of beverages, and it was often associated with barbarians. However, during my years of living in field camps and outposts in Gaul and Hispania, I acquired a taste for it; especially those beers brewed in Southern Germania and Upper Belgica.

Strolling along Hadrian Way, I also noticed the sidewalks and alleyways were cluttered with scores of the untouchables of the Empire – the crippled, the lepers, the blind, the infirm, and the lame – all looking for alms, drink or food.

I glanced at them – men, women, and children – wearing dirty rags. Some were exposing crusty sores and weeping scabs, and many were resting the shade, looking hopeless and despondent. Suddenly, a group of four or five children, shoeless and ragged, ran towards us.

Seeing them, Ricimer yelled, "Watch out. They're after our money." Grasping his sword, he stared directly at them. Apparently realizing we had guessed their motives, they ran back to the safety of the others.

I also saw several small groups of disabled men, probably former soldiers, wearing the remnants of their military uniforms. Many of them were missing limbs or appeared to be experiencing battle fatigue or some other mental disorder. Several others wore eyepatches, and a couple of them had lost an ear. Some extended their hands, imploring for handouts, while others stared at us in a menacing manner, as if we were the reason for their ailments – and perhaps we were.

We walked on. Occasionally, a prostitute would call out to us, offering her uniquely personalized services in return for a small fee. I could only imagine what aliments these scantily dressed solicitors of the flesh would bring along with their particular wares.

After a couple more short blocks, a large, brightly-colored wooden sign reading "Caesar's Golden Lance" announced our arrival at the tabernaria. The two-story building, graced with an ample outdoor terrace in the back, was full of guests.

"Here we are," Ricimer said as we walked through the opened front door of the tabernaria.

Because it was a warm late afternoon, the proprietor led us through the dark, damp public house and outside onto the terrace which was shaded by a sprawling sycamore tree. A large flowing water fountain was placed in the center of the garden, and a solitary statue of a bearded and helmeted gladiator (looking most ferocious with sword drawn) stood tall in the middle of the fountain. Most curiously, a steady flow of water gushed precipitously from his most impressive and enlarged genitalia. Shaking my head, I wasn't sure what to make of this warrior.

The proprietor eventually escorted us to an empty table situated beneath a wooden trellis – heavy with burnt-purple grapes. Once seated, slaves helped us remove our sandals, and then washed and dried our feet. Soon, a server, proudly showing off her ample bosom, took our beverage order. After that, she suggested, with a sly wink and a pretty little pout, that should we become interested in any of the establishment's other excellent offerings, she'd be most happy to indulge our every whim.

After she left our table, I looked at the patrons who were sitting at tables around the garden and observed, "Ravenna is becoming such an international city; people from all over the Empire are flocking here. Sadly, the Empire is no longer just for Romans."

Ricimer took a long drink from his beer. From the expression on his face, I didn't think he liked the intent of my comment very much. "The Empire was built for all people. You know, if the Empire is to have much of a future, it must continue to welcome immigrants, and incorporate them into the fabric of ordinary life."

I held my hands up and replied, "But aren't we reaching a breaking point here? Look, they're everywhere. You saw the type of people we just passed on the street. It's hard to walk down an avenue without being swarmed by these damned beggars. We can't continue to let just anybody in, can we?"

"I disagree. It's been Rome's most enduring legacy to integrate the best parts of the uncivilized world and mold them into a greater society. Those unfortunate few on the street are not good examples of a more pressing problem."

I looked around at the people sitting in the garden. He continued, "But there's such an anti-immigrant bias now – and it's so damn counterproductive. Don't most Romans know they weren't conceived under the Arch of Titus during Saturnalia? Huh? Most of our citizens hail from a foreign stock, and few of us have ancestors who rose out of the Tiber River a thousand years ago."

Sipping my beer, I nodded my head in quiet agreement. Ricimer continued, "Now the Senate is debating this horrible alien-expulsion bill. Damn it; the whole process makes me sick. The Senate is trying to close the doors to new immigrants, and it wants to disenfranchise many of the long-term residents who now reside peacefully in the Empire. It's pure madness!"

"Madness?"

"Yes, the passage of this type of legislation will certainly lead to trouble, and possibly, to civil war. Don't you agree?"

I uncrossed my legs and leaned forward in my chair. "Well, perhaps, but despite your arguments, we certainly cannot continue to let the large numbers of these barbarian hordes into the Empire. Our society is strained to the limits, and there's already so much poverty in the Empire. Enough is enough! Let's shut the door!"

Ricimer just shook his head in almost disbelief. Soon our server returned with another round of beer. Once she departed, I took a sip, put down my cup, and continued. "These immigrant populations are bringing all sorts of strange diseases along with them – why, we're just now getting over the last plague brought in by the goddam Goths – and most of these damn immigrants are uneducated, unskilled, and unsophisticated. Few of them even speak Latin."

"But it's always been this way — and Rome has always absorbed its immigrants."

I shook my head in disagreement and replied, "Maybe it was true in the past, but we cannot continue to take care of the world's unfortunate masses. Damn it, the treasury is depleted, and the army is underpaid and poorly supplied. We need to think about what's best for Rome. The Empire is in such terrible shape compared to just fifty years ago."

Apparently, Ricimer was unconvinced. "That's exactly why we need to continue to bring these people into the Empire peacefully. Rome is exhausted from its thousand-year reign. It desperately needs new blood, ingenuity, and above all, peace."

"So, you want to bring in even more barbarian hordes? What possible good could it do?"

Ricimer shook his head, "Julius, holding out the barbarian hordes, as you call them, will lead to forced and violent invasions. Can't you see our army cannot continue to be entrusted to dose these raging fires?"

He picked up his knife, tapped it a couple of times on his cup, and continued, "This ongoing assault on Imperial authority is precisely what Attila is doing now in Belgica. For him, its slash and burn, and he's a menace whom we might not contain this time. We don't need any more damn invasions. The Legions are stretched to the limits."

Ricimer briefly gazed around the garden and continued, "Whether we like it or not, groups of barbarians are continually drawn to our Golden Empire, and closing the door on them will only work for a short period. It's like a small brook; you can hold it back for only a little while before it grows to the point it overflows."

I just remained silent. Ricimer took another swallow of beer. He moved forward in his chair, wiped his mouth, and continued, "Jul, we have ample available land and abundant untapped resources in Hispania, and Western Gaul. We can settle them there. It's clearly to our advantage to bring them in peacefully, don't you think?"

I shook my head and replied, "Our supply of land isn't unlimited, and we must save it for our future expansion. We've brought in too many foreigners already, by God."

Ricimer was getting animated now. "No, I disagree; we need to settle them now before they knock the goddamn door down."

"Well, let them try and see what happens."

"No, that's Attila's plan. If we bring these people into the Empire peacefully in small groups, the settlers will eventually build cities and towns, create commerce, pay taxes, and consider themselves as Romans one day – just like all of the other groups of settlers who've been integrated during the last five-hundred years."

"You are a dreamer, my friend."

"Well, I've been accused of that before."

Ricimer stopped talking once again, took yet another sip, leaned even closer to me in his chair, and continued, "Just look at the people here in the garden. Like us, they want to live in stucco cottages with tiled roofs and eat off imported pottery rather than living under thatched roofs and on dirt floors."

"Uh huh."

"They want to experience the noble Roman dream: you know, enjoying fine wines from Italia and Dalmatia, well-woven cloth from Egypt and Carthage, delicate gold bracelets from Persia and Achaea, and spices and the other delights from the Far East the whole package. They want to be Romans – like us!"

Looking around the garden again, I could see an astonishing collage of people from all cultures, colors, and dress eating dinner, drinking wine and talking politics. After that, Ricimer began pointing out specific individuals and began speculating as to their possible countries of natural origin.

Then he said, "These dreams are impossible for tribal people who reside in mortal fear and abject poverty. Like you and me, they yearn to live under the protection of the *Pax Romana* so they can raise their children in peace and live full and productive lives."

I remained skeptical and replied, "But what about their leaders? Certainly, Attila and the other marauders aren't entering Imperial territory with an olive branch in their teeth. They've come to conquer, plunder, and exploit our nation. This is precisely why we're meeting with the Emperor tomorrow – to figure out a way to repel these goddam invaders. They are certainly not coming in peace but to line their pockets with our gold and to obliterate our way of life."

Ricimer agreed in part, saying, "Yes, the armies come to rape, pillage and burn; and invaders such as Attila must be forcibly vanquished or pushed back across the Rhine."

He paused again for a moment and looked directly into my eyes. "We must find a peaceful way to allow small groups of immigrants into our paradise, or they'll join the armies who are out to conquer and end Roman civilization."

I shrugged my shoulders; I was ready to conclude the argument and talk about something else. "Well, I don't know about that – but I do see your point."

Looking down at his now empty cup, he asked, "Do we want to be known as the generation who lost the heritage and culture which was passed down to us from the Greeks, Carthaginians, and Egyptians? Unless we make massive political changes soon, all will be lost, my friend. Mark my word."

I smiled and asked, "Well, shall we order another round?"

And we did.

As evening came upon us, we dined on plates of succulent pig and boiled cabbage followed by a bottle of a fruity white wine from the vineyards near Treverorum. Soon, the evening began to fall into a predictable pattern. A slave from a land far beyond the borders of the Empire began playing an unfamiliar string instrument and sang forlorn sounding songs in an unidentifiable dialect.

After that, several inebriated patrons – hailing from all corners of the Empire – began getting restless. As if on cue, a homesick merchant, soldier, or diplomat would burst into song, raise a solemn toast to some local deity or past lover, or issue an unwise call to arms or revolution.

As the political discussions were becoming much louder and more heated, fights started breaking out among rival groups, and the local constabulary agents were growing impatient. As morning and Emperor Valentinian would soon be beckoning us, I decided it was time to leave.

After paying the tab and exiting the tabernaria through the front doors, I turned back around and watched as Ricimer and our buxom server began climbing the stairs to the second floor. Clearly, his evening was not quite over.

Mid-morning, Ricimer and I reported to the Palace for our meeting with Emperor Valentinian. I must admit I was a bit nervous. Since the time that I began commanding the VII Legion, I had attended three or four meetings at the palace over the years, but they were scheduled solely for me to provide his general staff with routine updates regarding the VII Legion's capabilities and needs. This one was different. The Emperor was chairing the meeting.

After passing through several layers of security, we were ushered into a small holding room where the Master of Offices gave us last minute instructions regarding matters of courtship and etiquette in the presence of the Emperor. After the Master of Offices was satisfied we understood our ceremonial responsibilities, we were escorted to the meeting room.

Master General Aëtius, flanked by his primary subordinate commander, Field General Claudius Aegidius, and other senior members of his general staff, were already seated around a large wooden table. Shortly after we took our chairs to the right of Aëtius, the large brass doors opened from the residency, and Valentinian and his principal advisors were announced.

A court official, dressed in a bright ornamental costume depicting his official administrative position, entered the room first and bellowed: "All rise! Lord Emperor Flavius Placidius Valentinian Augustus, Pontifex Maximus, Dominus Noster, Princeps Senatus, and Nobilissimus Caesar bids you a warm welcome. Long Live the Emperor and the Empire for which he rules. Long live the Senate and People of Rome."

Flanked by an impressive entourage of festive courtiers, elaborately-appointed priests and bishops, well-heeled Senators and aristocrats, and at least twenty staff members, Valentinian entered the room and walked up to an ivory chair situated at the head of the table. According to their rank, the officers of state took their positions to the left and right of his chair.

After surveying the audience and nodding his head in apparent approval, the Emperor sat down. A few moments later, he looked up, and noticing we remained standing, he motioned for us to take our seats at the table or in a side chair.

Dressed in a long purple cloak and a white linen tunic which hung from his shoulders to his feet, Valentinian wore the jewel-encrusted diadem of Roman authority around his neck, tied loosely by a long silver chain. He displayed decorative rings on fingers of each hand and carried a richly decorated scepter. A large golden crown, set with pearls, topped his nearly bald head. He was the glorification of regal authority; *Ubi imperator, ibi Roma* – where the emperor is, there is Rome.

Standing about 5'6" and severely overweight, he was clean-shaven with large sad eyes, and he shared his father's prominent nose and ruddy cheeks. It was widely reported he was a spoiled, vain, pleasure-loving monarch who was heavily influenced by magicians, sorcerers and astrologers, and that he kept a harem of young women and boys at his personal disposal for all sorts of sexual games and degenerate perversions.

Yet, he was entrusted by the Senate to govern an already overstressed Western Empire and to repulse the invading hordes of Huns and Vandals from its territory. For a moment I wondered, what it was like to be one of the two or three most dominant men in the known world.

From my previous visits to the palace, I'd learned a lot about him. Born on July 2, 419, Valentinian III was the progeny of a long and impressive lineage. He was the son, grandson, great-grandson, cousin, and nephew (twice over) of former Emperors. While he officially ascended to the throne at the age of six following the death of his father, Valentinian did not assume authority until he was eighteen. Before that time, his mother, Galla Placidia, served as Regent.

I never met Valentinian's mother, but I'm told she was cruel and overly ambitious. Desperately wanting her son to become the Emperor, she plotted the deaths of many of her family members to achieve her purposes. His mother is also thought to have been involved in the deadly conspiracy against the Master General Stilicho and the subsequent execution of Serena – Stilicho's wife and Galla Placidia's cousin. When her son finally assumed the throne on his majority, Galla Placidia remained as one his top advisors and confidants.

Shortly after assuming power in 437 AD, much of the Western Empire began to fall away from Imperial control. While Aëtius pacified much of Gaul by defeating the Bagaudae and Burgundians early in Valentinian's reign, the Vandals had completely overrun the rich provinces in Western Africa, culminating in the capture of Carthage in 439. By 446, Western Hispania was in open revolt, and in the spring of 451, Attila was wreaking havoc in Belgica. By the time of our meeting, the Emperor had plenty of fires to put out.

Slowly, Valentinian arose from his chair, looked around the room, and began speaking. "Our scouts tell us Attila's army has commenced a scorched earth policy in Belgica, and he's currently encircling the city of Aurelianum in Northern Gaul. While we still hold the bridge crossing the Loire, and thus, we may have some limited access to the Loire Valley, the city gates have been shut, and Attila has begun the siege."

He paused for a moment and looked around the room. Satisfied all eyes and ears were on him, he continued, "Earlier this month, the Franks and other tribes joined forces with Attila; but, the Franks will live to regret this unfortunate alliance with the Devil. Mark my word."

Once again he paused for effect and continued, "We also know the other demon, Gaiseric, the King of the Vandals, is encouraging Attila to continue his onslaught. Then apparently the two of them plan to gobble up our territories situated between Gaul and Gibraltar. It goes without saying, Attila must be stopped immediately, and then we need to turn our attention to Gaiseric. General Aëtius, how do you plan to stop them?"

Aëtius looked at his three main subordinate generals – Ricimer, Aegidius, and me – shook his head in frustration and stood up to address the Emperor. "Majesty, the Legions have been stretched well beyond their capabilities. We desperately need more men and armaments. The government's failure to re-arm our Legions with state-of-the-art equipment has severely weakened our fighting force."

Valentinian responded, "Are you going to repeat those same tiresome arguments once again? Come, General, you can be more creative than that, can't you?"

"Majesty, with all due respect, they are legitimate arguments."

Hearing that, Valentinian screamed, "Oh, come now, General, its utter nonsense, and you damn well know it."

Aëtius didn't waver one bit; he looked again at his subordinate commanders and continued, "Furthermore, my Lord, much of our weaponry has deteriorated over the years or has become obsolete. The armies of Attila and Gaiseric are much better supplied, paid, and armed, and they outnumber us as much as four to one. Right now, the Legions aren't prepared to fight a major campaign in the West. Majesty, can you ask Constantinople for additional troops and provisions?"

Valentinian looked angry. Apparently not believing Aëtius' reply, he shook his head, waved his hands, and replied, "My dear General, as you well know that's exactly how we arrived at our predicament. With a payment of ten tons of gold, Constantinople has bought off Attila, and part of the peace settlement called for Attila to leave the Eastern Empire."

Valentinian shook his head and continued. "Emperor Marcian will offer us neither military nor financial support. They don't want Attila to change his mind and attack Constantinople again. The Eastern government has just survived a brutal siege by Attila. No, they won't help us. We are on our own, General."

Calmly, Aëtius asked, "Can you ask the Senate for more men and money, my Lord?"

The Senate was still the legislative body and the official Treasurer of the Empire. All revenue actions needed to be cleared through the Senate. Although once it was once a small deliberative body made up of thirty wealthy patricians from the city of Rome, it now had over three-hundred voting members. Also, several of those Senators were at political odds with both the Emperor and with other competing political affiliations within the Senate membership.

With this response, Valentinian became enraged – with his reddened complexion perfectly matching his royal purple cloak. I was somewhat afraid he might soon have a stroke.

He said, "Are you out of your goddamn mind, General? What, you suggest I should ask the Senate for more money? Those sorry bastards barely give me the time of day, and they can barely reach a quorum among themselves even on a mundane subject. When the Empire was expanding, and our armies could secure booty from our new territories, money was never a problem."

He stopped speaking, slowly looked around the room, nodded at his political and economic advisers, and continued, "However, we're losing territory now – thanks to your Legions' inefficiency and complacency, and your command's gross leadership problems. Tax collections are drying up faster than Lake Regillus."

Aëtius just looked at him without responding. Valentinian continued, "General, there's simply no extra money in the treasury to fund these campaigns. Tariffs and import taxes dried up once we lost the grain fields of North Africa to the Vandals. You wouldn't know much about that, would you, my dear general?"

Try as he might, Valentinian could not get Aëtius to react. The Emperor continued, "All of which is due, if I may add, to your Legions' almost comical inability to defend the Western Empire. By comparison, the Eastern Empire isn't losing its traditional land, import tariffs, and property taxes because of their failures and gross incompetence. Are they General? However, we, here in the Western Empire, are stuck with the likes of you and your feeble-minded confederates. However, all of us already know these facts. Don't we, General?"

Once again the Emperor sought the nods of approval from his general staff members. Upon receiving them, he resumed his verbal attack on Master General Aëtius. "We've devalued the national currency three times in the past decade, and because of this action, inflation has soared sky-high like a Roman Eagle. The Senate has taxed and taxed local businesses to the point where the owners have closed their shops and left the cities in droves."

Valentinian was red in the face. Pounding his right fist on the table top, he said, "Let me tell you a sad story, General. Five years ago, the Senate was persuaded by my government to levy a reasonable tax on the wealthy landowners, only to be subsequently voted out of office by their constituents – and the tax was rescinded quickly by the new incumbents."

I feared he might explode. He was visibly shaking and pacing slowly around the room; I was afraid he'd soon pound a wall or toss a vase. After a few moments, he shook his head and continued, "No, they won't attempt that again; and raising taxes to fund the invasion may have been our only reasonable source of additional domestic revenue. No, it's not an option. Christ, this is so goddamn frustrating!"

The Emperor shook his head a couple more times and replied, "My dear Master General, I'm afraid you'll have to save the Empire with the Legions you have left. Are there any other options you can offer me now, General Aëtius?"

For a short time, Aëtius stood silent – waiting for the Emperor to cool down. Then, looking directly at the Valentinian, he spoke in a quiet but firm voice, "Majesty, Rome still has one significant asset – with an exercise option which remains entirely within your sole command and control – which we can still utilize to help expel the barbarians. That's, land – hundreds of thousands of acres of available land – solely held in your name in Gaul, Belgica, and Hispania."

Once again, Aëtius stopped speaking for an instant, looked briefly at me, and continued, "Majesty, grant me the authority to negotiate directly with King Theodoric to encourage the Visigoths to join us in a joint military endeavor. I can also bargain with the Burgundians and other tribes, and I can persuade them to join our coalition."

Then he looked at Aegidius, Ricimer and me for our silent acquiescence. Upon seeing our nods of approval, he said, "If I can obtain King Theodoric's pledge of support, the Burgundians and some of the other tribes will probably follow suit. Majesty, they surely know they'll perish under a coalition between Attila and Gaiseric."

"You want me to give away more land, is it?"

"Yes, Majesty. To convince them to join us, I'll need to offer them something tangible – additional territory – in exchange for their services."

The Emperor seemed to understand this approach was the only realistic course of action to avert disaster. Slowly nodding his head affirmatively, I could tell he agreed with Aëtius' plan.

A few moments later, Aëtius concluded, "United as a cohesive fighting force, we might just be able to crush Attila before he can merge with Gaiseric. If, however, the Huns and Vandals join forces before we can defeat Attila, then all of Gaul, Hispania, and Belgica are doomed to fall from Imperial control. In that case, we'll be lucky to keep Italia and Dalmatia in our hands without additional Legions from the Eastern Empire."

Silently, Valentinian looked down for a few moments, and looking up, he again nodded his head in apparent approval.

"Our land is not inexhaustible, General. Please use it sparingly and efficiently."

CHAPTER V

The Catalaunian Plains, Gaul — June 21, 451

Master General Aëtius was as good as his word. In a short period of time, he was able to build an impressive coalition of barbarian partners totaling a combined army of almost 50,000 men. Utilizing his three Legions (approximately 25,000 Roman soldiers) as the primary battle force, Aëtius added teams of auxiliary military troops consisting of veteran mercenaries from the Visigoths, Burgundians, Britons, Saxons, and Alans. Although each one of the barbarian tribes formed its own regiment, Aëtius retained overall tactical control of these combined forces.

His enemy, Attila, commanded his personal army of 35,000 men along with the added armed contingents from the Ostrogoths, Rugians, Scirii, Franks, Thuringians, Bastarnae, Alemanni, Gepids, and Heruli tribes. His opposing forces equaled a total of about 55,000 men. However, they were ill-provisioned and far away from home, living mostly on what they could loot. To the contrary, the Romans and their confederates were well-supplied and close to home.

At the last possible moment, Aëtius was able to save Aurelianum from ruin. Attila's men breached the city walls during the previous day and were beginning to ransack the western portion of the city. As Aëtius' combined forces arrived on the hills surrounding the eastern side of the city, Attila quickly abandoned Aurelianum to seek a more advantageous location to fight the ensuing battle on the Catalaunian Plains.

The battlefield, the site of the ensuing fight, was located approximately twenty miles west of the city and was dominated by sharp slopes on its flanks which led to an impressive ridge. This ridge later became the central geographical objective of the mêlée; the forces which could control the ridge would be victorious.

To this day, I can remember the tragic and the heroic events of the bloody two-day engagement which followed. Arriving first, Attila seized the right flank of the ridge. Shortly after that, Aëtius' forces captured the left side. As the mêlée unfolded, both forces battled unsuccessfully to seize the high land in the unoccupied middle expanse between them.

Along the course of our strategic lines, the Visigoths were located on the northern flank. The Imperial forces defended the southern side, and the other allied tribes were situated together as a fighting group in the middle portion. On the front lines, the clash was bloody, brutal, and merciless resulting in a vicious and immobile stand-off. The Roman lines arched and curled, split apart, and then surged together again. As night fell on the battlefield after the first day of fighting, neither force had gained the upper hand; it was a draw.

On the morning of the second day, Aëtius ordered the Visigoth cavalry to circumvent Attila's defensive lines and attack them directly from the rear. In a coordinated and simultaneous effort, Aëtius and the other allied tribes mounted a fierce frontal attack on the Hun's defensive front lines. Short of provisions and exhausted from the carnage from the first day of the fight, Attila ultimately became trapped inside the confines of the Hun camp. Unable to mount an effective counterattack, Attila chose to break through the Gothic cavalry assault and retreat from the battlefield.

Commanding the VII Legion during the two-day engagement, my troops sustained an eighty-percent causality rate. Ricimer (leading the VI Legion) and Aegidius (commanding of the XXII Legion) suffered similar tragic losses. Attila's combined forces were likewise decimated.

Although our victory came at a steep price, we prevented the merger of Attila's forces with Gaiseric's Vandal army of over 30,000 men. A combined barbarian army would've been virtually unstoppable. Following the battle, Aëtius estimated his combined force sustained well over 25,000 casualties, including two of Rome's key confederates, King Theodoric of the Visigoths and King Plasurque of the Saxons.

With these crippling and devastating military losses, Aëtius was unable to mount an effective counterattack to annihilate the remainder of the invading forces. Attila, while defeated, was not vanquished. He'd live to fight another day. That day would come eventually but not without Rome paying yet another horrifying price in both blood and treasure.

Following the conclusion of the battle on the Catalaunian Plains, the remnants of the VII and XXII Legions slowly crept back into Aurelianum. This time there was no victory parade or viewing stands to cheer on our valiant warriors.

A majority of the citizens had fled the city to avoid the brunt of Attila's savage attack, and only a few residents were present to view the pitiful residue of the once gallant Legions slowly enter Aurelianum and secure the city gates and battlements.

There was even greater sorrow in Tolosa, the capital of the Visigoths. The newly-crowned King Thorismund, the oldest son, and successor of King Theodoric brought the lifeless body of their beloved former King home to a funeral pyre.

As soon as he was able to regroup, Ricimer, in command of the VI Legion, was tasked with the responsibility to shadow the retreating Huns until they slipped across the Rhine River and exited Roman territory. Once the border was secured and stabilized, Ricimer and what was left of his command withdrew to Treverorum to consolidate his forces. In the meantime, Aëtius took a small contingent of armed cavalry and returned to Ravenna to report to Emperor Valentinian.

A few days following the military engagement, I led a cohort of troops back to the Catalaunian Plains where we removed the bodies of our dead soldiers from the field. What had remained before our eyes was a grisly scene of blood, death, and destruction; a sight I'll never forget. Occasionally, we located a couple of combatants lying on the field of battle who were still holding on to life. Those fighters whom could not be helped were quickly dispatched.

Also, we gathered up the salvageable armaments, uniforms, and supplies, along with a few of our wounded soldiers. As a result, we carried several wagons full of useful material back to Aurelianum to help replenish our storehouses.

After a couple of weeks of refurbishment and healing in Aurelianum, I led the residue of the VII Legion back to our permanent quarters at Camp Aurelius Aegidius remained with the XXIII Legion to secure and rebuild Aurelianum. As a result of our Pyrrhic victory, the Western Empire was safe for now.

In the months immediately following the battle, I was plagued with a series of gruesome nightmares. While the particulars of each dream often differed, the chaotic scene in my mind remained the same. I was commanding my troops and helplessly watching as they were being butchered by the advancing barbarian invaders.

During these dreams, I could clearly hear their cries of pain and their pleadings for reinforcements, and I could visualize the chaos and confusion of the battlefield before me. In one dream, a veritable sea of blood was enveloping me. In another version, the barbarian attackers – portrayed vividly in my dream as menacing giants – were ready to devour me.

Sometimes my *aide-de-camp* would hear me screaming in my sleep and rush to my side. At other times, I'd awake from the nightmare in a cold sweat and lie in my damp bed for hours before sleep took me the rest of the way to morning.

As the ensuing days and weeks passed, many more of the soldiers in my command either died from their wounds or were released from military duty due to physical or mental disabilities. Soon, however, the remaining soldiers began performing the customary duties of Imperial soldiers while assigned to garrison – drilling, building, patrolling, and parading – and after a couple more months, life returned to a new normalcy.

Occasionally, new conscripts were added to our decimated ranks, and by early autumn, the size of the VII Legion grew to approximately thirty-five percent of its former strength. Although not battle-ready, our functional capability was adequate to protect Camp Aurelius from small bands of marauders or minor uprisings, and we were fully able to patrol and police the immediate surrounding area.

Placing my command in the talented hands of my Chief of Staff, Antoninus Lucan Agrippa, I took leave of my command in late September to rejoin my family in Nemausus and to ponder my future.

CHAPTER VI

Nemausus — October, 451 AD

Octavia was twenty-seven years old then. To me, she was even more beautiful than she was on the day I married her. As she matured over the ensuing nine years, her figure filled out to the point where she was, at the same time, more feminine and more voluptuous; and I loved her dearly.

Moreover, her smile came quicker, and she seemed more confident with herself, and the sweet aura of love appeared to pour out of her like an overflowing water-cistern during the springtime rains. Our union produced four children – Julius, Minerva, Claudius, and Caspian. Each of them was healthy, playful, and curious about the life which surrounded them. Sadly, my mother died in 447 AD, and by the autumn of 451, my father's days were clearly numbered.

It was early October, and the days were growing shorter as we approached the winter solstice. The weather had cooled considerably from the warm days of August, and the autumn rains began in earnest. The deciduous trees in our garden were in a full fall splendor, and a bright-orange harvest moon was slowly rising in the eastern sky.

Entering our bedchamber one evening, I noticed Octavia had lit the candles, and the bedcovers were pulled slightly over to the side. She held my hand firmly as we sat down on our bed. "Jul, I want to have one more child."

I couldn't tell whether it was a statement or a request. We both knew what happened previously, as she nearly died while giving birth to Caspian, our two-year-old boy-devil.

Looking deeply into her eyes, I replied, "Didn't the physician tell us that you shouldn't have any more children? Caspian's birth almost killed you, and you're now two years older. Do you think it's wise to try again?"

She pulled her hair over her left shoulder and gently stroked the side of my face with her right hand and replied, "I've fully recovered, and I'm much stronger now. Caspian's birth was difficult because it closely followed the birth of

Claudius. Having two big baby boys in successive years was just too much for me."

She stroked my cheek, looked into her lap, and said, "I'm ready now for one more child, and my body tells me that I'm fertile tonight. Let's place our fate in God's hands."

She kissed me passionately on my mouth, and rising slowly from the bed, she untied her sash and let her nightgown drop to the floor. Turning slightly away from me, she leaned over to blow out the candles on our sideboard.

"Don't blow out the glows." I implored, "Please let me look at you for a while."

Bashfully, she dropped her eyes to the floor, as if embarrassed by her nudity. She turned around, looked up, and gazed straight into my eyes, and I spent the next several moments admiring her magnificent nakedness.

She asked, "Which side of me do you find the most pleasing – the front or the back?"

"All of you; I love all of you."

Despite having four children, her body was still statuesque. Her skin was lily-white – as if she never ventured out into the sunlight – and her long brown hair was soft and silky as it fell over her right shoulder, barely covering her breast. Her legs were long and smooth, and her navel turned in ever so slightly. In the moonlight, she was far lovelier than any statue of Venus or Helen that I'd ever seen.

Moreover, she was all mine. Guardedly, I nodded; implicitly agreeing to her prior request. She turned away from me once again, blew out the candles, and lay down closely beside me on our bed.

Twice during the night, she woke me, and twice again, we joined together as one human entity. As the morning light entered our room, we had one last moment of intimacy. Later on at breakfast, she smiled at me in a way I'll always remember; as if she was telling me that I'd soon become a father again.

As the weeks passed, I began recovering emotionally from the hidden scars I received from the battle on the Catalaunian Plains. When I first arrived home on leave, my children could sense the stress I carried, and they kept an emotional distance from me. But slowly my mood began to change, and soon my head wasn't boiling over with military strategies, tactical maneuvers, and battle lines. My children noticed the positive change first, and soon I was no longer a stranger to them.

"I have my man back," Octavia told me one Sunday morning. "I wasn't sure I'd ever see you this way again."

She was right. I was calming down. Suddenly, the little noises and shadows didn't startle me as much. I was feeling slower, stronger, and self-assured. My stomach was not perpetually tightened, my pulse rate had diminished, and I no longer felt like I was on the verge of a light sweat.

Moreover, I realized for the first time in a while how different I was in Nemausus and around my family. I began to think differently; I no longer looked for the easy solutions to complex situations, and the feeling of uttermost dread was slowly dissipating. Moreover, I felt alive again.

As we entered the middle weeks of October, I continued to notice the inevitable change of seasons. The skies were greyer, and the sure signs of winter were quickly approaching Nemausus.

Sitting alone in my garden one late afternoon, I realized I had burnt myself out. The strength and enthusiasm I'd once felt for military life were gone, and there was nothing left. Furthermore, my expectations for the future were changing, and I realized it was time to make some important decisions regarding what to do next with my life.

A few days later, Octavia and I gathered up our children, and we drove our carriage out to one of our tenant farms located a short distance south of the city to enjoy a picnic lunch with Felix, Irena, and their kids. The weather was still warm, and as the children played together on the lawn, the four of us talked about the harvest and the coming of winter.

Later, Felix and I climbed to the top of a hill to look at the scenery unfolding below us. From the crest, we could see the whole valley. The October sun was hanging low on the horizon, and the countryside was brilliant in autumn colors. For a while, Felix and I sat together silently – sharing a bottle of wine. Although we later talked about our families and the complexities of the Roman world, my thoughts were of the future; what would I do next in my life?

In early November, I went to visit my father at his home on Tiberius Street. An older-appearing Josiah met me at the door and ushered me to the atrium where my father was seated in the afternoon sun. Shortly after my mother's death, he resigned his position as Minister of Finance and took over the responsibility of running the household and our tenant farms located in the nearby countryside. I'd come to seek his advice about my future.

"Father, I'm thinking about resigning my commission and placing my name in nomination for a seat in the Senate. I've come to ask your advice."

Just at that moment, Josiah came into the atrium carrying two cups of a warm ginger cider. My father took a sip, thanked Josiah, and responded, "Does your decision have anything to do with the battle on the Catalaunian Plains?"

I nodded affirmatively. "Yes, certainly in part. While the nightmares have diminished somewhat, they are still troublesome. It's time for me to seek out other options."

"What options?"

"Well, let me start with the army. With Aëtius remaining in command of the Western Legions, I've risen as far as I can in military service."

"But is it a good time to resign your commission?"

"Yes, I think so, Father. The Emperor doesn't have the resources to rebuild the army to its former strength, and Rome still has three other talented field generals in Ricimer, Marcellinus, and Aegidius to defend the Western Empire with what remains of our remaining forces. But we may have one too many generals right now."

I stopped for an instant and took a sip of cider, "My children are growing up, but I barely know them. Father, I never planned to make the military my career. I think it's time for me to leave."

He reflected for a moment and asked, "I know the battle took an enormous toll on the Legions. How vulnerable are we now?"

"Well, we're in pretty bad shape, and Attila has escaped our grasp. I assume he'll rebuild his forces and come after us once again someday soon, maybe next summer. Furthermore, Gaiseric knows we've lost considerable capability, and I suspect he'll make another move on the Empire shortly, too."

"So, I'll ask you again; is this the right time to leave the service of Rome, my son?"

It was a question I'd pondered over and over. "Father, I don't think my staying or leaving the Legion will have much of an impact on Rome's future."

"No, why not?"

I told him that without additional men and arms from the Senate or substantial support from Constantinople, the legions' capability to protect the Western Empire had significantly diminished. I pointed out while we retained the capacity to put out minor fires in the provinces, the legions would be unable to respond effectively to major uprisings or massive invasions.

"For the Western Empire to survive much longer, Aëtius will have to continue to muster military support from our barbarian partners in exchange for more Roman territory." I explained, "Right now, only Aëtius has the political influence and personality to form new alliances. I can do much more to help Aëtius and Valentinian in the Senate than on the battlefield."

My father smiled. "Well, I believe you've already made up your mind." I smiled and nodded my head.

For another hour or so, my father and I talked about politics, religion, and most preciously, our time together when I was a young boy. It was always the best part of my visits – the spontaneity, the humor, and the intellectual challenges. Most importantly, I felt the love between a father and his devoted son. I still miss him so much even after all these years.

As the afternoon wore on, I could tell he was tiring. Kissing him on the forehead as I left, I returned home to Octavia and the children. It was one of the last times I ever saw him.

I returned to Camp Aurelius four days later to initiate my separation from military service. My Chief of Staff, Antonius Lucan Agrippa, did not seem surprised at my decision. Shaking my hand, he said: "We'll miss you, Sir. Rome is forever in your debt. What will you do next, Sir?"

Tribune Agrippa was a promising young officer. He reminded me of a similar young man who reported for duty in June 442 AD, and I prayed he'd have a long and illustrious career. Unfortunately, he died heroically in battle the following spring when Attila crossed the Rhine and attacked Italia.

"First, I need to take care of some urgent family business, and then I may try my hand at politics."

He nodded approvingly, and after a short pause, he asked, "Shall I gather the men, Sir?"

"Yes, I need to need to say my farewells."

Although it occurred many years ago, I can still recall much of my brief remarks to those brave survivors of the battle on the Catalaunian Plains. Tribune Agrippa called the men into a formation, and then standing on a raised platform on the drill field, I addressed my troops for the final time.

"After nearly six years as your commander, I've decided to surrender my commission and seek out other ways of serving Rome away from the battlefield. Throughout our many campaigns in Gaul, Belgica, Hispania, and elsewhere, you've steadfastly displayed unsurpassed courage, fortitude, and resilience; often against overwhelming forces and resources. You, my beloved VII Legion, have shown like a beacon in the night. In the name of Rome, you ferociously took the fight to our enemies and triumphed."

Briefly stopping to regain my composure, I continued, "It isn't necessary for me to reiterate the stories and accounts of our hard-fought campaigns, to remind you of your wounds and your sacrifices, or to mention your losses in terms of friends, comrades, and above all, your innocence. You hold these memories deep in your souls."

Turning away, I looked at the autumn covered hills beyond our camp for a moment. Facing my men one more time, I concluded. "You will always command a deep and abiding place in my heart. Wherever my journeys will take me, I will forever tell my family and my colleagues of your triumphs, struggles, and glories. I will always hold you – the officers and men of the VII Legion – deep in my heart. Farewell."

At first, there was silence as many of them looked at each other wordlessly. We'd fought the Franks along the Rhine, the Vandals in Hibernia, and the Bagaudae in Belgica. We'd fought together from Germania to Hispania.

Then all of a sudden, the men of the VII Legion roared their approval, and lifting their spear shafts and raising their chins ferociously, they began striking their shields hard against their armored knee-plates — the highest tribute they can bestow on their commander. The sound was overwhelming. Tears formed in my eyes and I thought I'd go deaf as the racket rang out on the drill field and throughout Camp Aurelius.

Upon leaving the grandstand, I rode out of Camp Aurelius for the last time and traveled to Aurelianum to meet with General Aegidius. He was thirty-seven years old: tall and hearty, with a sturdy chest and piercing eyes. His hair was dark brown, with early streaks of grey, which tumbled off his brow and curled richly on his shoulders like a pile of autumn leaves blown slowly by the wind. Solely on merit, courage under fire, and hard work, he rose steadily through the ranks from a junior officer to the position of a field general.

He listened carefully to my reasons for surrendering my command and commission, and upon concurring with my assessment of Rome's immediate needs for military resources, he agreed to handle the matter for me with Aëtius and Valentinian.

Putting on my battle uniform one last time, I rode back to the Catalaunian Plains with a small group of soldiers. I was amazed at what I saw there. The battlefield was picked clean by scavengers — birds, animals, and humans — so the site of the ghastly horror was almost unrecognizable to me. In the five months which elapsed since the conclusion of hostilities, the local farmers returned, plowed the fields, planted wheat and barley, and were busy harvesting their crops.

Although there was almost no trace left of the battle, I was able to locate the precise location of our last (and ultimately successful) stand against Attila's final assault. Dismounting and getting down on one knee, I wept bitterly at the reminiscence of the slaughter which occurred before my eyes during those two fateful days in June. Making my peace with God and with my fellow slain comrades, I arose from this hallowed ground and rode back to Aurelianum to surrender my sword, crest, and ampule.

Within a few months of my departure from military service, the VII Legion was formally dissolved. The remnants of my previous command were attached to the XXIII Legion under the authority of General Aegidius. Thus, the long and storied history of the VII Legion – the once-legendary Legio VII Claudia Pia Fidelis – ended as a mere footnote in history books.

Shortly after I returned to Nemausus, I filed the proper papers with the city government to place my name in nomination for the Senate. Our city magistrate, Tiberius Nerva Cinterro, possessed the authority to choose our region's representative in Rome, and his selection would be made in January. With my military background and family connections, I believed I'd have a good chance of being selected.

Established around 700 BC, the Roman Senate, or Curia, remained the world's oldest continuously serving deliberative body. In its traditional role, the Senate sent and received ambassadors, appointed officials to manage and govern the provinces, declared war, and negotiated peace treaties and alliances. Most importantly, the Senate appropriated funds for public use. Although the Senate could not propose legislation, the chamber had the authority to approve or disapprove bills proposed by the Emperor, a provincial consul, or a private citizen.

Since the time of Emperor Augustus, the membership of the Senate was limited to three-hundred members who served for renewable two-year terms. While all Senators must be citizens, many of the incumbents arose from provincial aristocracies whose ancestors may have fought against Rome at an earlier time.

A week after I received my appointment to the Senate in late January, 452, Josiah unexpectedly knocked on the door of our home. There were tears in the old man's eyes. "Sir, you need to come to your father's house immediately," he implored. "Please hurry, Sir."

My father was dying. As I sat by his bedside and as I held his hand, I talked to him as he went in and out of consciousness. Although I was unsure whether he could hear me, I told him my favorite memories about growing up in Nemausus, my time in Rome while attending the Academy, and my many years away in the service of the Western Empire. At appropriate intervals, Octavia and my children, and my brothers, sisters and their families came to his room and made their tearful farewells.

When he was able, he gave us specific instructions concerning the disposition of his property, a summary of his achievements and perceived failures, and his hopes for his children and his grandchildren. In the late afternoon, Archbishop Paulus Octavius Oronoco came into my father's bedchamber to hear his final confession and to administer the last rites. By the time the Archbishop left my father's bedchamber, any hope for his recovery had been abandoned.

Early in the evening, he awoke from an interrupted sleep, looked at me, and smiled. After briefly gazing around the room at the family and mourners who assembled at his bedside, he breathed his last breath. My father was gone.

For a moment there was silence in his bedchamber, and then I heard a sound arising out of me which I'd never heard before. Coming from the depths of my soul, I uttered an ancient, primeval sound of both grief and terror.

I collapsed on my father's chest and wept for a long time. Even to this day, I experience a sense of intense pain and loneliness as I relive the loss of the man who was most central to my life. He was my father, my mentor, my best friend, and my confidant. His role has never been eclipsed or replaced.

After I closed his eyes and kissed him one last time, the attendants removed his body from his bed, washed him, and anointed him in the old traditional way. While my family, like many Romans, was fully Christianized, we held on to many of the ancient rituals, rites, and ceremonies.

In keeping with the old custom, the attendants dressed my father in his finest toga and placed a wreath on his head. After that, he lay in state in the atrium of his home for eight days – with his feet pointed toward the door. A 'Charon's obol' was placed on his mouth, which was meant to be used as a payment to the mythical oarsman, Charon, who would ferry my father across the water which separated the land of living from the world of the dead.

Following the conclusion of the eight-day period of mourning, my father's body was carried by a wagon to the Church of St. Perpetua, formerly the Temple of Gaius Caesar, for sanctification. It was also the last day I'd ever see Master General Aëtius alive. Following the blessing of the body and the prayers of salvation and deliverance, Aëtius stood up and spoke in glowing terms of his longtime Minister of Finance.

He began, "I've loved few men in my life, and none more than Claudius Gaius Donnimus." He reminisced about their twenty-five-year alliance, my father's expertise and loyalty, and his lifelong service to Rome. Finally, it was my turn to speak.

Dressed now in the attire of a Senator of Rome, I cleared my throat and began the eulogy: "My father was a noble Roman. He was born in the final days of the rule of Emperor Theodosius the Great, and he was the son and grandson of generals. As a boy growing up in the Capitol, my father heard magnificent stories from visitors and merchants who gathered from all over the civilized world. He dreamed of all the places he'd visit one day: a noble Roman."

"After receiving his commission in the Legions, he served for ten years as an officer on the general staff of Master General Stilicho, and he fought gallantly for Rome in many far-off places throughout the Empire, such as in Dacia, Thrace, Germania, and Hispania: a noble Roman."

"He was a husband, father, brother, grandfather, uncle, and a trusted friend who served as an example to everyone whom he encountered: a noble Roman."

"He told me a man's best memorial to his wife was their children: a noble Roman."

"He was a man who gladly shed his blood and valiantly fought our enemies with all his strength and intellect: a noble Roman."

"And after leaving the legions, he continued to serve the Emperor for over twenty-five years while in the service of our beloved Master General Aëtius – long after my father's body grew too old and too feeble to fight on the battle-field: a noble Roman."

Standing on the top step of the ancient church, I stopped speaking for a moment and looked out at the large crowd who assembled in the plaza below.

Feeling intense sadness at the sight of my father's body lying in state just before my podium, I took a deep breath and continued my eulogy. "I remember as a child, he told me never to be satisfied by success or discouraged by failure; rather, each instance of life contained a message for me to learn. He said the worst sadness in life is not failing, but rather, not trying. He admonished me to reach for the heavens, and to dream of making our world a better place: a noble Roman."

As a tear rolled down my cheek, I concluded, "Strong, valiant, unafraid of failure, and unbending in his beliefs, my father lived each day as if it was his last day on earth. He was my hero, my inspiration, my best friend, and my confidant. He was a noble Roman."

After I sat down next to Octavia and my children, a priest came forward, anointed my father's body with holy oils. The priest walked slowly around the casket seven times, swinging a small ampoule of holy incense and chanting the prayers of repose and sanctification.

When the officiant concluded the final benediction, the pallbearers stood up, lifted my father's coffin from the stand, placed it firmly on a cart, and wheeled his remains a short distance to the funeral hall, which was located directly behind the church. As he was finally laid to rest in the family crypt next to my mother, his soul began its celestial journey.

Traditional Roman belief holds that the soul is immortal, and following a person's death, the soul will be judged before an appropriate tribunal. The virtuous will be sent to Elysian Fields for rest and repose, a celestial banquet, and amalgamation with the gods. Those few men who had lived extraordinary lives, such as Augustus, Hadrian, and Scipio, would become gods themselves.

Those who lived a wicked life, however, are directed to the nether world called Tartarus to suffer eternal chastisement. Virgil describes this place in *The Aeneid* as a gigantic place deep inside the earth, surrounded by the flaming River Phlegethon and with triple walls to prevent sinners from escaping.

As the Empire became slowly Christianized, the fundamental dogmas changed slightly to refer to the places of everlasting duration as heaven and hell. The Church also adopted the belief that the greatest of the deceased mortals are elevated to sainthood. Although the official religion of the Empire changed from being pagan to Christianity, many of the underlying philosophies remained mostly the same.

Later that evening, I met with Aëtius for the final time. He looked weary, and there seems to be something pressing on his mind. After presenting my family with condolences and personal messages from Ricimer, Aegidius, and others, he turned to the business of the Empire.

He said, "Although we walloped Attila on the Catalaunian Plains, he was able to limp away across the Rhine. Presently, Ricimer is shadowing him, and we fully expect Hunnic invasion come springtime. If Attila's forces grow much larger in strength, we may not contain him. Jul, the Empire is in great jeopardy and could fall."

I shook my head in disbelief. Could this result possibly be true? A few moments later, Aëtius continued, "If that's not bad enough, King Gaiseric and the Vandals are consolidating their presence in North Africa. We think they'll soon cross the Straits of Gibraltar and enter Southern Hispania. Thus, we may face a two-pronged attack."

"Can it be that bad, Sir?"

Aëtius looked around to see if anyone was listening to us. "Yes, it is. The area from Cyrenaica to the Straits contains some of the richest and most fertile lands in the Empire. We need to retake these provinces soon so the grains and taxes, which we desperately need, are funneled back into the Empire. Unfortunately, we cannot exist much longer without the Port of Carthage under our control."

"Sir, I understand Carthage is the key to revitalizing the Western Empire."

He asked, "Have you ever been to Carthage?"

"No, Sir."

Aëtius looked down, took a deep breath, and slowly shook his head. "On many occasions, I've seen the splendor of Carthage first hand. I can't begin to express how deeply I love the city and its rich heritage. It has the best harbor in Africa – perhaps in the entire Mare Nostrum. Did you know the port can easily handle a thousand ships a day?"

"That's a lot, Sir."

"Yes, it is, and the harbor is splendid – beautifully proportioned with massive marble monuments from as far back as the Phoenician times. You know, it's even more breathtaking than Alexandria, and from its docks and anchorages, Carthage used to ship well over a half a million tons of grain per year into Ostia. Jul, we must take it back. We must take it back soon."

I remained silent – just trying to imagine Carthage and the province of Mauretania.

Then he said, "Africa is one of the most advanced areas of the world. Not many people know that the region around Carthage contains over twelve-hundred miles of paved roads, vast irrigation networks, and lush green valleys. Before the Vandals' invasion, we only needed one Legion to secure the entire region from Leptis Magnus all the way to Volubilis. By contrast, Syria and Palestina need four Legions."

Once again, I shook my head and replied, "How can I help, sir?"

He smiled, "Can you convince the Senate – better yet Valentinian himself – to try to secure military troops and revenue from Constantinople? We're in bad shape – as you well know. Even now, I cannot pay our soldiers on a regular basis – much less convince barbarian armies to come to Rome's assistance again. Yes, we are in dire need, my friend. The Senate needs to allocate some more money to ensure the Legions' survival."

"I report to the Senate in two weeks. I'll do my best, Sir. You have my word."

Aëtius smiled, patted me on the shoulder, looked around once more to ensure nobody was overhearing our conversation, and said, "Then there's the matter of Valentinian. He's getting much harder to work with. I know you remember well his madness in Ravenna last May. Without a doubt, he's been getting worse every month. Julius, and I say this confidentially, one day we might have to, umm, neutralize him. Of course, I'm talking treason. Can I count on your support?"

Somewhat in a state of shock, I slowly nodded my head affirmatively and replied, "Yes."

Although we talked another twenty minutes about my father, our battles in the name of Rome, and our dreams for the future, I couldn't dismiss his suggestion of high treason. After I embraced him and shook his hand one last time, he walked out into the Nemausus night. I never saw him again.

However, his reference to "treason" haunted me for a long, long time.

CHAPTER VII

The City of Rome – April 452

Traveling to Rome by boat, I left Octavia and our family in Nemausus. Serving as a senator was only a part-time job, and I didn't wish to uproot my family from the usual routine of their daily lives in Gaul. However, I missed my family immensely.

I arrived in Ostia, the Port of Rome, shortly after sunrise on the 12th of April, and I marveled at the vast stone warehouses and mighty wharves of this bustling anchorage. It was a bright morning, and the ship shuddered as it struck against the pilings at our berth in the harbor. I'd not been to Ostia since I graduated from the Academy.

There was a cavalcade of activity going on before my eyes. The shipwrights, chandlers, caulkers, sailmakers, and carpenters were arriving for another day's work. Merchants and traders from all over the Empire were selling their cargoes of grain, cotton, linens, marble, and spices.

Stevedores and sailors, speaking in dozens of languages, were likely giving orders, taking orders, or exchanging information on prices, weather conditions, pirates, politics, and the latest gossip. Slaves were busy unloading shipments from the arriving boats, and local tax collectors and customs agents were boarding the vessels to calculate tariffs and to guarantee the validity of their manifests.

Upon disembarking my ship, passing through the military checkpoints, and gathering up my meager belongings, I quickly found a man with a small cart who agreed to transport me north to Rome. It took me a moment or two to become used to the steadiness of land after three days at sea, but once I boarded the cart, I settled down for the twenty-mile journey to the former Capitol of the Empire.

Driving up the heavily rutted Via Ostiensis, I was amazed by the types and sizes of the loads of imported trade which were heading toward the city. On every side of me, carts creaked and rattled. Almost ten years had passed since I last rode up to the Eternal City, and with every passing mile, I could see prosperity and commerce still thrived in this part of Italia.

As the springtime day was winding down, my driver crested a long hill, and we stopped for a view of the city. My first glimpse of Rome that afternoon was both startling and magnificent. Stretching out in front of me for seemingly endless miles under a blue sky, the grand and ancient city emerged.

The panoramic scene almost took my breath away. I saw the finest villas were built on the surrounding hillsides, and I noticed how the Tiber River stretched out like a silver thread of blue and sparkle as it meandered like a snake through the vast metropolis. A few miles ahead of us, between the Vatican and Janiculum Hills, I could see the outline of Hadrian's Tomb at the bend of the Tiber River.

While gazing at the view, I recalled Emperor Hadrian constructed the Imperial mausoleum in 139 AD, and there lay his remains and those of several of his succeeding emperors and royal families. In 217 AD, the shrine was full and subsequently sealed following the burial of Emperor Caracalla. Almost silently, I uttered the old pagan prayer, "May the earth rest lightly on them."

Coming down the hill by way of the Cornelian Way, we crisscrossed through Agrippina's Gardens to the intersection with the Via Triumphalis. Taking the road, and passing by the marble Pyramid of Caius Cestius, we entered the city walls through the Aurelian Gate, a massive edifice made of tan Etruscan marble.

Once we were passed under the gate, the scope of the massive city was dazzling. Suddenly, temples, theaters, arches, and statues were positioned everywhere. Nowhere in the Empire – except maybe in Athens or Constantinople – could one see such an impressive sight. The street was paved with granite and was so wide fifty citizens, standing abreast, could pass by at the same time without touching. And the entire area surrounding me was mobbed with people, animals, and noise. The sound was almost deafening – joyous and threatening at the same time.

On our way winding toward the north, we circumvented the Circus Maximus, passed the Septizodium (named for the seven planetary deities, Saturn, Sun, Moon, Mars, Mercury, Jupiter, and Venus), and rode under the Acqua Claudia Aqueduct all the way to the Flavian Amphitheatre. Circling the arena to the right, my driver finally dropped me off at Trajan's Baths where I'd reside until I found a permanent place to live.

During my years serving in the Senate, I often took the trip from Nemausus to Rome. However, I always marveled at the beauty and magnificence upon my return to the Eternal City.

Although no longer the Capitol of the Western Empire, Rome was still its principal religious and spiritual center. And oh, what a splendid sight it was to behold! Everywhere I looked when walking around the city, was the evidence of its splendor.

In 330 AD, the Emperor Constantine ordered an inventory of the buildings and monuments within the Capitol. The resulting document reflected Rome had, among other things, forty triumphal arches, twelve forums, twenty-eight public libraries, twenty-five basilicas, one-thousand bathhouses, one hundred temples, fifteen Egyptian obelisks, and sadly, forty-six brothels. It was the wonder of the world!

Eleven aqueducts – some well over sixty miles long – supplied water to the bathhouses and over 1350 strect fountains. Also, the general populace was spectacularly entertained at four amphitheaters (including the Flavian Amphitheatre, which held over 50,000 spectators), three hippodromes for chariot races (one facility capable of holding over 400,000 people) and four large public theaters (the largest, the Theatre of Pompey, had over 25,000 seats).

And despite the fact the city was still teeming with well over five-hundred thousand inhabitants in 452 AD (down from one and a half million during Emperor Trajan's reign), I was thrilled to see acres of public parks, woodlands, and open areas surrounding the churches, public baths, and grand monuments. In addition, most of the private buildings were painted white with red terracotta rooftops. Even in decline, it was such a beautiful city!

The sack of the city of Rome in 410 by Alaric and the Visigoths was gradually fading from the memory of the inhabitants. Thankfully, Alaric did not destroy the Holy Places, such as the tombs of Saints Peter and Paul, or level the massive Aurelian Wall, which was subsequently restored and refortified. Even with the passage of forty years, the city hadn't completely recaptured the might and magnificence of his former self when it was undisputed the Capitol of the civilized world.

After a two-week search, I finally purchased an apartment in a small building located near the Theatre of Marcellus. It was a short pleasant walk from my flat to the Forum where the Senate House, also known as the Curia Julia, stood.

The Curia Julia, originally an Etruscan temple constructed in the late fifth century BC, was rebuilt by Emperor Diocletian in 305 AD following a devastating fire. Despite its importance in the overall management of the Western Empire, the interior of the Senate building was surprisingly austere. The building enclosed three rows of seats encircling the inner chamber with seating capacity for up to three-hundred Senators. To establish a quorum, a minimum of fifty senators must be present on the floor.

A statue of the goddess Victoria, standing on a globe and extending a wreath, had been erected at the far end of the hall. The marble statue, the personification of victory, was placed there by Emperor Augustus in 31 BC to celebrate the military power of Empire. Even during the Christian period, remnants of the pagan past were found everywhere around Rome.

The throne of the Emperor was located in the center of the hall, and to his right and left were chairs for his principal advisors and assistants. Also, a podium was placed in front of the throne so the speaker could directly address the Emperor. Despite the fact that Emperor Honorius had decided to move the Capitol of the Western Empire to Ravenna in 408 AD, the Senate, for reasons of its own, elected to remain in Rome.

I'd serve as a senator for the next two years.

As is the custom in the Senate, I was assigned to a senior senator to learn the process and the procedures of the legislative body. My mentor, Gaius Gallus Gallipolis, had already been a member of the Senate for well over thirty years. Bald and somewhat overweight, he soon became more than a mentor to me; rather more like the father whom I'd just recently lost.

Gaius' office was located in the Forum Romanum on the second floor of the Basilica Julia. Sometimes while waiting for him there, I'd look out his windows and watch the steady flow of people meandering down the Via Sacra

– beginning from the impressive Arch of Septimius Severus to my extreme right, passing by the Basilica Amelia directly in front of me, and eventually veering off toward the Arch of Titus and the Flavian Amphitheatre.

On a typical day, the avenues were crowded with a wide variety of merchants, slaves, soldiers, priests, and all types of government bureaucrats. There were Italians, Greeks, Egyptians, Carthaginians, Nubians, Jews, Dacians, and many other citizens and visitors of all colors, creeds and natural origins emanating from all over the Empire and beyond – each one dressed in the distinctive and often colorful fashions of his or her native lands.

During my first months as a Senator, Gaius taught me the essential functions of senatorial life, such as: initiating legislation; selecting the right committees upon which to serve; how and when to vote; and most importantly when to sit down and keep quiet. He also taught me many valuable lessons about matters of law, philosophy, bureaucracy, timing, and above all, being patient with the slow and often painstaking deliberative legislative process.

He explained the Senate was split ideologically between conservatives and liberals and both ideologies were equally patriotic. He said conservative senators were more rigid in their thinking and their approaches to problem-solving. He often stated that they saw life primarily in terms of black and white, talked in simple declarative sentences about political and moral issues, and were often more result-oriented.

He mentioned the liberal senators, on the other hand, were often more curious, saw life in many shades of grey, and were commonly long-range thinkers. Furthermore, he counseled that liberal senators often spoke or wrote utilizing nuance and possibilities, tried to see the big picture, and were often more open to experimentation, forgiveness, and inclusion.

He also noted each faction saw the world differently, and each affiliation was necessary to solve Rome's long-term and short-term problems. He advised me to listen carefully to the views and political positions of each side, fully understand their particular viewpoints, and take the necessary time to arrive at a definite opinion or judgment.

Finally, he also cautioned me to keep my own counsel; beware of cliques, gladhanders, and political parties; exercise extreme restraint in money matters; keep backslappers at an arms' length; avoid gossipers and supposed benefactors of all types; and always remember the Emperor's spies were everywhere.

Perhaps most importantly, we taught me to listen. I distinctly remember him telling me, "Remember always the wise words of Epictetus, who reminded us that we have two ears and one mouth so we can listen twice as much as we speak."

We soon became fast friends.

Over those first weeks and months in the Senate, Gaius told me many color-ful stories and provided curious anecdotes which were aimed at molding my techniques and establishing my place alongside my fellow Senators. There's one account which I'll always remember.

We were sitting in his office on a crisp February day, and he told me a sto-ry about his former mentor, Tacitus Marius Lucinius. Gaius said, "Senator Lucinius was a lawyer by occupation, and it was customary for established attorneys to employ apprentices and train them in the finer points of the law. One particular apprentice, named Euathlus Olcious, agreed to pay Lucinius a certain sum of money when the young lawyer won his first case in the Imperial Courts. However, the young man later attempted to avoid paying the costs of his apprenticeship to Senator Lucinius by never making a court appearance."

I responded, "Sounds fraudulent to me, I daresay."

Gaius smiled and continued, "Well, Lucinius eventually brought a lawsuit against his former apprentice in an attempt to recover the costs incurred in advancing the student's legal training. Olcious was shocked by the writ and stormed into Lucinius' office, demanding the writ be withdrawn. However, Lucinius told his former intern that he now faced a legal dilemma. Lucinius explained,

> If you lose the matter, the judge will award me the money I seek. If on the other hand, you win the lawsuit, you will have won your first case, and you will owe me the payment according to our agreement. Either way, I'll collect the sum of money you initially agreed to pay me.

Lucinius has always maintained the story is true," Gaius concluded, "but I'm not so sure of its veracity."

We enjoyed a good laugh. Whether it was true or not, from his stories, advice, and insights, I learned the basics on how to be a better senator and perhaps, a better citizen, too.

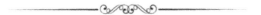

One afternoon, Gaius and I decided to go for a short walk from the Forum to a sidewalk café located on the plaza facing the Pantheon – the great temple erected by Augustus in 27 BC to honor all of the gods and goddesses. It was an early May afternoon, and after we found a shaded table, he ordered a jug of Tirolian red wine.

Suddenly, he began reciting poetry – perhaps his own verse:

> *Who has not loved shall love by tomorrow's dawn.*
> *For the springtime is new and full of song, and it brings new life.*
> *In spring, the songbirds love to mate and sing together.*
> *The forest unfolds its tender leaves in a renewing rain,*
> *And those who have not loved shall love by tomorrow's dawn.*

Then he laughed heartily, took a sip of wine, and continued in a booming voice:

> *Tomorrow the Queen of love under the forest's shade*
> *Shall join fair lovers with the boughs of myrtle trees.*
> *Tomorrow she leads her chorus in song and dance.*
> *Tomorrow Dianna shall rule from her sublime throne.*
> *Who has not loved shall love my tomorrow's dawn.*

Then he laughed again and looked at me, saying, "You seem so distant today. What could possibly be the matter? We'll not have such a glorious springtime afternoon like this one for long, my friend. This grand city is a damned inferno in the summertime, you know."

I was a bit preoccupied. We'd recently been told by the Emperor's representative that Attila's army was on the march again. This potential apocalypse was weighing heavily on my mind that lovely afternoon.

From the reports I'd received earlier in the week, I mentioned to Gaius that Aëtius was busily preparing for the Hun's offensive. In the attempt to defend

Imperial territory, I noted that Aëtius was only able to assemble a marginal defensive force – garrisoned near the Rhine River – which consisted of a significantly weakened VI Legion augmented by a few ragged elements from our remaining barbarian partners.

"Having fought Attila last year to a draw," I said, "and knowing the sorry state of our Legions, I fear the end of the Empire may be near."

Gaius chuckled, took another sip of the tart red wine, and replied: "The barbarians have been at the gates of Rome for well over three centuries now. We've always found a means to drive them back. Julius, my young friend, don't be so despairing."

Like my father often did, Gaius patted my hand and looked me square in the eye. "You surely know the methodologies of our imminent demise are always in front of us, and I'm sure you recall the admonishment of Sophocles:

> And ever shall this law hold good that nothing which is vast enters into the life of mortals without a curse.

So don't be glum, my young friend."

"Me? Now, who's the doomsayer?"

He smiled, patted me softly on my left shoulder and said, "No, while I'm really quite cheerful, I fully understand the Empire won't last forever; like the great Kingdoms of Egypt, Babylonia, and Carthage, Rome will surely fall one day. If not from an invading army, then the Empire will succumb from disease or pestilence, or by civil war, or perhaps, from a curse from the heavens; but surely not on this lovely afternoon."

"That's reassuring, I guess."

Gaius nodded affirmatively, and after taking a small piece of cheese out of the bowl on our table and placing it in his mouth, he continued, "Yes, all good things must end – but all in a timely manner. You know dark and depressing thoughts, such as yours, often remind me of Socrates who once lamented that all of us – our friends, our lovers, our families, and even our enemies – are already sentenced to death. And most of us will die in most unpleasant ways."

"Even more happy thoughts! What will we talk about next; an onset of some great plague or pandemic?"

As he smiled at me, an attractive young girl passed us, her baby held tightly in her arms. "Julius, let's not spend afternoon speculating on about what may, or may not, be the cause of our eventual demise one day."

He lifted his wine cup and tapped it to mine. Smiling, he said, "Attila has added just one more possibility to the eventual result. Unfortunately, death isn't just a possibility; it's a certainty – but probably not during this peaceful afternoon. Agreed?"

I laughed and allowed my eyes to follow the shapely physique of the young woman as she walked past the Pantheon and on her way to perform her particular task that day. I thought of Octavia carrying one of our children.

Then I replied, "How can **you** be so morose yet pretend to enjoy such a marvelous day; you know, all your talk about death and cataclysm."

He reached over and patted my hand; he knew I was not yet convinced. "Yes, the overall prognosis for man and his creations has never been rosy. Jesus has told us that He's coming soon, and He may come back to earth in fiery judgment long before Attila raises his sword against the Aurelian Walls; but who knows? Empires rise and fall; and earthquakes, flood, and pandemic come along whether we are ready for them or not. These events aren't within the control of us mere mortals."

He stopped talking for a moment and casually looked around the beautiful piazza. "The Bible talks of creation, where God created this beautiful world from nothing in only seven days, and the Bible also tells us about the end of time. Furthermore, there are so many stories in mythology about beginnings and ends, and the prospects for humankind are no exception. Although all men initially grow robust and tall, we'll all soon decay and grow old, like me. But, Julius, remember without death and decay, there's no possibility of new life, growth, and change."

Once again he stopped talking and collected his thoughts. "The rose grows out of a seemingly dead vine and blossoms into the delight we see each spring. As summer comes, the plant wilts and brown spots form on its green leaves. As autumn arrives, the leaves turn brown and fall – and soon winter seems to take the very life out of the plant. Deep under the winter snow, however, there's a bud – a spark of life – which with the return of the sun and the spring rains, grows again to become the rose. My friend, we are part of a never-ending cycle."

"Gaius, that's an excellent comparison – the so-called circle of life; but is it worth protecting and preserving? In the end, we all turn to dust and ash. Is there really any point to it all?"

He looked off as if to see something which may have never been there. He concluded, "Yes, there are many things worth defending. All around us, we can see acts of charity, heroism, and bravery. Also, our shared values, aspirations and accomplishments, the essential elements of our collective civilization, are worth preserving and defending; and the gods have chosen Rome to do it."

He shook his head, brushed a few of his remaining longer hairs from his brow, and concluded, "As a former pagan and a scholar of the world's religions, I've learned all cultures celebrate the harvest and then rejoice in the fertility of the springtime. As a Christian nation now, we believe almost the opposite; from decay and death comes the real promise of everlasting life. It's an interesting twist, I must say."

He smiled, slowly shook his head and said, "So much has changed over the past fifty years, and I don't know whether the Christian understanding is correct or not; however, one day soon I hope to find out for myself. Until then, Julius, let's enjoy the here and now. Let's prepare for the worst, but enjoy the gifts the Lord has given us – today, in the here and now."

We clicked our cups of wine together, and for the next several hours, the two of us sat and talked at our table in the advancing shadows of the Pantheon – laughing, arguing, and enjoying just being alive in Rome during the springtime of 452 AD. Times like those are often some of my most cherished memories of Gaius – the times of being spontaneous, energetic, and bewitched by his wit, anecdotes, and eternal optimism.

I was sitting alone in my office one warm June afternoon when Romulus, my secretary, knocked on the door and advised me a courier arrived with a parchment for me. After signing for the document, I broke the seal and unrolled the parchment. It was from my sister, Placida.

Dear brother,

I write to inform you that Octavia died last night, just after giving birth to your son. I know you planned to be here for the birth, but the baby came early. It was a difficult delivery for Octavia, and she lost a considerable amount of blood. We named the boy Cassius, in honor of her father, and the baby is with me now. My husband and I will also gladly keep Julius, Minerva, Claudius, and Caspian at home with us until your term in the Senate is over. It's a sad time for all of us, dear brother. I am still weeping. The children send their love. Oh, I am so sorry I couldn't have sent you better news. Stay strong.

Love always, Placida.

I must have reread the parchment twenty times, and I wished to the Lord Jesus on countless occasions this horror was just another bad dream. Somehow the pressing business facing the Senate and people of Rome was no longer important to me. After dismissing Romulus for the day, I walked aimlessly for hours through the hot and crowded streets of the city, and I eventually found solace in the office of my mentor, Gaius Gallus.

After offering me a cup of wine, he let me ramble on for the next thirty minutes, never interrupting me or challenging me on anything I'd mentioned.

Once I finished speaking, he said, "I think I know somewhat how you must feel. My wife, Edna Clarita, died almost two years ago, and I still miss her every day. You know, it's almost funny; I miss things about her which used to annoy me when she was alive; such as, how she used to tell me when I needed a shave, a haircut, or a clean tunic – or how she used to pester me about my weight, my language, and my regimen."

Looking at the expression on his face, I realized we shared a common pain.

He continued, "Oh, how I regret all of that now. Along with the big things which go without saying, there are so many little, mundane, everyday things I miss about her such as, our early morning talks, our walks along the streets of Rome, and how she carefully listened to me ramble on about my day in the Senate. I didn't realize until I lost her how much I'd relied on her advice about a particular piece of legislation or an Imperial decree. Even now, when something momentous happens in the Senate, I say to myself that I need to mention the matter to Edna Clarita."

He was close to tears – as if her death happened only a few days ago. I reached out and touched his arm in an attempt to soften the blow. I replied, "You've mentioned it to me before. I know you miss her dearly."

He looked at me with tears in his eyes. "Julius, she's constantly in my dreams at night. Sometimes these dreams bring me great happiness, and sometimes they bring great sorrow. You know, I wish I could talk to her one more time, and tell her just how much she meant to me and how much I still love her and miss her. My dear friend, I know precisely how you feel today."

Standing at his second-floor window, I was staring at the Forum below, watching the endless parade of people walking by.

After a moment, I turned back to face him. "Over the years of our marriage, I've spent too much time away from home in the service of the Western Empire. Even now, I'm here in Rome when I should've been by her side in Nemausus. Damn it; I regret my lengthy absences so much now. You know, we planned to share a long life together, and I promised her once my term with the Senate was over, we'd leave Nemausus and live in a villa somewhere on the south coast."

So many things that could've been and so many things which should've been flooded my mind. I said, "And you cannot begin to imagine how much I regret our decision to have one more child. From the instance I agreed to it, I questioned our sanity. The physician told us clearly Octavia was lucky to have survived Caspian's birth, and we should have no more children. If only I'd . . . "

Gaius looked into my eyes and replied, "Don't blame yourself, Julius. You cannot undo the past. It is what it is. Trust in God and accept that even this tragedy has a purpose in God's divine plan."

We spoke for hours well into the night. As dawn broke over the Eternal City, I was all talked out. After that, he offered me the opportunity to spend several days at his villa near Palestrina. Somewhat reluctantly, I agreed.

But I found little peace among the lush fountains and warm baths of his country villa. The pain was almost unbearable. I even recall even spending time at Edna Clarita's tomb, talking to her about my wife. Octavia was my rock and my sounding board. She was my lover, my wife, my conscience, and the mother of my children.

For days on end, I couldn't imagine life without her. I'm not ashamed to admit

I cried myself to sleep for much of the next week, and I always awoke with a hollow, burning sensation deep within the pit of my stomach. On many occasions, I longed for death and deliverance from my pain, and I often questioned the benevolence, goodness, and wisdom of God.

However, my mourning and self-pity ended abruptly when word reached Palestrina that Attila, the Scourge of God, and his hordes surprised Aëtius by not striking once again at Gaul. Rather, his army entered the Empire by marching over the Alps and attacking Northern Italia. By the time word reached Palestrina, Attila had besieged and overwhelmed the city of Aquileia on the Italian border with Dalmatia, and he was moving toward Mediolanum and Ravenna. Perhaps even Rome was in his sights.

Upon being briefed by Romulus on the dire situation, I concluded I needed to go back to the city at once. With Aëtius and Ricimer still waiting for the Huns to strike in Northern Gaul, there was little Roman military capability in Italia to thwart the impending oncoming tide of butchery, slash, and burn.

As soon as the word spread that Attila and his army had begun their march south, the city of Rome began filling up with refugees from all parts of Italia. From the plains of the Po Valley to the high hill towns of Calabria and Tuscany, there was a buzz of fear and looming horror. In preparation for a possible siege, the Senate authorized the immediate repairs to the ancient Aurelian Wall, the vintage city fortifications which were first constructed by Emperor Aurelian in 271 AD.

Enclosing an area of approximately 5.3 square miles and a circumference of twelve miles encircling the city, the walls were 52 feet high, and they contained 383 towers, 7,020 crenellations, and 18 main gates. The walls were once believed as impregnable. When constructing the fortifications, however, the builders didn't anticipate an invading army would attempt to commence a prolonged blockade of the city.

Most marauding forces simply were not provisioned for extended operations. The Huns, however, were experienced in siege warfare. Their army had encircled Constantinople for almost two years, and Attila recently blockaded (and later destroyed) the cities of Verona and Aquileia. A siege of Rome was now a real and pressing danger. In 452 AD, the city's garrison consisted of only about twenty-five hundred soldiers — far too few to defend the walls adequately.

Although Alaric sacked Rome in 410, the Goths were let into the city with a promise not to destroy the Imperial buildings or to kill the populace. Actually, the city hadn't been forcibly conquered in well over six-hundred years.

Among the unexpected refugees to the relative safety of Rome were Emperor Valentinian, his immediate family, and much of his entourage. Although Emperor Honorius had believed Ravenna was easier to defend than Rome, Valentinian apparently thought otherwise.

Soon after he settled in the official residence on the Palatine Hill, he summoned four Senators to meet with him to discuss the perilous situation — Senators Gennadius Avienus, Memmius Aemilius Trygetius, Gaius Gallus Gallipolis, and surprisingly, me.

Just like the meeting with the Emperor in Ravenna one year earlier, the four of us were quietly seated around a rectangular table when the big bronze doors opened, and Valentinian entered the room. This time, however, there was little pageantry — it would be all business that day. The Emperor looked tired and worried; his color was not good, and he looked uncomfortable.

After we'd taken our seats, he cleared his throat and said, "Once again, Master General Aëtius and his incompetent staff have been outfoxed by the devil, Attila. While our idiot General was waiting for the Huns to strike again in Northern Gaul, the Huns — predictably, I may add — marched over the Alpine passes and leveled the city of Aquileia."

Valentinian stopped speaking and stared at us for a few moments. "Can you believe such stupidity?" He appeared angry.

After slowly shaking his head and deeply exhaling, he continued, "After leaving Aquileia with not one stone still standing on the next one, Attila and the Huns quickly controlled the main roads along the Po Valley. After that, they burned Padua, Vicenza, Verona, Brescia, Bergamo, and Placentia in rapid succession."

He briefly conferred with an aide and then said, "At last check, he's camping outside the gates of Mediolanum. Once he's done with Mediolanum, my intelligence officers tell me that Attila has his eyes squarely set on Ravenna. He'll probably march onto Rome. Gentlemen, he must be stopped before he leaves the Po Valley."

Pausing again, Valentinian pushed aside a few strands of hair which had fallen onto his face, adjusted his crown, and slowly exhaled once more. He seemed clearly frustrated with this predicament. Turning to his left, he uncovered the map board and pointed to a map of Italia and the surrounding Alpine regions.

He continued, "Here's my plan for destroying Attila. General Aegidius, with a contingent of less than two-thousand men, is currently situated between us and Attila's force of over twenty-thousand men. Aegidius is merely shadowing the Hunnic bastards. Utilizing slash and burn techniques, he's purposefully destroying our villages and fields. On my order, Aegidius is attempting to deprive Attila of the necessary supplies he needs to continue the march toward Ravenna."

The Emperor stopped for a moment and conferred once again with one of his military advisors. "Furthermore, Aegidius has been instructed not to engage the main Hunnic army unless forced to do so. His primary job is to harass the Huns and to slow their military advance south."

Perhaps for effect, he glanced at the notes he held in his left hand. "Also, I've ordered General Aëtius to gather up what remains of the VI Legion in Northern Gaul and to proceed around the Alps to the north and strike at Attila's base-camp on the upper Danube River. Perhaps we can get Attila's attention this way. But Aëtius will not have the Visigoths to help him this time; they cannot be expected to fight for Italia as they fought for Gaul."

Valentinian stopped talking again and conferred briefly with a staff member once more. "At the same time, Emperor Marcian is sending troops from Thrace to strike Attila's home territories from the east. I believe our three-pronged strategy is sufficient to force Attila to reconsider his efforts at ravaging the remainder of Italia and to return north to his homeland."

For a moment, the Emperor stopped, stretched out his arms, leaned on the table, and mumbled something none of us could hear to his staff. "Senators, I need you to ride north, meet with Attila personally, and convince him to withdraw. Pope Leo has already agreed to go along with you."

After briefly looking down at the notes on the table, he turned to another one of his advisors and quietly asked for advice on a matter.

Then he looked up again and addressed me. "The reason I'm asking you to go on this journey, Senator Majorian, is because you courageously fought Attila on the Catalaunian Plains last summer. Perhaps he'll listen to a former adversary, or maybe some of his warriors will feel endangered by your presence. As far as I know, you are the only commander to have defeated his men on the battlefield."

I nodded in acceptance of my instructions.

The Emperor concluded, "The future of Rome depends upon you five men. You must convince Attila to turn back and give up his ambitions of conquest. To aid you in your mission, I'll provide you with a contingent of cavalry and with a strongbox of gold and jewels to help entice the bastard to leave the Empire. I know it's a risky undertaking. Furthermore, I'll allow one or two of you to decline the mission. However, at least two of you must go north with Pope Leo."

CHAPTER VIII

Mincio, Italia – July 452

Two days later, we departed the city of Rome through the Porta San Lorenzo, and we followed the Via Tiburtina north and east toward Tivoli. Earlier in the morning, Senators Trygetius and Gallipolis opted out of the peace mission because of pressing health reasons, leaving Pope Leo, Senator Avienus, and me to represent the Emperor.

His Holiness, Pope Leo, in full papal dress, rode behind our coach in a jewel-encrusted papal wagon. He was surrounded by a large contingent of priests, Church dignitaries, and ecclesiastical attendants – each carrying crosses, banners, or censers – who prayed, chanted, and sang hymns during most of the journey north to the Po River Valley.

As we entered into the once lush valleys of Umbria and Tuscany, I cringed at the scene of the ravaged and burned landscape. To deprive Attila of the forage, food, and supplies he needed to sustain his army on its way south, all of the buildings were burned to the ground, and the crops, vineyards, and orchards were destroyed. The farm animals, which couldn't be moved from the vicinity in time, were slaughtered and left rotting in the fields.

It was a horrible sight. The smell of burning buildings and crops and the stench arising from the carcasses of the decaying animals reminded me of the aftermath of the battle on the Catalaunian Plains. It was a scene I had hoped I'd never see again.

Tired, sick, and sore following an arduous three-day journey from Rome, we arrived at the military encampment of General Claudius Aegidius near the city of Mincio. Following refreshments and a short rest period, he briefed us regarding what we should expect when we arrived at Attila's headquarters – located near the south shore of Lake Garda.

The following morning, we'd meet with the devil himself.

Under a white flag of truce, Aegidius arranged a small contingent of armed cavalry to guide us across the grasslands and meadows to the outskirts of Attila's camp. At the entrance of the enemy encampment, several armed Hun guards received us and dismissed the Roman contingent. From this point forward, we traveled with our enemy escort for the final two or three miles to the belly of the beast – the heart of Attila's bivouac.

The Hun encampment was massive. It stretched as far as my eyes could see along the south shore of Lake Garda. Everywhere I looked, I saw campfires, small groups of enemy combatants, and hundreds of soldiers' tents scattered along the lakeshore. The layout and organization of the camp, however, did not conform to the strict structure, discipline, and security of a typical Roman bivouac. I'd long understood barbarian camps were often loosely designed and poorly configured.

But something was clearly wrong here, and for a moment I couldn't put my finger on it. Soon, I discovered the cause. It was the smell emanating from all around us – and not the typical or familiar stench from soldiers' latrines, rotting garbage, or the spoiling remains of slaughtered animals. Something terribly wrong was lingering in the putrid air of the Hun camp – it was the plague.

Often during my military career, I'd experienced the telltale signs of disease, pestilence, and rampant infections. The local commanders of the Legions were always mindful to prevent these outbreaks. All of us knew well that nothing potentially more crippling to an army than the occurrence of disease. And there it was, clearly present in Attila's camp.

As we rode deeper into the bivouac, I saw piles of corpses were stacked everywhere along the road. Also, I saw and heard moaning soldiers begging for assistance as the medics were sorting out the living from the dead and dying. God's vengeance was clearly being manifested in the encampment all around us.

Upon descending from our wagons and horses when we arrived in front Attila's tent, we were ordered to prostrate ourselves on the ground. With a sounding of horns, cymbals, and drums, the flap opened, and a huge man walked out of the royal tent. All of our eyes were fixed upon him.

King Attila, then in his mid-forties, wore a reddish-brown jewel encrusted cloak which covered him from his neck to just below his knees. Slowly, he walked over to the Roman contingent, lying face down in the mud at his feet. Looking up at him, I noticed his hair was long and streaked with grey. With a prominent nose and dark skin probably from too much time in the sun, his piercing brown eyes stared down at us with a fierce determination.

He wore heavy gold earrings and sported multiple tattoos on his massive forearms. He displayed rings on each finger of his hands. A rumpled red beard, also streaked with grey, fell from his chin all the way to his upper chest, and an elaborate helmet of gold topped his head. In his right hand, he held a large Persian flat sword.

Around his throat, a necklace held a disturbingly looking creature bronze resembling a lion or tiger – perhaps it was a talisman – and a tarnished badge representing a former Imperial commission was attached loosely to his robe. Despite his piercing brown eyes, Attila's face was a perfect blank, and it was impossible for me to guess what he was thinking. I can picture him perfectly in my mind to this day; he was that impressive.

Approaching us slowly from his tent, he stopped at the location directly in front of one of the young priests. He gently raised the boy off the ground to his knees, and with a swift blow of his sword, severed the young priest's head from his trembling body. Both parts fell with a thud and splattered in the mud.

Laughing a hearty laugh, Attila took a few more steps forward, placed his huge right boot squarely on the head of Senator Avienus, and asked us in perfect Latin, "Why has the Pope of Rome come to meet with me? And why are he, and these influential Senators, lying in a pig sty at my feet? Is this any way to greet a mighty King?"

We lay still on the ground, not knowing what to do next.

Then he roared, "I am Attila, the King of the Huns, the son of Mundzuk and the grandson of Uldin. My armies have battled you swine from the mountains of Dacia and the gates of Constantinople to the plains of Germania and Gaul."

With great fanfare, he noisily cleared his throat, spit on the ground, and continued speaking. "Though once I commanded Legions and fought fiercely to preserve your heritage and grandeur, you arrogant bastards treated me like a leper. By your incessant greed and insulting behavior, you drove me from your vile and collapsing Empire as surely as an old woman chases a rat from her cellar. You spat on my people, raped and enslaved our women, and devastated our homes, vineyards, and farms."

He looked at the body of the slain priest and smirked; "Now you travel here from the grand city of Rome in your best vestments, tunics, and togas to beg me to spare your civilization from the punishment it so greatly deserves."

Laughing heartily, he said, "How many people have you killed or conquered? How many men, women, and children have you enslaved? How many homes have been burnt to the ground, cities have been leveled, and religions which have been desecrated and destroyed in the furtherance of your old pagan gods? Now, a new religion is festering in the Roman heart, and the leader of your elaborate superstition lies dormant in the mud here in front of me and is ready to beg for Rome's deliverance."

He stopped speaking once more and spat on the ground once more. "You plan to offer me some meager tribute of gold, silver, and jewels. You will whisper your hollow promises of future collaboration and peaceful cohabitation."

Once again, he stopped talking as we gazed at us lying on the ground at his feet. "How dare you approach the great King of Huns with these gimmicks, lies, and charades? Where is your Emperor? Why is the great Valentinian not with you today? Where is the great Master General Aëtius? Are they cowering in Ravenna or Rome, or have they turned tail and sailed for Constantinople?"

Then he yelled, "Mark my word; Rome's thousand year reign is finished. And Rome won't rise again!"

He turned to one of his lieutenants and whispered something to him in his native tongue. Soon, a detachment of Huns appeared, picked us off of the ground, and dragged us to a holding tent. There, we waited for six hours, not knowing our fate.

After that, one by one, we were taken from the holding tent to meet with Attila. Finally, it was my turn, and when I entered his tent, Attila was standing with his back to me. Turning around, he looked at me suspiciously and smiled as he looked at the dried mud which was still splattered on my tunic. Two generals, who fought each other to a draw almost a year prior, faced each other as opponents once more.

I remember his tent was plain and utilitarian for a field commander; necessarily large but simply furnished. There were two large wooden tables along the walls, a few chairs, and several large chests. Maps and ledgers were strewn on the table tops, and a foul odor filled the air. A smoky clay oil lamp dimly lit the interior, and in the center of the room, two couches were set around a low rectangular table.

"I remember you well," he said "from the Catalaunian Plains. My forces threw everything we could muster at your position, but you didn't run. Had we broken through your line during the first day, I'd be having dinner with Gaiseric today in Tarragona. Your men did well."

I wasn't certain how to react, if at all. "It was the worst two days of my life, Sire," I replied. "Not until the end did I dare hope for survival, much less for victory. By the conclusion of the second day, my men were exhausted. My supplies were gone, and there was nothing left to throw at you. Unfortunately, we let you go back across the Rhine to safety. If only we could've taken the offensive once more, we wouldn't be meeting today in your tent."

For a few moments, he glared at me. I could see the anger in his eyes, and I wondered whether he'd kill me on the spot. Soon his demeanor softened, and wearily, Attila sat down on a chair behind his desk. Obviously, he knew he was in a desperate situation.

Feeling a bit relieved, I replied, "Sire, I see clear evidence of plague in your camp. How widespread is it?"

His eyes met mine. I could tell he was worried. He replied, "For three weeks, we've been watching more and more soldiers die because of this monster. I can barely assemble a company of men to go out and forage for supplies. As you must know, your friend, General Aegidius, is burning and destroying the fields to our south, and we've exhausted all there is to plunder from our east and north. I have a real dilemma now. Do I strike at Ravenna or do I go home and try to fight you another day?"

I didn't answer.

He continued, "I hear from the fat Senator in the other tent that my old friend, Aëtius, is moving his army against my stronghold from the west, and the demon, Marcian, is striking my homeland from the east. Because I've no place to go but south, I'll strike with all of my vengeance at the heart of the Empire – the city of Rome. It's my only viable option."

I exhaled. "Sire, I've seen plague before – and no, you aren't going south any-time soon. Your army is in no condition to wage an attack. Furthermore, Aegidius will shadow you from here to the walls of Rome, and he'll strike out and cut at you all along the way. There'll be no supplies for your men on the road, and should you even make it all the way to Rome, you must be prepared for an extended siege. From what I've seen this morning, you are incapable of doing that."

I stopped talking for a moment, not knowing whether it was wise for me to continue. However, I said, "The city is well supplied with food and water, and without the necessary siege equipment, the Aurelian Walls will hold you out for months. Given enough time, Aëtius and Marcian's troops will join together and come after you from the north. You're now in our crosshairs, Sire. It's you who must seek terms from us."

Attila sighed and looked at me. "So, what would you have me do? Beg for terms of surrender? Offer my men into slavery? Or should we die nobly in one last great fight to topple the great city of Rome? Of those choices, I like the last option the best."

I hesitated, knowing I didn't have the authority to propose another alternative. I decided to offer him another approach. "Take your army and go north. The Emperor will guarantee you free passage out of the Empire. Only death and disgrace waits if you continue on your path south. Perhaps one day, we'll meet again on the field of battle as allies and not as combatants. That's your best choice, Sire."

He asked me to sit, and we talked for a while about our youth, our families, and our battles. I'd almost forgotten as a young man, he grew up in the Court in Constantinople. For a while, we sat together in an eerie silence as two trou-bled soldiers feeling the wind of change passing us by. I think both of us knew the collapse of each of our empires was quickly coming.

My time with him was over. Bowing, I left him, and his men escorted me back to the tent with the others. Dinner and wine were brought to us, and then night and another full day passed before we learned Attila was going back to his homeland.

Ravenna and Rome had been spared.

Two months later, the Scourge of God and what remained of his army crossed the Danube and exited Roman territory for the final time. There were several competing theories regarding the reason why Attila decided to give up on his plan to attack Ravenna and Rome.

Senator Avienus attributed Attila's decision to the Emperor's wise three-pronged plan: 1) ordering Aëtius to send the VI Legion east into the Hun's homeland; 2) while at the same time, moving Marcian's forces west from Thrace; and 3) at the same time, commanding Aegidius' forces to deny Attila food, shelter, and supplies from the south. With military operations threatening the heart of the Hunnic homeland and the denial of provisions to the south, Avienus argued the Emperor's grand strategy forced Attila to terminate his invasion plans and return home.

Conversely, Pope Leo believed Attila did not fear the might of the Legions as much as he dreaded the power and magnificence of the God of the Christians. Leo reported to the Emperor that Attila was fearful he'd share the fate of Alaric (who died shortly after sacking Rome in 410 AD) as divine punishment for Attila's slaughter of so many innocent noncombatants when he obliterated Mediolanum and the other Italian cities in his way.

Interestingly, the Pope also reported Attila had spoken of a huge man – dressed in priestly robes and armed with a sword and visible only to Attila – who threatened him with death. Because Attila was a superstitious person, the Pope surmised Attila decided to abandon his southern campaign and return to his homeland out of fear and superstition.

I believe, however, Attila's decision to abandon his Italian peninsula campaign was dictated by overwhelming logistical and strategic realities. It was evident to me supply shortages, and a devastating outbreak of the plague significantly reduced the useful capability of his military forces. The Huns simply didn't have the bureaucratic machinery of its Roman counterpart for providing his Army with the necessary logistical support for an extended military campaign.

With Aegidius burning and slashing the countryside to his south, Attila would've been unable to obtain the food, horses, and supplies which were necessary for his troops to undertake siege warfare. It would've been impossible for him to capture Ravenna and Rome.

Another factor may have been Attila's army already acquired considerable quantities of plunder from its earlier operations. The addition of another strongbox of gold and jewels provided by Valentinian may have also helped convince Attila to return to his homeland. For both of these reasons, I suspect it was more reasonable for Attila to conclude peace terms with Rome than to wage war to the south.

Shortly after Attila returned to his Palace north of the Danube, our spies reported he planned to regroup and strike at Constantinople again. However, on the night of his marriage to his fifth wife, Ildiko, he suffered a severe nosebleed and choked to death in his bed.

Ironically, the Scourge of God failed to name his successor, and soon after that, several of his sons battled each other for control of the Hunnic Empire. At the same time, many of the other tribes, loyal only to the persona of Attila himself, left the loose confederation. In short order, the once mighty Hunnic Empire collapsed.

With the passing of Attila and the demise of the Hunnic Empire, Valentinian felt secure enough to envision life without his Master General. The citizens of Rome construed the death of the Hun King as the dawn of a new era of Roman power, prestige, and prosperity. Suddenly, Valentinian was popular again with his subjects.

After leaving Rome for Ravenna to great pomp and fanfare in early September, the Emperor summoned Aëtius to the Court in Ravenna on the pretense the General would present the Emperor with a 'Status of the Army' report. Egged on by the powerful and devious Senator Petronius Maximus, the Emperor abruptly became enraged with Aëtius, charged down from his throne, and publically accused Aëtius of high treason.

While the Master General was attempting to the calm down Valentinian, the Emperor drew a sword from his scabbard and repeatedly stabbed the unarmed general to death. The man who had saved Rome from doom and peril on numerous occasions suddenly stumbled and died on the floor of the Court.

An onlooker, Senator Sidonius Apollinaris, reportedly later said to Valentinian, "I am ignorant, sir of your motives or provocations, Majesty; I only know you have acted like a man who has cut off his right hand with his left."

For over thirty years, Master General Aëtius was instrumental – by his sheer military genius and through his uncanny ability to form political alliances with several barbarian partners – in keeping the Western Empire viable and substantially intact.

A usual round of bloodletting quickly followed Aëtius' death, including the summary executions of his chief of staff and much of Aëtius' inner circle, many of whom I'd served with for many years. Due to Valentinian's increasing paranoia, I often wondered whether the slaughter of Aëtius loyalists would eventually reach all the way down to Ricimer, Aegidius, and me.

Thankfully, the purge only lasted a couple of months, and I slept lightly during that time with a sword stashed safely under my bed. Even if the Emperor conjured up some illusions the three of us were co-conspirators in a treasonous plot to assassinate him, the Emperor still had an Empire to run. As the weeks and months went by without an arrest or provocation, I began to sleep a bit more soundly. The crisis had passed.

Next, Valentinian needed to find a new way to deal with the remaining obstacle to the Western Empire's fiscal and cohesive integrity – the Vandals. King Gaiseric had already conquered Carthage, much of North Africa, and a significant portion of Southern Hispania.

The Vandal King and his massive army now placed their eyes squarely on the islands of Sicily, Sardinia, and Corsica, and perhaps, on the city of Rome itself. Thus, Valentinian still needed to deal with the foremost adversarial forces still taking aim at the wealth and influence of the Western Empire. With Aëtius dead, the task at hand suddenly became much more challenging.

CHAPTER IX

The City of Rome — May 454

Shortly after returning to Rome from Mincio, I took the familiar two-day voyage from the port of Ostia to Massalia, and then I rode a coach on to my home in Nemausus. In a pervasive state of grief, I spent many days by myself at the mausoleum of my dear wife, telling her all about my time in Rome and speaking of my deep and abiding love for her. To this day, I cannot begin to describe the sense of unbearable pain and constant sorrow I experienced while sitting beside her final resting spot.

But it was also a time of great joy and pride. I held my baby son, Cassius, in my arms, for the first time, and I savored the reunion with my other sweet children, Julius, Minerva, Claudius, and Caspian. They were such a blessing to me, and I was saddened to leave them again.

Until I finished my term of office in the Senate, Placida agreed to rear my children in her home. We agreed the city of Rome was no place for a widowed man to raise his young family.

Over the next two years, I took every available opportunity to get away from Rome and spend precious days with my young family. But it seemed like one crisis or another would call me away from Nemausus too soon in order to tend to the business of the Empire. Often, the days spent back in Rome became weeks and the weeks became months, as I delved deeper into the challenges and disappointments of government.

There were matters of taxation and revenue; the problems of the poor; the arming and training of the legions whose ranks had been decimated by war, retirements, supply shortages, and sadly, corruption; and the governing of the provinces, principalities, and territories within the Empire. The latter were becoming increasingly difficult to control.

Some other issues which were taking up my time included the frequent incidence of plague, famine, and pestilence, the role of slavery and manumission, the longstanding problems inherent in immigration issues, and in all such things involving matters of national security, foreign intelligence, and power politics. Also, there was the increasing and disturbing role of the Papacy in the overall governmental affairs.

All in all, I stayed busy in Rome; but my heart, however, remained in Nemausus.

During my years as a senator, Ricimer commanded the VI Legion which was stationed in Treverorum, a city in Gallia Belgica. In 287 AD, Diocletian chose the city as the capital of the western part of the consolidated Empire, and once fortified, the city became prosperous and prominent.

From his base in Treverorum, Ricimer attempted to make a life for himself as a local dignitary. In 452 AD, he married a woman from a wealthy Roman family, but she died in childbirth less than a year later. Unfortunately, their son died of complications due to dysentery about two months after his wife's death. As far as I know, he never remarried.

I also heard his younger brother, Olaf, died in 453 AD as a result of the wounds he sustained on patrol during a Berber ambush near Sabratha in Africa Proconsularis.

From briefings on the Senate floor, I'd learned Belgica and Germania were in frequent rebellion during those turbulent years, and it seemed Ricimer spent much of his time putting down local insurrections and dealing with local chieftains. Like Aëtius, Ricimer became adept in negotiations and quelling hostilities with the barbarian nations situated on Rome's porous frontiers. Due in large part to his fierce tenacity and natural resourcefulness, Ricimer helped keep Rome firmly in control of its Northwestern cities and provinces.

Aëtius also presented Ricimer with a great honor. In the late summer of 454, and at the head of a Roman Army, Ricimer peacefully entered Galicia for negotiations with his older brother, King Gustave. It was first, and I think the only time, Ricimer returned to his homeland since being sent away to Rome by his father King Rechila in 426 AD at the age of eight. He was welcomed back by his former countrymen as a conquering hero.

When possible, Ricimer and I communicated with each other from time to time by letter and courier. It would years, however, before I saw him again.

One evening in early May, I decided to walk down to the Tiber River to cleanse my mind of the arguments and issues which had been debated in the Senate over the previous weeks. It was finally a warm, clear evening. After more than a week of soaking spring rains, it was great to spend a few minutes outside.

Dodging mules, small carts, and wagons, and picking my way through the winding alleys and crowded streets of the bustling city, I passed the massive Theatre of Marcellus and the Porticus Octavia. I turned west and began my walk along the Tiber River. Once or twice, tough-eyed men carefully watched me, and I decided it was best to walk on rather than confront them. Unlike the paved streets of the business district, the river walk was uneven and winding.

Off to my left, I could see the Ponte Cestio – the bridge which connects the Insula Tiberina to the right bank of the Tiber. According to tradition, the island was formed in 509 BC after the expulsion of the last king of Rome, Tarquuin the Proud. As the legend has, it the people arose from the tyranny of nearly three-hundred years of living under the rule of monarchs. They slew the tyrant and threw his body into the Tiber. The story continued that his body settled onto the bottom where dirt and silt accumulated around it and eventually formed the island.

Stopping for a moment, I could also see the ancient temple to Aesculapius, the Greek god of medicine and healing, standing tall in the middle of Tiber Island. I'd learned the Temple was established on the island in 291 BC in the aftermath of a grave pestilence. After that, the island and the temple acquired a sacred character associated the cult of the god of medicine who was rumored to give its physicians 'secrets known only to heaven.' After standing for almost five-hundred years, it was still a magnificent structure.

Walking slowly along the quiet river bank and alone in my thoughts, I suddenly heard a muffled scream. Quickly rounding a corner, I saw two men robbing a woman. Instinctively I yelled, "Move away from that woman!"

But the men only glared at me and continued their assault. Soon one man snapped back, saying, "It's none of your concern. Now get about your business."

Then he slapped the woman hard across her face. She fell limply to the ground, and I was certain she was now unconscious.

I screamed out again, "Stop!" I cautiously stared at them, but they paid me no heed.

As I began to approach them, the first man released the woman and came charging at me, followed closely by his companion. Taking my knife from the belt under my toga, I ducked his initial punch from the first man, and thrust my blade deep into the area just below his ribcage and angled my weapon up toward his heart. Crying out fiercely in pain, he promptly died on the spot.

The second man produced a short knife, and raising his hand above his head, he attempted to deliver the blade into my neck area. Reacting quickly, I threw up my left arm just in time to stop the downward thrust of the weapon and promptly kneed the man in his groin area. He fell to the ground, winced in pain, rolled over, and stood up to face me once again.

I smirked at him and yelled, "The odds are even now, my friend. Show me whether you have the gumption to attack a Roman officer."

Upon deciding that turning and running was probably the better course of action, he glared at me one more time and vanished into the night.

The woman, who was now slightly disrobed and bleeding heavily from her head, lay still on the ground. Placing my fingers on her neck, I could still feel a strong pulse. Picking her up in my arms and firmly putting pressure to the impacted area to stop the flow of blood, I carried her from the river walk back to the Porticus Octavia and gently set her down on the stairs which led up to the old temple. By the time a physician arrived, the bleeding had almost stopped.

After he washed and bandaged her wound, we gave her some water. Breathing better now, she looked up at us. I asked, "Who are you, madam?"

"Ursula. My name is Ursula, sir."

Ursula appeared about 5'4' tall, and her long golden hair fell in gentle waves to just below her shoulders. She had bright blue eyes, and I surmised she was about twenty-five years old. Although her facial features seemed Germanic or Belgic in origin, she had only a trace of a foreign accent. With so many foreigners living in Rome, her presence in the city was not at all unusual.

"Do you live around here, Ursula?"

She was still breathing heavily. "Yes, I live with my father in Transtiber Quarter. It's just a few blocks across the Pons Fabricius on the left bank, Sir." She pointed in a southerly direction. "We live on Constantine Street, about a block or two from the bridge."

"You have a nasty cut on your head. Do you know the men who assaulted you?"

"No, I've never seen them before. My father is a tailor by trade, and I help him with his deliveries. I think the men were after the money I carry."

However, I suspected the thugs might've been after something else completely. "Shall we contact your father?"

Probably still in a mild state of shock, she exhaled and replied, "Yes, if you would, Sir."

Though innocent at first, I began seeing Ursula on a more frequent basis. One late afternoon, we agreed to meet at a small tabernaria near the Quadrifrons to share a bottle of wine. For the next several hours, we talked and enjoyed our time together. I told her about my life and career, and I still vividly recall how she touched my hand as I told her about Octavia's death and my children in Nemausus. Eventually, I told her many things I'd never said to anyone else before; talking to her was so damn easy.

Also, she told me of her life – much of which was untoward and shocking. She had been a slave for many years, and she talked about her struggles to gain legitimacy in an often unforgiving Roman world. She also spoke about the life shared with her father in the rooms just above his tailor shop on Constantine Street. Only later did I learn the horrors of her former life in servitude.

As the weeks passed, I began seeing on almost a daily basis. Over a glass of wine at an outdoor café or during a stroll through the market stalls in Trajan's Forum, we'd discuss my role in the Senate, or we'd explore a matter involving politics, economic issues, or a social imperative. No subject seemed beyond her intellectual grasp.

Although not always familiar with the minor intricacies of a particular topic, her natural curiosity made up for any lack of knowledge. There was little she wouldn't want to discuss, and this fact alone was quite unusual for a woman coming from her station in life. She intrigued me so much.

Soon we became lovers. In bed, she had no equal, and her passion for love-making was obsessive, overwhelming, and mesmerizing. Her energy seemed boundless, and her sexual appetite was almost irrepressible to me. She was as beautiful naked as any woman I'd seen before or ever imagined in my sweetest dreams. Her skin was feather soft, and it was as pure and white; it was scented in such a way as to bring out the passion in me so quickly. Never before or since have I caressed such smooth skin. Soon, she moved into my flat.

During those days while serving in the Senate, my mind could never entirely escape her – though I tried hard at first – and I found myself on many of my afternoons lying next to her in our soft down feather bed. I simply couldn't get enough of her, and with each passing week, our bond became deeper and fuller. Octavia, although still on my mind, had been dead for almost two years. Ursula, however, was a profound, tenacious, and abiding pleasure for me in the present. I became alive again.

CHAPTER X

One Sunday morning in late June, Ursula and I were sitting on my second-floor terrace enjoying our breakfast. My apartment was located near
the Theatre of Marcellus, and our balcony provided a sweeping view of the
Tabularium and Temple of Capitoline Jupiter. We were talking about the events
of the previous week when we heard a commotion on the street below.

A wealthy patrician was viciously beating one of his slaves. The patrician, well-
dressed and heavy-set, was also screaming insults at the terrified boy kneel-
ing before him. Young, blond-haired, and muscular, the slave was clearly of
Germanic descent. Although it was evident to me the slave could've easily
overcome his much older assailant, he simply knelt obediently in front of his
master, and took the brutal punishment without making a sound or offering
any resistance.

Although I wasn't immediately sure regarding the circumstances of what the
boy had done to enrage his master, it later became apparent the young slave
pulled his master's cart too fast, and in doing so, caused the patrician and his
wife to experience discomfort and annoyance.

The patrician screamed, "I told you to go slow, you insolent bastard. My wife
and I are being bounced all over the road like marbles in a jar."

Stopping only to strike the poor slave over and over again, the master said, "If
you ever do that again, I'll castrate you with a dull knife. Do you understand
me?"

Following further insults, a series of brutal lashes, and several swift kicks to
the boy's stomach and groin area, the master ordered the slave to pick up
the cart and continue the journey home. What surprised us the most was the
seeming indifference of the people who passed them on the street. Although
several of them turned their heads to watch the assault, they continued on
their journeys seemingly unconcerned.

"How can Christians just ignore such abuse?" Ursula asked, "Where's their humanity? Don't they have eyes which see and ears that hear?"

I just shook my head. "I don't know. Perhaps they don't want to become involved in the personal business of the owner and his slave. Or maybe, this type of punishment is merely part of these onlookers' normal lives. I suspect most of them have slaves of their own, and perhaps, the abuse isn't abnormal. My family, however, would never treat any of our slaves that way."

Soon the patrician climbed back into the cart with his wife, and we watched as the poor slave picked up the handles of the cart and began a slow walk down the street in front of us. Interestingly enough, I heard the patrician yell, "Faster, you damn idiot. Faster, we'll never make it home."

Until that morning, Ursula and I hadn't talked very much about the circumstances involving her enslavement and her later manumission. I carefully avoided the subject because I was apprehensive about what I might learn from her on this cruel subject. I was well aware my family owned slaves for several centuries, and I suspected I was often somewhat indifferent about the slaves under my direct control both in my households and on our family tenant farms. Slavery was a common practice in the world which we lived in, but now I was deeply in love with a former slave. The woman who had borne the burdens of Roman dominance and society's immoderations was sharing my bed.

I sensed it was time to broach the subject. While rubbing her back, I said, "Tell me what it's like growing up in Belgica. How did you become a slave?"

She turned her head and smiled at me. "Nobody has ever asked me this question before. Yes, how did all it begin?"

She took a deep breath, "Well, my people are Burgundians, and we lived together in a small farming village. One day when I was eight years old, the soldiers attacked our village, and my family – and many others – were killed or captured. Julius, the survivors were rounded up like cattle, and later separated into distinct groups based on our age, our physical condition, and our gender."

She shook her head and frowned. "Seeing the commotion today brought back so many painful memories to me. So I'll tell you everything, my love. But it's not a pretty picture."

She gently took hold of my hand, looked me in the eyes, and continued. "For several days, we were neither fed nor given anything much to drink other than dirty water. I guess they did it to weaken our spirits. One of the young girls who were with me died in a cold, damp cattle pen. Perhaps, she was one of the lucky ones. Rain fell on us, mud was everywhere, and there was no dry place to lie down. We were cold, hungry and frightened."

She stopped for a moment again. Then I said, "If it's too painful for you, please tell me no more."

"No, you need to know these things before we can go forward with our relationship. You must know the truth about me."

She poured herself another glass of wine and rose up from her chair to leave the balcony. Taking my hand, she led me back to our living quarters. "I never saw my mother or my brothers again. I found my father five days later. By then, my mother and brothers probably were sold to slave traders and bound for who knows where."

"Oh, Ursula, I'm sorry to hear that."

"A few days later, I was stripped of my clothes and given a filthy tunic to wear, and we walked, chained to each other, for several days until we arrived in Lutetia. Several people died along the way either from hunger or thrust – or just from the shame. Several others died as a result of the constant beatings we received by the sadistic guards, and a few were executed after they tried to escape. The journey wasn't only exhausting, but it was also humiliating. On the morning after we arrived at our final destination, we were bathed, fed, and dressed in cleaner clothes, and marched to – what I'd find out later to be – the central slave market."

She stopped once again and began crying softly. I held her tightly in my arms and stroked her hair. "Once we arrived inside the slave market, we were stripped naked and paraded into a large room. All of the slaves who were present to be auctioned off that morning were led onto a raised wooden platform – where we stood together side-by-side facing the buyers."

I could tell immediately this was hard for her. Looking out a window, she continued, "Although we were treated as pigs or cattle – or something worse – we were human beings. Just a few days prior, we were living peacefully in a small community and went about our daily lives. Standing with me on the platform,

I guess there were fifty or more men, women, and other children. All of us, including me, displayed small wooden signs hung around our necks, telling the buyers about our ages and attributes. Our hands were tied tightly behind our backs, and we were naked."

I was familiar with the harsh practices of the slavers. On several occasions, I'd attended these auctions to purchase slaves for my household operations and farming businesses. The auctions were never pleasant. Human beings were being degraded, ridiculed, and beaten. Families were separated, and even when confronted with strict orders to be silent, mothers and fathers screamed when their sons and daughters were taken from them.

Slavery had always been the norm in the civilized world, even under Christianity. There was nothing I could about the institution of involuntary servitude except treat our slaves in a humane fashion and provide them with a realistic opportunity for manumission. I suspect that these slaves knew they were dealt a very bad hand, but I also believed these same unfortunate people would place Romans into slavery if the tables had turned in their favor. Yet, it happened to a woman whom I loved deeply, and this made all the difference to me.

She continued with her story. "Because I didn't know the local dialect, I couldn't understand the words they were saying; but believe me, I knew their intentions. Several men came up to me and eyed me as if I was a strange beast or a creature from a different world. Several others touched me."

She gritted her teeth and shook her head. "Julius, I was only eight years old, and until then, no man had ever seen me naked. I felt degraded and ashamed. God, how I wanted my mother! I'd never been so violated in my life."

I held her hand; I couldn't fully grasp all that I was hearing.

She said, "It was then when I first saw my father. While I was still standing on the platform, he was being led into the room with a chain around his neck. He was naked, too. I'm not sure when it was when he first saw me, as all of the men were looking down, chained together. Once he recognized me, he screamed out my name, and he was severely beaten for his outburst."

I stood up and walked out to the balcony; I felt so ashamed, and my views on slavery began to change that day. After shaking my head, I came back into the room and sat back down on the couch. She was still pacing.

She continued, "Aside from the outburst from my father, none of the other slaves showed any emotions at all – except, perhaps, fear. Each one us knew even at the age of eight — why we were in this room. I wondered what would become of me. Would I end up as a servant in a patrician's home? Or would I go to a farm or worse, to a mine?"

She was wringing her hands and breathing quite quickly. Soon she came back to the couch and sat down next to me. "What about my father? I wondered what would happen to him. While he was educated and a tradesman, I questioned whether he'd be sold to someone who would use his talents or whether he'd end up in a quarry or some other hellhole. Those most unfortunate slaves, who suffer their fates under the worst of conditions, die after only a few years of beatings, starvation, and emotional abuse."

"So, what happened to you? I know you and your father were later reunited here in Rome."

"Yes, a wealthy slave merchant bought forty of us at the auction that morning – including my father and me – and after a three-week march without shoes, we ended up here in the city. We were kept separate from each other, and nobody knew he was my father. It was safer for me that way."

She took another sip of wine and continued. "A few days later, after we were fattened up and washed, we were auctioned off again in the central slave market here in Rome. As luck would have it, my father was placed in a tailor shop which was located less than two blocks from the home where I later worked as a domestic slave."

She tried to smile but couldn't; she just shook her head and continued. "My eventual owner, Tiberius Arugulas Cervantus, branded me with a hot iron on my right breast – the breast you kiss sweetly at night – and once I grew to be a girl of twelve or thirteen, he molested me regularly. My shame was overwhelming."

She stopped abruptly as if the retelling of her ordeal was becoming too much for her. "If I dirtied the sheets, he'd slap me and force me to clean them while his stench was still blanketing me. You know, I ended up having three abortions and one miscarriage in less than five years. I was barely healed when he was at me once again. You cannot begin to understand how much I hate the man. One day I'll kill him, I swear. I curse him!"

I held her close to me and asked, "So, how did you become free?"

"My father's owner was much more generous and sympathetic than mine. My father became highly skilled at his craft as a tailor, and he was permitted to keep some money from the profits of his master's business. When his master died unexpectedly about two years ago, the terms of his owner's Will freed my father from bondage. He was also given the title to his master's tailor shop. Once freed, he automatically became a citizen, and shortly after that, he approached my master to purchase me."

"Did your master understand the relationship between you and your father?

"No, my master didn't know I was the daughter; he'd never have sold me to my father. I suspect he'd have rather slit my throat than give me away to my father."

"So what happened next?"

"My master was led to believe my father wanted to purchase me and place me in a house of prostitution. Thankfully, my father was superb at his deception; he called me a whore, a slut, and he debased me in front of my master. After being offered a good price for me – much more than my master assumed I was worth – my master sold me to my father."

"Oh, Ursula."

"A week later, the manumission requirements were completed, and I was freed. It was a happy day for both of us."

We sat in silence for a long time. "It was only by pure luck we ended up on the same street in Rome. We never found out what happened to my mother or my brothers. I pray they are alive and free somewhere in the Empire, but I fear. . . "

She cried a long time in my arms. "So, Julius, do you still want me in your bed after hearing all of those awful things?"

"Oh, Ursula, my poor Ursula."

I held her close in my arms as we wept together.

From the earliest of days of the republic, slavery was a fact of life in the Roman world. In 330 AD, the Emperor Constantine commissioned a population survey of the entire Empire. The results revealed that although Italia's slave population amounted to about forty percent of the total population, the Empire as a whole counted just fewer than five million slaves   or about fifteen percent of the total population.

While most slaves performed manual labor or domestic services, other slaves were employed as highly skilled jobs or professions, such as teachers, accountants, and tradesmen.

A few days later, the subject came up again as we were eating our evening meal. Ursula asked, "You're a Senator. Isn't there anything you can do to help these poor people?"

"I don't know. Generally, the state doesn't interfere with the master-slave relationships. Except in extraordinary cases of cruelty or exploitation, a master can decide to treat his slaves kindly or could choose to torture, mutilate or even execute his slaves; but the times are changing."

"How so?"

"Well, as the Empire has grown, several laws have been enacted to help the status of a slave."

I told her that in 43 AD, Emperor Claudius ruled that if a slave was abandoned by his master, the slave became free. Furthermore, approximately twenty years later, Nero granted slaves the right to pursue complaints against their masters in court, and about a century after Nero's decree, Antoninus Pius ruled an owner who killed a slave without just cause could be tried for homicide.

I said, "And there's a recent law which provides a slave can volunteer for military service and receive his freedom after only having ten years of honorable service in either the army or navy."

She smiled. "Well, I guess there's been some progress over the years; but it's not enough."

"Now, there's a bill currently pending in the Senate which prohibits Christians from being slaves. I'm not certain how it would be applied – if enacted – to pagan slaves who later converted to Christianity, though. I recall that a few months ago, Pope Leo pointed out at least three former popes had been slaves. So things are changing even more."

Still, I could tell Ursula wasn't satisfied with my answers. She asked, "Didn't you mention yesterday about a change in the use of manumission – you know, freeing a slave?"

"Yes, there's some movement in the Senate on this matter, too."

I told her manumissions are a lifeblood of our civilization as the best members of the slave population, once freed, are integrated fully into Roman life. I said, "While Augustus limited the number of slaves which a citizen can free in his Will, the proposed Senate legislation would lift the percentage to a number up to fifty percent of the master's household slave population. In large estates, it could end up as a great number of slaves."

I stopped and thought for a moment and said, "And I'm aware of another bill which would free the children of slaves once the child attains his twentieth-first birthday. These are certainly positive developments."

"Why can't Rome just eliminate slavery altogether?" she asked. "It's unfair, and it's such a hideous practice. We're primarily a Christian nation now, aren't we?"

"I don't know about a total elimination of slavery happening anytime soon. So much of the wealth in the elite classes stems from the ownership of slaves. Also, it's a substantial revenue matter for the Empire."

"Really?"

I told her the Emperor receives a 5% tax on the sale or the inheritance of all slaves, a yearly tax of 2% must be paid on the value by the owners, and a considerable fee is gathered for enacting the process of the legal manumission of former slaves.

"And most of the public buildings, roads, and aqueducts throughout the Empire have been constructed using slave labor at a fraction of the cost of using paid citizens to do this work," I said. "Yes, slavery should be curtailed and better formulated. Yet, I doubt it'll ever completely disappear."

We sat in silence for a long time, reflecting on what each other mentioned. Finally, I asked her, "During the time you lived with your master, did you ever see your father?"

"Only at the slave church and only a couple of times a year."

"How did your father treat you whenever you met him?"

"Well, he made it clear to me early on that we must keep our relationship a secret because my master would prevent us from meeting should he find out. My father said, however, one day he'd come for me; however, I'd have to be patient."

I thought about it once again. "It must have been painful for both of you – being abused by your master and with your father unable to help you."

"Yes, I often cried when I'd see him, but it was a great comfort to know my father was there for me. I spent many hours dreaming about how he'd come to my master's house someday and rescue me. It got me through some terrible times."

"Tell me about the slave church."

She replied, "Well, it's a small building not far from my master's house. During the week it was used as a slaughterhouse – mostly for sheep. Although the building was in bad shape and smelled terrible, it was vital to our slave community."

"How so?"

"It was the only place where we could go and enjoy a modicum of freedom. We could talk to each other, embrace each other, and sing hymns, and a slave priest conducted the religious services. It was often our only moment of peace."

"A slave priest?"

She smiled. "Yes, Father Maltychosis was captured during a raid in Crimea. His captors didn't know he was a priest, and he kept it to himself. Once he was sold and taken to Rome, he let his new masters know of his ordination."

"If it were me, I would've mentioned it much earlier."

"Well, he told me that he was afraid to tell it to his captors because they weren't Christians."

"Well, that makes sense, I guess."

"Later, he told the officials in the slave market about his status, and he was sold to the Pope. After a while, the Pope allowed Father Maltychosis to hold services for the slave population only – but not for other Christians. The Pope, as far as I know, hasn't decided to free him."

I shook my head, stood up from my chair, and paced the room for a while. "I know the Church emphasizes the belief slavery is a natural state; I recall Paul, and perhaps even Jesus, spoke of slaves being obedient to legitimate authority."

"Perhaps so; however, our priest preached a different interpretation of the Holy Scripture. He said the Old Testament prophets, especially in the Book of Exodus, advocated liberation from bondage. He pointed to Moses as the prime example of freeing enslaved people from captivity."

I touched her hand and said, "I guess you can find several different interpretations within the contents of the Bible."

Ursula nodded her head. "I remember the last time I was in the slave church; it was just before my father purchased my freedom. Father Maltychosis told us that Jesus himself took up the mantle 'to set the oppressed people free' and his liberation philosophy eventually led Jesus to his death on the cross."

"Do you miss attending the slave church?"

"Yes, and once in a while I still try to go there, but they always turn me away. They're afraid of informants being among their ranks, and that their masters will attempt to re-enslave me."

I sat silent as she continued, "The slave church gave us a chance to talk among ourselves. We could pray, ponder, organize and debate. There we were free of many of the restrictions our masters placed upon us."

She stopped talking for an instant as if to gather her thoughts. "It was the one time in my life as a slave I felt safe, loved, and protected. I hear the masters now plan to close the slave church. I suspect they're afraid of our liberation philosophy."

"I hope it doesn't happen. Slaves should feel safe in church."

She told me that when the Church was young, it was the one place where the underbelly of society could go and be a part of something good and holy. In the early days, few of the aristocratic families converted to Christianity, and it was not until Emperor Constantine's conversion that the Church's social standing changed for the elite class

I took her hand. "Well, now the Church is the dominant religion in the Empire, and the Church has helped alleviate some of the brutality toward the slaves."

"Yes, Julius, there's been some change; now the once oppressed Church is now the oppressor. From what Father Maltychosis told us, the days of toleration are over. The Church is demanding strict orthodoxy; there's only one acceptable doctrine."

We talked about how heresy is outlawed by government action, and how gentle people are being persecuted for their beliefs all over the Empire. I recalled how hundreds of innocent believers had been slaughtered as a result of these mind-numbing doctrinal disputes; such as, whether the Holy Spirit proceeds from the Father and the Son or just from the Father.

"It's madness," she said.

"I agree. Too many have been slaughtered over theological concepts which can't be proven or disproven."

She nodded her head in agreement. "In the early days, the Church was much more Jewish in its approach, and much more tolerant and philosophical regarding simple disagreements in beliefs or rituals. Now, the Church clearly is much more pagan than Jewish."

"What do mean – the Church is more pagan than Jewish?"

She told me the Apostle Paul understood that the future growth of the Church depended upon a large-scale conversion of the Romans. Furthermore, he knew most Gentiles would never accept many requirements of the Jewish Law, such as male circumcision and the adherence to the strict dietary laws. So, Paul made these Jewish mandates optional for its new converts, and he talked more about the notions of love and salvation rather than the precepts of obligation and ritual. She stated what Paul and his successors have done in their preaching is to adapt Christianity in such a way as to absorb the old pagan order.

She laughed and squeezed my hand. "That's what we were taught in the slave church. Let me give you an example; the early Christian Fathers knew Jews could never accept the teaching of God mating with humans. To pagans, however, the practice was well-accepted; the traditional gods often mated with humans. It was easy to sell this concept to the Romans."

I took a sip of wine and looked out at the Forum Romanum in the distance. As usual, she was making sense. She continued, "In my little village, each house had their own god; now every house in Rome has its own saint. In pagan times, men of high standing could become gods after they died; now, they can become saints. And like the goddess, Minerva, we now have a woman in the hierarchy of Christian theology, the Virgin Mary. Jews would never have allowed any of this to happen."

She stopped for a moment, took my hand, and said, "Ancient temples, once consecrated to a particular god, are now Christian churches, and these buildings are now consecrated to a particular saint. Father Maltychosis taught us the vestments, incense, ceremonies, and hierarchy of priests and bishops appear much the same now as they did during the reigns of Tiberius and Trajan. Only the words are different."

We sat and talked for another couple of hours about these and other subjects, and I promised her that I'd talk with my mentor, Gaius Gallus Gallipolis, about enacting new legislation providing better treatment of slaves.

I don't know whether our conversation about slavery and the Church was another turning point in our relationship, but the passion she demonstrated over dinner that evening was later carried on in our bedchamber later that night.

Ursula was one of those few women I'd ever met who wanted to be in charge in the bedroom. She knew what she wanted, and she often asked for it. She was neither ashamed of her body nor bashful in her requests for intimate satisfaction.

While we were making love, she talked relentlessly, telling me how she felt, and asking me what I wanted from her. She was never embarrassed to ask me to satisfy a particular need or to show me the right ways of pleasing her. Watching her face, I could tell the precise moment when she was fulfilled, and timing myself with her rhythms, sighs, and grimaces, I often reached my summit then, too.

Those were good days.

A few days later, I met with Gaius in his office in the Basilica Julia. I mentioned the scene on the street in front of my apartment, and I brought up the issue regarding the legal status of slaves in the Empire. I asked, "Can it be improved? It seems such a key blemish on our culture."

He shrugged his shoulders and thought for a moment. "We hear rumors of exploitation from time to time; however, there's little information regarding how widespread the abuse may be. It's clearly in the owner's best interest to treat his slaves humanely, you know. I remember Seneca wrote if a slave was treated well by his master, he'd perform a better job than a poorly treated slave."

Then I told him more about Ursula and her story of going from freedom to slavery, and to freedom once again. He shook his head, "Over the years, I've become much more stoic about the concept of slavery, and as you know, I've freed almost all of my slaves. Even saying this, I'm appalled by the actions of cruel slave-owners."

"But can't we as a society do more for these captives?" I asked. "Certainly, the Senate can do more to help these unfortunate people."

"Yes, all laws can be changed except one: the law of unintended consequences. Many of our statutes sound magnificent when first enacted but later turned out much different than what the lawmakers first intended. Even freeing scores of slaves may have unintended outcomes."

I agreed. During my brief time in the Senate, I'd read several proposed bills which sounded reasonable on first reading but would have ended up as disastrous legislation in the long run. "But isn't it time," I asked, "to rethink the issue of slavery?"

"Perhaps; as Rome has grown older and wiser as a civilization, we've expanded the meaning of freedom beyond all prior conceptions of personal liberty which were ever known in antiquity. The leaders who championed what they knew in their hearts as right and just, eventually triumphed. Maybe we need to look at slavery again."

He explained that over the past millennium, Rome established three equal branches of government, and each of these branches – the Emperor, the Courts and the Senate – granted new rights, privileges, and responsibilities to its citizens. "Our forefathers, in giving these liberties to us a little bit at a time, didn't presume to understand the extent of freedom in all of its dimensions. Over centuries of struggle, things have gotten better."

We talked about how Roman law has evolved over the centuries, and he said, "The Senate and the Courts, and various Emperors at times, have entrusted to future generations the obligation to redefine and to expand these rights. We need to revisit these matters regularly."

Turning to the issue regarding the expansion of citizenship, we talked about that in the early days of the Republic, when only a few Italians could enjoy the rights of citizens. Over the years, the government has granted citizenship to millions more of its people – including to freed slaves.

I said, "But often these rights ebb and flow as the political winds blow in various and competing directions, don't they?"

"Yes, the rule of law has always been interpreted differently by succeeding generations. In the long view of history, it's been expanding rather than contracting."

He stopped speaking for a moment and looked out his window. "My friend, no society is perfect. We've lived through centuries of struggle, and along the way, we have made laws, expanded coverage, and set limits – but always we've moved forward. Yes, things have certainly gotten better."

Gaius explained the rule of law is essential to maintain social order, especially as the size of the middle class has expanded throughout the Empire. To prosper, he mentioned citizens need to understand the process of delicately balancing 'security' against the concepts of 'freedom and fundamental fairness' when dealing with their government and with one another. Hearing that explanation, I smiled. Gaius was always at the forefront of enlightened and progressive thought.

He continued, "A civilization needs specific and enforceable limitations on government and its officials to preserve peace and stability. In this way, we remain free, and we can grow stronger and prosper as a nation."

I smiled and said, "I guess that's the reason why you keep reading and rereading those dusty law scrolls on your shelves."

"Yes, I do, and you should read them, too. The trick, of course, is finding the correct and the binding rule of law. It's often a time-consuming process, my friend."

At that moment, there was a knock on the door, and Gaius' assistant entered. "Sir, there are soldiers here from the Emperor to see Senator Majorian."

"Well, send them in."

Shortly thereafter, an officer of the Imperial Guard entered with an entourage of three armed soldiers. After saluting, he said, "Senator Majorian, the Emperor would like to see you right away. Can you please come with me?"

"Is Valentinian in Rome or are we going to Ravenna?"

"Sir, he's staying at his residence on the Palatine. Can you come with me now, Sir?"

I looked at Gaius and winked, "Well, we mustn't keep the Emperor waiting."

A few moments later, we left Gaius' chambers, walked down a flight of stairs, and exited the Basilica Amelia. Turning to the left, we walked passed by the Temple of Antoninus and Faustina, and under the Arch of Titus, and then we turned right onto the Clivus Palatinus – the road which connects the Forum to the Palatine Hill.

After passing through several levels of security, we passed through the gilded halls known as the Aula Regia and the Lararium, and eventually into the Triclinium. In each room, several men stood on guard, and around their necks, each one wore a large golden badge on a chain identifying the level of their authority. The soldiers were tall and powerfully built – the Emperor's personal guard.

Upon leaving the Lararium, our escort led us down a darkened corridor, our footsteps making no sound on the thick Persian carpets which covered the floors from wall to wall. We were now deep into the inner sanctum.

The Triclinium was the last main room in the palace. It was large and extravagantly decorated, with Corinthian columns and contained a frieze depicting the founding of Rome by Romulus and Remus in 753 BC.

I marveled at the other decorations on the walls; everything a riot of color and sophisticated detail. There were brightly painted shields displaying the numbers of the various Legions, marble statues and busts of famous Romans and Greeks, stuffed African animals and ferocious beasts, vases of roses and other colorful plants, caged birds with exotic feathers and tropical markings, and intricately carved furniture from all over the world.

Valentinian, seated at a large table at the rear of the room, saw us, and he motioned us forward. We bowed deeply before him, as he said: "No courtship today, Senators. Please have a seat. There's an important matter I need to discuss with Senator Majorian right now."

After signing and stamping the document which he'd been reviewing, Valentinian handed it to his assistants. They bowed, turned to the right, and abruptly left the room. After exchanging a few pleasantries with us, he stood up and paced along the length of the far wall for a minute or so. Something weighed heavily on my mind.

"I need a new Master of Soldiers," he said. "The bastard, Aëtius, was plotting treason against me, and as you well know, he was summarily executed in Ravenna last autumn. I understand we've located and dealt with all of his co-coconspirators, and I want you to know I was happy to learn neither of you was a part of the treasonous plot against me."

He stared directly at me for several moments; perhaps, he was trying to determine whether my expression would yield some information about my loyalties. "Julius, I want you as the next Master of Soldiers. Will you accept the commission?"

I was shocked at his proposal. I replied, "As you well know, Majesty, I've left military service and now serve my constituents as a Senator. Surely, there are more worthy and talented men in the Empire to serve as the Master General."

"No, there are not, and after consulting long and hard with my advisors, I've selected you."

"Majesty, Generals Ricimer and Aegidius are certainly more capable than I. Each one currently commands a legion, and each one has considerably more experience in the field than I do."

Valentinian shook his head. "Yes, each one of them is clearly capable, and each one has served the Empire courageously and consistently over the years. But, Senator Majorian, they are barbarians. After Stilicho, we cannot have another barbarian as Master of Soldiers. We need a Roman to fill the position. I need someone in command who can help placate Aëtius' troops, many of whom have become hostile to my authority."

He hesitated for an instant, and took a breath in order to choose his words carefully. "You are the one, Julius. It's you who can bring the legions back under Imperial control. I want you to agree to accept the command. Of course, I will not force the role upon you; however, you'd do Rome and me a great service if you'd accept. And I'd consider it a great personal favor. We . . . I, need you in that position."

"Majesty, may I think about it for forty-eight hours?"

Valentinian looked a bit crestfallen at my answer but nodded affirmatively.

After a few more moments of light conversation, we bowed to him and quickly left the palace. The offer was a great honor; something I'd often dream about when I was first commissioned as an officer in the Legions. It was certainly an opportunity which I'd not anticipated when we entered the palace earlier in the afternoon.

While I was prepared to decline the offer, I'd need some time to consider the consequences of denying the Emperor his first choice as Master of Soldiers. Either way, my life wouldn't be the same after that afternoon.

CHAPTER XI

A small commotion rouses me from my thoughts. It's the changing of the guard; it must be midnight now. The Captain of the Guard, a young officer of about twenty-five years of age, has ordered the current contingent of soldiers to attention as a new group of men replaces them.

The young soldier approaches me with a torch in his right hand. Stopping in front of my cell, he holds the light high and gazes in at me. "Well, I see you're still with us, Sire."

I nod at him, and he goes on to the next cell.

A few minutes later, it's quiet once again. From the few torches illuminating the dark, dank prison, I can barely see the worried faces of the prisoners who will probably share my fate come morning. Like them, I've no realistic hope of avoiding execution. Ricimer knows well if one goes after the Emperor, he needs to kill him or face a similar fate himself. Once Ricimer placed his treasonous plot into motion, the dye was cast. There's no going back now. Ah, the dark desires of men.

A priest came by my cell a few hours ago to hear my confession and absolve me from my sins. While I thanked him for his time and compassion, I declined both. On several occasions, I've requested a meeting with Ricimer, but he has given me neither the courtesy of an appearance nor an explanation for my confinement. I'd like to hear the reason for my imprisonment directly from his mouth.

CHAPTER XII

Treverorum, Belgica – December 454

At the time I was appointed as Master General, Count Ricimer still commanded the VI Legion from Treverorum, a large city on the northwestern edge of the Empire. To soothe his rumpled feathers and his deep disappointment at not being selected as the Master of Soldiers, I decided to journey to see him.

Founded by the Celts in the 4th century BC as Treuorum, the city was conquered by the Romans in the late 1st century BC and renamed Augusta Treverorum. The city later became the capital of the province of Belgica, and in 454 AD, it was one of the five biggest cities in the known world with a population of approximately 100,000 residents. It was, however, a long way from the city of Rome; and not just in distance but also when comparing the cultures and traditions.

After meeting with Valentinian in the Palace on that September afternoon, Gaius and I walked directly back to his office in the Basilica Amelia to discuss the merits of my proposed appointment. We talked for hours, and he led me to the conclusion I should resign from the Senate and accept the Emperor's commission. Then, it was time for me to talk the matter over with Ursula. I knew it would be a tough sell.

As we often did after long a day in the Senate, Ursula and I sat together on the couch in my apartment, holding hands, as I recounted the battles, compromises, and negotiations which made up my day. She listened quietly as I told her about being escorted by a contingent of soldiers to the Palace to meet with the Emperor. I mentioned his gracious offer, my subsequent discussions with Gaius, and my decision to accept the commission.

"Julius," she said, "I'm so proud of you, but what happens to us, to me?"

"Fairest, you can come with me."

She smiled, shook her head, and kissed me on the cheek. "I cannot go with you to the edges of the Empire as your concubine or mistress, and it would be unseemly for you to marry a former slave. So, no, you must go on without me. You've made no promises to me, and I'll not hold you back."

I took her other hand in mine. "You are now my whole world, and should you not agree to come with me, I'll remain in the Senate."

Getting down on my knees, I looked up into her eyes and asked, "Ursula, please marry me."

I saw tears well in those eyes. "No, my prince, I won't marry you. Being a slave was bad enough; as you well know, I was raped and . . ."

She wept uncontrollably as I held her in my arms and rubbed her back. "No, I cannot marry you. It will only lead to disgrace. Too many men in Rome have seen me, and dishonored me, perhaps some of the same people whom you serve with in the Senate today. This is why I rarely agree to go out with you in public; someone may see you and me together. I cannot be your wife, and I won't be your concubine."

"Ursula, please listen to me. Please hear me out. After we are married, we'll leave Rome and go far off to distant places in the Empire where no one will know you and no one will ever know these horrible things you've told me. You'll never have to come back to Rome again. This I promise you."

She shook her head again in a negative fashion. "No, our marriage cannot happen, ever."

I argued further, "Once my time as Master of Soldiers is over, we'll live the rest of our lives in Nemausus, among my children and my family. No one will ever know you were ever a slave. I promise you this, my darling. I promise."

A gleam of hope appeared on her face. "Are you sure, Julius? Are you really sure? I don't want you to hate me someday because of my past. I don't want you to be ashamed of me should someone recognize me or tell stories about me."

"I could never hate you."

I kept holding her in my arms.

Then she said, "I don't want your family to despise me or pity me. I could never live in shame again. I'd rather die, and I don't want you to marry me just to do the honorable thing. We can part ways now, and I can return to my father's business. You've been good to me, and you owe me nothing."

We talked for hours, and eventually, we agreed to talk more about it later. The next morning, she consented to marry me only if the slave priest, Father Maltychosis, was the officiant at the ceremony, and only if her father and Senator Gallipolis were the only witnesses to our sacred union. I quickly agreed.

Three days later, we were married in my apartment in a private ceremony. Within the week, Gaius, by virtue of his power and status in the Senate, convinced the Church to free Father Maltychosis from slavery. I learned later Father Maltychosis spent the rest of his life attending to the needs of the poor and desperate people who resided in the slums of Rome.

Gaius also presented a private bill to the Senate which permitted me, a member of the senatorial class, to marry a freed slave – a practice which had been disallowed by Emperor Augustus in 26 BC. Then Gaius buried the provision deep in an appropriations bill which nobody ever took the time to read.

After spending the next thirty days in Ravenna, consulting with the Emperor and his military advisers, Ursula and I, along with a small contingent of cavalry, began our journey to meet with the four principal field generals who commanded the legions which defended the Western Empire.

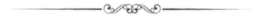

In early October, we began our journey west toward Treverorum. Over the years, I've always been amazed by the resourcefulness and foresight of our forefathers in constructing and maintaining a system of main thoroughfares which traversed the course of the Empire.

Over the preceding seven or eight centuries, Roman roads had been the physical infrastructure which was vital to the maintenance, expansion, and development of the state. As such, these roads provided the Empire with an efficient means to facilitate the overland movement of armies, civilians, commerce and communications throughout the nearly two million square miles which comprised the Empire.

During the reign of Emperor Constantine, his accountants determined the Empire built well over fifty-thousand miles of stone paved roads throughout the

Empire, stretching from Hadrian's Wall in Northern Britannia to the shores of the Persian Gulf in Mesopotamia. At that time, his managers also calculated the Empire constructed no fewer than twenty-nine great military highways radiating from the Capitol, and the Empire's one-hundred-thirteen provinces were interconnected by three-hundred-seventy-two lesser paved roads.

On our way west, we traveled along the ancient, yet still grand, Via Cassia toward the city of Mediolanum. When we were able, we stopped at many of the military installations and fortifications which protected the Western Empire, and we assessed their level of readiness and functionality. After speaking directly to the local commanders, I noted some of the installations attained only a minimum degree of military readiness whereas some of the other facilities still had a long way to go to accomplish their missions.

Each of these installations, however, needed considerably more men, armor, and structural improvements to become or remain battle ready. I always heard the same complaints from the local commanders: months of back pay owed to their troops; frequent desertions; shortages of construction materials and exorbitant labor costs; unsafe drinking water and dry wells; and crumbling walls and battements. However, there was no money in the budget those days for such things.

While meeting with Aegidius and his general staff in Mediolanum, we engaged in a frank discussion about the operational integrity of the imperial armies. He noted, "With the death of Attila, we've survived our biggest threat yet. No, I don't believe the Huns can – or will – reorganize. Now we need to look west and south; that's where our next problems will arise."

"Are you talking about Gaiseric and the Vandals?"

He stood up and pointed to a map. "Yes, certainly the Vandals, but we also need to be cautious in our dealings with the Goths, the Franks, and the Burgundians. Aëtius developed a unique personal relationship with these tribes, and his execution raises new concerns about their continued fidelity and allegiance to Rome."

"Yes, I need to keep it in mind. By the way, Valentinian mentioned the matter to me, too."

"Well, I've no doubt he's worried. Valentinian isn't popular with these people – in fact, they despise him."

"I suspect you're right; any recommendations?"

"Maybe Ricimer can deal with these tribes, and I'd consider that approach if I were you. At one time, you may have been able to work with them. As the Emperor's handpicked agent, you'll need to re-establish your credentials. So, be careful; I'd expect trouble."

I nodded in agreement. "I agree, and I know the tribes are too valuable as allies and much too dangerous as enemies. It'll be my first order of business, I assure you."

A few moments later, Aegidius stood up. He said, "Now we'll need to turn to a delicate issue, the matter of royal succession. The Emperor is now in his mid-thirties, and some people seriously question his manliness."

"Yes, I've heard the rumors."

"I know it may seem somewhat awkward, my friend, but you need to convince His Majesty to produce a male heir or designate a successor. Valentinian is the last surviving male member of the Imperial house. Although he has two daughters, should he die, Rome needs a man to succeed him on the throne."

Aegidius stopped for a moment as if to find the precise words to finish his thoughts. "At this stage of our national vulnerability, we certainly need to avoid a dynastic war. Should the Emperor die without a male issue, the House of Theodosius is at an end, and we can expect chaos in the Western Empire. I'm not – in any way - suggesting treason here. We need to find a formula to avoid a disastrous war."

Somewhat embarrassed, I smiled and replied, "I'm unsure how to approach Valentinian on such a delicate matter, but I'll think about it. I know when Theodosius II died in Constantinople a few years ago without a male heir; Marcian married the emperor's sister to avoid a fight for succession. Maybe you or Ricimer could marry Valentinian's wife when he dies?"

At that suggestion, we both laughed for a few moments. Although Valentinian's wife, Licinia, was the daughter of the late Emperor Theodosius II, she was clearly no beauty. Smiling he said, "I don't think I'd want to go quite that far in service to the Empire."

Then Aegidius raised one more problem. "Now that Attila's empire has disintegrated, we're facing the problem of refugees flooding into the Empire – as individuals and in small groups. They've decided life south of the Danube is more promising than the confusion and struggle that's going on north of the river."

"Are they still coming in? I assumed it has slowed to a mere trickle."

"Yes, they still cross the frontier in droves, and Julius, I cannot continue to feed these people. There's a famine in Northern Italia, and unless the immigrants are fed, housed and employed, there'll be some unpleasant difficulties facing us before springtime. Hungry people will often resort to crime and insurrection."

"I understand. Just do the best you can, my friend. The Imperial Treasury is currently at a low ebb. Do your best."

Ursula and I stayed in Mediolanum for another week. During that time, she began experienced bouts of morning sickness, and she also presented a familiar glow about her.

"Yes, I'm pregnant. I hope to give you another son."

I smiled, "Do you want to go back to Rome? Your father or Gaius can help you until I return. Mediolanum is the easiest part of our journey. It's a long way from here to Treverorum, and winter is fast approaching."

"No, my prince, I want to be with you. And I want to have my son born in Belgica – where I was born and where some of my family may still live today. Also, I want to find my village and take our son there."

"I'm not sure your village even exists today; it may have been burned to the ground."

"Even if it was destroyed, the river still flows, and the great ocean isn't far away. My ancestors' spirits still reside there in the lush valleys and the vast forests. I want my son to see these places."

I asked, "But how do you know the child is a boy?"

"Women know these things, my sweet. He talks to me already."

We left Mediolanum in mid-October and hoped to cross the Alpine passes before winter arrived. After saying our farewell to Aegidius, we traveled west through the rolling hills of the wine country of Northern Italia, through the tall grasslands and meadows still bright with the last flowers of the year, and through the dense forests with ancient trees which were just beginning to change color. The weather was dry and the air so clear we could see the Alps. Those towering mountains separated Roman civilization from barbarism and divided our world of enlightenment from the realm where ignorance and savagery prevailed.

The journey west, and then north, was as difficult as I'd expected. While stopping along the way for rest and the opportunity to inspect the crumbling imperial forts and installations, our small group traveled up the ancient Via Domitia across Franco-Saxon territory and went by boat along the Danube to the small city of Vienne in Northern Germania.

The autumn foliage was breathtaking and the days were getting shorter as we approached the winter equinox. After leaving Vienne in an early-season snowstorm, we traveled on a minor road through the Pennine Alps, and we turned northwest in the direction of Treverorum where we'd spend the winter.

Along the way, we observed that the peasants who were residing in the countryside still adhered to the vestiges of their old pagan cults. They were venerating Thor or some other local god just as seriously as we worshiped Christ and the Saints. Superstition still ruled in the dark valleys and thick forests of Germania. Their fear of demons, man-wolves, and winged goddesses appeared to influence the daily lives of those ordinary people. Even the few priests, who operated the small Christian churches in those quaint hamlets and rural outposts, practiced a strange combination of Christianity and paganism – as if to appease all potential deities.

Despite the snowstorm, the dreary winter weather held off until the very last portion of our journey. Toward the end, the skies darkened, almost as grey as paving stones, and the wind, once soft and mellow, turned into a gale. The forests were dense, and the branches of the trees almost met over our heads – shutting out what little light which filtered through the clouds.

The horses became troubled and whinnied and reared against our forward route, and our escort soldiers grew uneasy and apprehensive as their eyes darted from left to right, looking for an ambush or an opportunity for rest and relief.

As we were climbing over our journey's last mountain passes in mid-November, the snows were deep and unrelenting. The road became a narrow pathway pounded in the snow, and our horses picked a cautious route between the drifts to find their way down the steep slopes and through the seemingly impenetrable forests. Had we waited another week to finish this portion of our journey, the mountains would've been impassable.

We often rode in silence, listening to the horses' hooves crunching in the ever-deepening snow. Finally, the signs of civilization began appearing all around us, and once we crested the last hill in our journey west, we saw the rooftops and smelled the wood smoke of the place where we'd spend the long cold winter of 454-455.

Treverorum was a welcome site; but after our nearly three-month expedition from the palm trees, green grasses, and warm breezes of the city of Rome, it was dark, smoky, and foreign to us. Even though the city had been in Imperial hands for almost five hundred years, it was clearly a Frankish city now in customs, dialogue, and appearances. As I rode into the grand city on the Moselle River, I wondered whether Rome would be able to retain this outpost of the Western Empire for much longer.

Under a threatening sky, the color of tarnished silver, we entered Treverorum through the Porta Nigra, which was one of the four gates standing on each side of the roughly rectangular city. After leaving our cavalry escort at the fort immediately outside the city gates, our local military guide accompanied us down Augusta Street to the official residence of the Master of Soldiers.

Our new home, an ancient two-story stone house built high on a hill during the reign of Emperor Diocletian, was luxurious by local standards. The main living quarters were located on the second floor of the residence with the kitchens, stables, supply rooms and slave quarters situated on the first floor.

As we entered the great room, a log fire was burning brightly in the fireplace. Ursula smiled and walked over to one of the larger windows, threw back the shutters, and gazed out at the city below us. "Julius, I'm finally home. After seventeen years, I'm finally where I belong."

In a little girl fashion, she wrapped her arms around herself and gazed out at her new – but somehow familiar – surroundings. She exclaimed, "I recognize these smells; the air; this setting. These people look like my people – the way they dress, the way they walk, and the way they gesture at each other. You've made my dreams come true; oh, what a fantastic feeling!"

I smiled and encircled my arms tightly around her waist and asked, "Do you think your village is very far from here?"

"No, I'm sure it is not too far away; you know, I can almost sense it. One day we'll shall go there together. One day soon, I hope."

Wrapped up in each other's embrace for ten minutes or more, we looked out the window and gazed out at the sprawling city encircling us. It was growing late in the afternoon, and the large flakes of wet fluffy snow were falling and blowing into the 'great room.'

The alpine breeze was also blowing softly through her long blond hair and brushing it softly onto my face. After a while, our cheeks were rosy from the sharp bite of the frosty air. As she began shivering, I kissed her and closed the shutter tightly, and we sat together for several minutes more in front of the blazing fireside.

Following a knock on the door, the two slaves who were assigned to our home entered the main living room with our evening meal – consisting of grilled pork, boiled cabbage, freshly baked wheat bread, and a large urn of local red wine.

The male slave, Cluny, was a young man in his late twenties from Ethiopia. He had blue-black hair of an Egyptian hue – perfectly straight and almost reaching his waist. Although he was proficient in the Frankish language, his ability to speak Latin was negligible. However, Ursula was able to communicate to him in through an awkward combination Burgundian – a language which was strikingly similar to Frankish – Latin, and hand gestures. Soon they were both laughing.

The female slave, Elmina, was from the highlands of Caledonia, and she was probably about fourteen years old. Tall, with long curly red hair, her skin was white as the snow piling up on the sill just behind the shutters; her Latin was good.

Initially, both Cluny and Elmina served us our meals with their eyes lowered and with no expression on their faces, except one which indicated strict obedience. Because of Ursula, both of these slaves would soon, however, become active members of our family.

After dinner, we decided to go for a walk and become more acquainted with our new community. Being familiar with the city, Cluny led us through the parallel and perpendicular streets of Treverorum. During this time of the year, it was totally dark by suppertime, and when we began our stroll, there were only a few people still out.

The recent snowfall had dropped about one inch of snow on the streets, and our boots made a crunching sound as we walked along toward the main town square. From time to time, a puff of wind blew a swirl of snow around us, and it made me appreciate we weren't in sunny Italia anymore.

Ahead of us, there was a wide street lined with many closed and shuttered shops. As we walked, there was little noise emanating from the sleepy town except the sound of water flowing from the local fountains, which were fed from an aqueduct towering high above us.

As I looked through the partially closed shutters, I could see families sitting together at tables or nestled around their fire hearths. In one home, I saw a young boy playing a lute while his sisters were dancing around him in a circle.

We passed a couple of tabernarias which were full of men enjoying a few beers after a day's work, and on one corner, we walked by St. Rita's Church where a choir was practicing for the next Sunday's services. Curiously, a few people passed us carrying freshly cut evergreen trees and garlands.

Cluny told Ursula that the following Friday was St. Nicholas' Day, and he mentioned the city fathers were preparing for the annual celebration in the main square. Many of the local people had already decorated their homes with local greenery and large pinecones, a practice which predated Christianity.

Cluny eventually led us to the Aula Palatina, a massive government administration building built by Emperor Constantine around 310 AD. Containing many government offices, the building served as my headquarters during the long winter. As walked around the darkened city, Cluny also pointed out several other public buildings, such as the Baths of St. Barbara, the even larger Circus Amphitheatre, and the modest forum.

Following a city tradition dating back to the time of the Celts, we ended our tour by tossing a coin (for good luck) from the large stone bridge which crosses the Moselle River just inside the massive city walls. In the end, the winter of 455 was the coldest one in fourteen years.

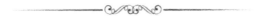

Awakening from a deep sleep later that evening, I sensed Ursula wasn't lying in bed beside me. Looking up, I saw her naked profile standing at the window and looking out at the city. It had stopped snowing, and the once-cloudy sky was replaced by a full moon which was shining directly upon her.

Silhouetted in the moonlight, she looked almost mystical. Her long blond hair fell like a veil down to the middle of her back, and her voluptuous hips were lily white and curved as if mimicking a statue of the goddess, Venus.

I called out softly, "Ursula, what are you doing there? You'll catch your death of cold."

As she turned sideways to respond to me, I could clearly see a slight bulge rising in her abdomen; her pregnancy was just beginning to show.

In the soft moonlight, she was even more beautiful than I'd remembered, and she aroused such a passion in me that I immediately slid out of the covers, walked to the window, picked her up in my arms, and carried her back to bed. Soon, she began kissing me deeply and passionately. I tasted her tongue on my tongue, and a wave of desire entirely enveloped me.

Rolling on top of her, she wrapped her legs around my hips, and we soon joined as one human entity. Lying together later in the warm glow of the fire's remaining auburn embers, we held onto each for a long time as we watched the shadows dance on the ceiling above us.

Later on, she asked me to recite a poem for her. After taking her into my arms, I brushed the hair out of her eyes and kissed her mouth. Recalling a verse from a poem by the great poet, Catullus, I said,

> *Let us live, my darling, and let us love.*
> *And let the words of the aged, ever so proper,*

Be worth less than nothing to us.
For the sun may set and rise again;
But when our short time is done,
We'll sleep for an everlasting night.
Now give me a thousand kisses to remember you.

We made love again, and as the hearth-light dimmed and the starlight grew in a greater luster, we fell asleep in each other's embrace. I'll never forget that magical evening, especially in light of the events which would soon follow.

The following morning, I reported to my headquarters detachment in the Aula Palatina. I remember that evergreen boughs decorated the walls and rafters and coal-burning stoves cut the early winter chill. Count Ricimer was already waiting for me in my office. I hadn't seen him since the morning following the battle on the Catalaunian Plains in 451 AD.

We sat in my office with a pile of maps and parchments scattered on the table between us. The morning light was streaming through the ancient windows, and a marble statue of Emperor Gratian looked disparagingly down among us.

After a few minutes of small talk, he looked at me in a disparaging fashion and said, "I must tell you that I was mad as hell in not being appointed as Master of Soldiers. I almost resigned my commission. I deserved the job, you know."

"Although I argued for your appointment, Valentinian wanted a Roman to fill the position. After Stilicho, he said . . . '

Ricimer slammed his fist on the table. "Yes, but that was well over fifty years ago, and the Empire has changed considerably since then. Julius, unless Rome accepts this new reality, the Western Empire will disappear. I recall we had a similar talk at the tabernaria in Ravenna during the night before we met with Aëtius and the Emperor. In my judgment, things have just gotten worse – even with Attila gone."

"I guess you know Aegidius was also disappointed at being passed over."

"Screw Aegidius!"

As he described in detail about the many years of service he'd given to the

Empire, Ricimer was as angry as I'd ever seen him. We ranted and fumed about the battles he'd fought against the many enemies of Rome, his loyalty to the ideals of the Empire, and the sacrifices he'd made to advance the directives and decrees of Valentinian only to be passed over for the position of Master General solely because of his barbarian heritage.

He screamed, "I am as Roman as anybody else in this goddam Empire. Screw Valentinian and his royal court of madmen, ass-kissers, and magicians." Apparently, these feelings had rested heavily on his mind for several months, and he told me once again he was devastated by the Valentinian's decision to select me rather than him. Yes, he was livid!

After another thirty minutes or so, however, he began to settle down, and we talked about the recent deaths of his wife, his only child, and his brother, Olaf. Still racked with strong emotions, he bowed his head; and then looking back up at me, I could see a deep sadness in his eyes. For the next several minutes, he was silent as if he was still sorting out the details of these tragic and painful deaths in his head.

Suddenly, as if he'd finally closed the chapter of this part of his life, he smiled as he told me all about his triumphant return to his homeland at the head of a large Imperial contingent, and his reunion with his older brother, Gustave, and the rest of his Galician family. Overall, he seemed proud of this feat, and he reminisced about the many other achievements of his career as a Roman officer.

Eventually, we turned to the matters of pressing business. I asked, "So, how are things in Belgica?"

Ricimer took a deep breath and said, "The military district is calm for now but just a month ago, a small band of Alemanni warriors, maybe as many as two-hundred of them, invaded Germania Superior from Raetia. I dispatched Count Burco with the First Cohort, and luckily he was able to drive them back over the Rhine. They'll come at us again in the spring."

I stroked my chin and asked, "How about King Gunderic and the Burgundians; what's going on there?"

"Well, they seized large portions of Gaul just west of Lugdunum, and they are now threatening to take the city itself. The King recently told me in order for the Burgundians to remain federated with Rome, the Emperor must cede control of the Gallic territory south to the sea. He says this gesture would represent payment for their service to the Empire in fighting Attila."

Ricimer paused for a moment. "With the arrival of the recent migration of large numbers of Burgundians to Gaul, we Romans are now few in number here, and they are many. I think Rome can only retain control of this province with their help."

I shook my head and replied, "I agree, but just between you and me, we must keep a sharp eye on King Gunderic. On the one hand, Ravenna is concerned with his political intentions; however, on the other, they've been among the most loyal federates of the Empire. We need them act as a buffer between Italia and the Franks. So we face a real dilemma there. And what about Theodoric; what's his status now?"

"King Theodoric and the Visigoths? Well, you'll need to talk to Avitus about them. I think they're friendly, but I'm uncertain about their loyalty to the Empire."

"Okay."

"Furthermore, Avitus cannot be trusted; he's very cozy with them. I predict he'll make a play for the Throne should something happen to Valentinian. I'd watch him carefully, Julius. He is not your friend."

Our meeting went on for several more hours, and over lunch, we talked about our early days as junior officers in Gaul working under Aëtius. Following a glass of wine, Ricimer asked me about Ursula.

"She has helped me overcome Octavia's death," I said. "I think I told you that Ursula is Burgundian, and she wants me to help her find the place where she lived as a young girl. And, my friend, she's pregnant. Our baby is due in late March or early April. So, we'll remain here for the winter and spring. By the way, can you arrange for me a meeting with King Gunderic? Maybe he can help us locate Ursula's village."

"Yes, I'll arrange it."

Early Friday evening, Cluny, Ursula, and I followed a large crowd of people walking up Augusta Street to the main square of Treverorum. It was December 6 – St. Nicholas' Day. It was quite a sight to see!

The town square was illuminated by hundreds of torches, and the city fathers strategically placed several tall pine and cedar trees all around the plaza. As the festivities began, the Bishop gave a short welcoming speech, and thereafter, hundreds of children started decorating the evergreen trees with ribbons, bows and wooden cutouts of all kinds.

In an attempt to keep the people warm on this cold and snowy evening, the city fathers lit bonfires in sand-traps, and vendors erected long rows of stalls and tables to sell the mounds of homemade cakes, cookies, and pies to the families who gathered there that evening.

Many other townspeople, carrying long garlanded and decorated pine-poles, were singing and cheering as they walked around the tables and stalls, and children ran and dashed in every direction – laughing with excitement and anticipation. A light snow was falling, and soon the trees – and many of the participants – were almost totally covered white in the newly fallen winter snow.

In my judgment, the Franks, as a group, were the most attractive people in Europe. They were tall and fair-skinned, often with blond hair and blue eyes. However, I've been told they were confrontational, and they loved to battle. They also drank way too much and sang too loudly. Unlike many Italians of my day, the Franks took great pride in military service.

Ricimer told me at our meeting earlier that morning St. Nicholas' Day was a reconstituted remnant of a pagan celebration which originated from a much older time when the Celts celebrated the winter equinox. In the revised Christianized version, St. Nicholas was portrayed as a Christian bishop (appropriately wearing a tall bishop's hat and an ornate red cape, and carrying a silver mitre) and the Bishop was accompanied to the square by his nemesis, the cruel Knecht Ruprecht.

The devilish looking elf walked tenaciously around the plaza with his entourage of little demons, and he inquired of the children whether they'd been saying their prayers. If not, the character, which represented evil incarnate, shook his bag of ashes at them, or beat them softly with a stick. The good children were given a special treat, ranging from sweets to marbles or some other small toy, and the Bishop would hug and bless them.

After looking around the city square for a few minutes, it became apparent to me that paganism remained the predominant religion in this part of Belgica. Although Emperor Constantine issued the Edict of Mediolanum in 313 AD (which finally legalized Christianity in the Empire), the transition to Christianity was moving slowly in this part of the Roman world.

Between 313 and 391, both paganism and Christianity were legal religions of the Empire when Emperor Theodosius the Great passed legislation which prohibited all pagan worship in the Empire. While no longer a state-sponsored religion, it was evident the ancient pagan theologies still thrived in Treverorum.

Hand-in-hand, we walked around the square marveling at all that we saw before us. As we stopped at a local stall to purchase some freshly baked cakes and *glühwein* (a hot mulled wine), Ursula heard a sound which caused her to leave my side and dash quickly to the stall next door. Apparently, two of the vendors were speaking in Burgundian. After a few moments, Ursula began talking with them in her native language, and soon, I could clearly see tears of joy running down her face.

Taking me by the hand over to the next stall, she said, "Darling, these are my people. They live not far from the town where I was born – in Atria. One woman has recently been there – several times, she says. She said she might even know some of my family."

I held Ursula tightly as she wept with joy. She asked, "Can we go there soon? Maybe one of my sisters is still alive. Please, can we go there soon?"

Nodding affirmatively, I was lost for words as her joy filled us both with emotion. Ursula and Ederle (as the other woman called herself) talked for almost an hour as Ursula tried to absorb everything Ederle was saying.

Finally, she turned back to me and said, "So we'd remember our native language, my father and I spoke Burgundian at our home in Rome. There was only one other man whom I knew in the entire city who understood Burgundian. Darling, I doubted I'd ever use it again. I'm glad now my father made me remember these words. Perhaps he was thinking about this very day."

Looking to my left, I saw a Frankish man pointing at Cluny. The people in northern climes rarely saw a black man, and every once in a while, someone came up and stared at Cluny – or touched him – or asked him about his circumstances. One person shouted that Cluny was one of the devils, but his big toothy smile soon convinced the bystanders that Cluny was just a man after all.

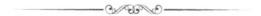

The hard winter came. The Moselle River froze over, the snow drifted to fill the creek-beds, and the Belgic world was cold, silent and snow-covered. Throughout the long and bitterly cold nights, we could hear wolves howling in the dark forests, and the midday sun was pale as though its power had been sapped by the penetrating northern wind. Spring came slowly to Northern Gaul, and it never came too soon.

In short order, our lives fell into familiar patterns. Ursula managed our household including the purchase of food and wine, and by overseeing our overall living conditions. She also participated in official Church activities, and she helped organize (and later operated) an orphanage for Burgundian children. She rarely, however, was seen with me at any local festivities or national celebrations out of fear she'd be recognized by those who may have known her in her prior life in Rome.

On the other hand, I spent most of my working days in seemingly never-ending meetings with the members of my military command or in discussions with our Frankish counterparts. Three days a week, messages were received and supplies were delivered to my headquarters (by way of *cursus publicus)* from the Valentinian and from subordinate staff officers who were scattered within the confines of the Western Empire.

Each message needed to be read, answered, and implemented, and many of these Imperial commands or subordinate requests were either as fanciful or preposterous as to be almost laughable had our general military situation not been so dire. During the winter, I often lamented my decision to give up my plush Senate seat and return to active military service. How I missed Rome and sunny Italia on these bleak winter days!

Also, it must have snowed nearly every other day that winter, and in those cold, dark weeks from December to late January, the sun didn't rise until mid-morning and it set in the early afternoon. Except for Church services on Sunday morning, I rarely saw Ursula in the bright sunlight.

I'd never been so cold. Even during my early military career in Southern Gaul, the weather would break after a few days of blizzard conditions. In Treverorum, however, the winter never ceased for long during those dark and stormy months. Our wood fires could only produce sufficient heat to warm a small room, and even our horses and livestock were showing the telltale signs of frostbite and hoof rot.

Soot was everywhere; soot from the candles, lanterns, and fireplaces. It covered our tables, our charts, and armaments, and it accumulated on every sill or flat place in the Aula Palatina. At least during those miserable winter months, there was plenty to eat and drink, and soon the grey winter days were somewhat longer.

As a consolation, we knew because of the unrelenting conditions, the barbarian tribes were limited in their opportunities to ransack our villages or invade imperial territory. In retrospect, the harsh winter of 455 was also the last winter when there was little barbarian activity in the northwestern portion of the Empire, and it gave us time to resupply.

In early February, the weather turned somewhat warmer, and I believed there was a brief opportunity for us to attempt the five-day trip south to Lugdunum. The main connecting road, the Via Agrippa, had been cleared of ice and snow south from Treverorum, and Ursula, Elmina, and I – in an elegant carriage drawn by four white horses – began our journey along with a large contingent of cavalry and supply wagons. Although Ursula was in her seventh month of pregnancy, we were relatively confident she could withstand the ordeals of another long ride.

Leaving Treverorum under a clear sky, the temperature was slightly above freezing, and a gentle northwestern breeze was blowing. Traveling through their hamlets and boroughs, I'm sure the local people viewed us as a wondrous or mysterious sight; with sixty uniformed cavalrymen carrying colorful banners and flags and multiple wagons and coaches. We tried to average about twenty miles per day, and we'd stop for the night at a Roman installation or outpost.

The road, though paved, was bumpy, and Ursula often became nauseated. Every once in a while, we'd encounter a snowstorm or icy rain, and the temperature inside our coach was only a bit warmer than the air outside.

To pass the time, we'd talk about our future and our past. I remember asking Ursula what she knew about her tribe and their origins. She said she knew only the little bit which her father told her about her family and their village. She asked me, "What do you know?"

I smiled and kissed her. "Well, several centuries ago Pliny the Elder wrote that your people immigrated to the Baltic island of Bornholm from Scandinavia in the first century AD. Around the mid-2nd century, they settled along the frontier in an area just west of the Rhine River in Northern Germania."

We looked out the window and saw a peasant family walking toward our wagon. A little boy with blond hair and a shaggy cap waved at us. We waved back.

Then I told her that in the late 3rd century, her ancestors crossed the Rhine and began raiding towns in Northern Belgica. Although they were eventually subdued, Emperor Septimius Severus permitted them to settle peacefully in the area where her family had resided.

She asked, "So what caused the trouble between my people and your people?"

"Well, the Burgundians lived peacefully under Roman protection until approximately fifty years ago. However, following Stilicho's withdrawal of Imperial troops from the region to Italia to fight Alaric and the Visigoths, your people began to conduct raids into lower Belgica."

"Were we at war with Rome?"

"Well, no; but the acts were viewed as treasonous by the Court in Ravenna. Although your tribe was nominally federated with the Empire, the situation soon was regarded as an intolerable assault on our sovereignty."

"An assault?"

"Yes, then, as I recall, Valentinian ordered Aëtius to send in the VII Legion, my old command, and after a brief period of fighting, the uprising was brought to an end in 436. Of course, it was long before my time as an officer."

"Is that when my father and I were enslaved?"

I stopped for a moment. I didn't want to upset her. "Yes, I think so – but since that time, your people have been one of our strongest allies."

I told her as partners with Rome over these last several decades, the Burgundians fought bravely alongside Aëtius, especially in the battle against Attila on the Catalaunian Plains in 451.

"We now owe a lot of thanks to your people," I said. "They are clearly one our most valued allies."

"Is this the reason why we are going to meet with King Gunderic?"

"Yes, as Rome's fortunes have faltered, the Burgundians' star is rising. We need to convince the King to remain federated with Rome while at the same time, being careful not to give away too much Roman territory in Gaul to him."

"Okay."

"If the Vandals attack us from Hispania, as we expect they will someday soon, we'll need the armies of the Burgundians – along with the Visigoths and other tribes – to push King Gaiseric back into Northern Africa."

CHAPTER XIII

Lugdunum, Gaul – February 455

In 43 BC, the Senate ordered Munatius Plancus, the governor of Central Gaul, to establish a city for the settlement of Roman soldiers who were retiring from active service in the Legions. Increasingly, the city became referred to as Lugdunum.

The name of the city is apparently taken from the name of a Celtic god, Lugus ('light') and the word dúnon (the Celtic word for 'hill-fort'). Later, General Marcus Vipsanius Agrippa recognized Lugdunum's strategic position on the natural highway from northern to south-eastern Gaul made the location a natural communications hub. Eventually, the city was selected as the starting point of one of the principal roads, the Via Agrippa, which meandered throughout Central Gaul and Northern Belgica.

Over the ensuing centuries, Lugdunum became a center of business and commerce, partly due to its location at the convergence of two navigable rivers, the Rhone and the Saone. Two emperors were born there (Claudius and Caracalla), and the Burgundian refugees, fleeing the Roman suppression of their rebellion in 436 AD, were resettled by Aëtius in the area around Lugdunum.

We entered through the massive city gates of Lugdunum during the warm and sunny afternoon of February 16, 455. The morning snow was almost completely melted, and the Rhone River was free of ice. We were escorted to the Imperial Barracks by the captain of the resident guard, and after enjoying an evening meal with the local Roman commander, we turned in for the night in a spacious upstairs apartment in the visiting officers' quarters.

Ursula's nausea worsened considerably during the last leg of our journey, and she was grateful to sleep on a fine goose-down bed for the first time since we left Treverorum. Later on that week when Ursula felt better, we met with King Gunderic.

Shortly after succeeding his brother, Gundahar, to the throne in 451 AD, King Gunderic joined forces with Aëtius against Attila during the battle on the Catalaunian Plains. Blond and dressed in his crimson cloak and wearing his royal crown, Gunderic was a tall, heavyset man in his early forties with an explosive laugh and a quick temper.

Ricimer warned me the King had little patience with or compassion for those people whom he considered as either weak or bombastic. Despite his current federation status with Rome, it was believed that Gunderic had long harbored thoughts of empire and prominence.

A couple of days later, Ursula and I rode out of Lugdunum to meet with King Gunderic at his palace which was situated about ten miles west of the city. Like Treverorum, I secretly wondered, as we exited Lugdunum through the southwestern gate, how long the city would remain in Imperial hands. While still nominally Roman, the population was now primarily Burgundian, and I'd been informed that Latin was rarely spoken in public except in an official capacity.

Riding out under a clear Gallic blue sky, I also knew well Gunderic expected Rome to cede a large area of land to him as payment for past services to the Empire. As Master of Soldiers, I assumed the King understood I did not have the authority to cede Roman property. However, I was worried about our visit.

After going through the formal procedures and local curiosities which were involved in the proper courtship and pleadings in his realm, we met with the King and his Council shortly after lunch. As I bowed deeply before the King, he said in a loud voice, "Master General, have you come before me to deliver the lands which were promised by Aëtius in return for our help in defeating the Huns?"

"Sire, I've no authority to cede imperial property to you or any other sovereign. Only Emperor Valentinian has the power."

"Valentinian – the wretch – he murdered my friend, Aëtius. I spit upon the Emperor, and I spit on you for being his stooge."

"Sire, I come here not to defend the Emperor's participation in the Master

General's death. Aëtius was my friend. I served under him for nearly ten years, and my father attended to him for well over twenty years. His death caused me great pain, and to this day, I wish it was Aëtius who still held the legal title which I now hold."

I paused for a moment, waiting to see whether the King would respond to my statement. Hearing none, I continued, "No, Sire, I come before you and your gracious court to elicit your help in combatting a shared enemy, King Gaiseric and the Vandals. They'll soon march north again."

"Gaiseric is not my concern; you should talk to the Visigoths. My concern is the land we were promised in exchange for the shedding of our blood and wasting our treasure."

"Sire, Attila was your enemy, too. Had Aëtius and his coalition failed to prevail on the Catalaunian Plains, we'd be standing now in Hunnish territory. Attila wasn't a friend of the Burgundians."

After asking Ursula and me to sit with him and his ministers at the table in the royal hall, we talked at great length over our mutual concerns and aspirations, trying to find areas of common ground. Soon, however, his attention turned to Ursula.

"Your wife, my friend, she's quite a beauty. I've been told she's blood of my blood. True?"

At that point, the King turned away from me and began conversing directly with Ursula in their native language. Speaking directly to a woman (other than the queen) was highly usual in the proper royal setting, and the exchange between them caused a low murmur of disapproval from the other courtiers seated in the ceremonial hall.

From the tone of their conversation, however, I could tell it was a positive development. Once or twice, the King and Ursula looked at me and began laughing – knowing well I couldn't understand a single word they spoke to each other. Uncharacteristically, and I'm sure most improperly, suddenly both of them arose from their chairs and warmly embraced each other. Gunderic kissed her on her cheek, and she curtseyed to him.

Finally, he turned to me and said, "Master General, I'll help your wife find her home and her family. I understand the child she's carrying is half-Burgundian. That, my dear friend, is a good sign, and is helpful to our relationship and subsequent discussions."

"Thank you, my Lord."

"Tomorrow, I'll personally escort you and your bride back to her little village – Atria. It's only about a three-hour ride from here. Maybe she'll find some of her family there. Who knows?"

By then, a big smile formed on Ursula's face. Causing another murmur of displeasure, she embraced King Gunderic once again. Tomorrow, she'd be going home.

Several hours into our journey to Atria, King Gunderic told us that Ursula's village could be seen from the top of the next hill. Rounding the corner and climbing a steep grade, we finally looked down and saw the village of her birth. It was a rustic collection of approximately twenty to thirty small buildings which were sitting on three parallel muddy streets. Ursula immediately climbed out of the coach and ran a few steps forward to have a better view of the village.

"There it is. There's my home – it's on the middle street, the second house from the end. That's my home; oh, my God!"

"Are you sure?"

"Julius, I lived there for eight years, and I've seen it in my dreams many times. Yes, we're in the right place. Oh, I can't believe I'm finally home. At last, I'm home!"

After getting back into our coach, the caravan, consisting of two coaches and a cavalry escort of twenty mounted soldiers, continued the short journey down the hill and stopped in front of the only inn in town, The St. Regis. The King's advance party had arrived in Atria a couple of hours before us to make all of the proper arrangements for the King and his entourage.

Upon exiting the carriage, we dined on a meal of succulent roast lamb, boiled carrots, hard bread, and a sour malt beverage called 'mead.' Following the end of the meal, the King rose out of his chair and said to Ursula, "There's someone here who's been waiting to see you for a long time. She says her name is Olga and she's your sister. Constable, please bring the woman in now."

Ursula held her hand to her mouth in a failing attempt to suppress a cry of pure joy as a tall peasant woman in her mid-thirties was led into the dining room. "Oh my God, Olga; oh my God, it's you!"

Ignoring royal protocol, Olga rushed straight into the open, reaching arms of Ursula, and they embraced for a long time, crying softly in each other's arms.

The King and I spent the next several hours discussing matters of state while Ursula, Olga, and Elmina left The St. Regis and walked down the muddy street to Olga's home. By late-afternoon, we began our three-hour journey back to Lugdunum. It would be dark by the time we arrived there. A few moments after our trip back began, I asked Ursula about her afternoon with her sister.

"Well, Olga and I spent most of the time catching up on the missing eighteen years. She's married to a tanner, Rolf, and has four living children?"

"Fairest, you're an aunt. That's so wonderful. Tell me, how did she avoid being captured and sold into slavery?"

"It was just pure luck, I guess. A week before the assault on our village by the Romans, Mother sent Olga to stay on her grandmother's farm and help with the harvest. She was there when Aëtius arrived with the slavers."

"Did they also attack your grandmother's farm?"

"No, I guess because the farm was so isolated, they missed it. Once the soldiers left Atria and the village was safe, Olga came back and rebuilt her life there."

Ursula stopped talking for a moment and took a deep breath; she had tears in her eyes. "Olga told me much of the town was burned to the ground, including our home, and only a few townspeople survived the rampage; a few lucky ones who ran and hid in the woods and a few old men and women who witnessed the attack. I guess these old folks were of no value as slaves and were left there to die."

"That's awful; I'm so sorry. Did your sister ever learn anything about the whereabouts of your mother and your brothers?"

Once again Ursula stopped speaking. She just stared out the window into the forest. "No, she hadn't heard anything about anyone else in our family before today. She was relieved, however, to learn our father is still alive and that he's now free."

During our conversation, I was almost ashamed of being a Roman. Not only did my country enslave her and her family but the principal antagonist in the assault was my friend and mentor, Aëtius.

Apparently feeling my sorrow, she said, "I don't blame you. Slavery has been a part of humankind for endless centuries. Even the Burgundians now have slaves."

Although Elmina was silent during our journey, I knew well she was listening to our entire conversation. In another uncharacteristic move, Ursula reached out and squeezed Elmina's hand.

I remained in Lugdunum for a couple of weeks, meeting with King Gunderic and receiving emissaries from other tribes and other places throughout the Western Empire. Occasionally, a messenger arrived from Ravenna with instructions and questions from the Emperor, and I'd prepare a package for the courier to take back to the Court.

Also, emissaries arrived from the military headquarters of the four principal field generals under my command: Generals Aegidius, Ricimer, Avitus, and Marcellinus. They reported information concerning their weekly field operational strength, their resources and needs, their activities and situations, and other information I'd need to answer their inquiries and to run the military operations from my temporary headquarters in Lugdunum.

News moves slowly in the winter and travel is weather-dependent. I'd often wish there was a speedier way to send and receive information and military intelligence.

Because Ursula was in her eighth month of her pregnancy, she was unable to venture beyond Lugdunum and the immediate surrounding countryside. However, the business of the Empire called me, and I needed to travel south to Arausio and meet with General Avitus before springtime arrived.

Therefore, I decided to place Ursula in the care and custody of King Gunderic in the relative safety of Lugdunum. If all went well, I planned to go back before Ursula gave birth of our child.

CHAPTER XIV

Arausio was founded in 35 BC by the veterans of the II Legion, and shortly, after that, the city became the capital of the province of Narbonensis. The historian, Pliny the Elder, once described the city of Arausio as follows:

> *Arausio is a miniature Rome, complete with many of the public buildings which would be familiar to any citizen of the Empire, except the scale of the buildings was reduced to accommodate a much smaller population.*

Over the next few centuries, the city prospered, but it was later sacked by the Visigoths in 412 AD. Following their capitulation by the XXII Legion under the command of Master General Stilicho two years later, the Visigoths were peacefully settled in the immediate area of the city. By the time of our arrival that winter, Arausio, like Lugdunum and Treverorum, displayed the distinct feel of being a barbarian city. The Visigoths were clearly in control.

After a tedious two-day ride along the Via Agrippa, my entourage entered Arausio through the ancient Arch of Augustus, which had been constructed in 14 BC to honor the veterans of the Gallic Wars. The Arch was now part of the massive defensive walls which surrounded the city. It was a beautiful early-spring day, and the countryside was just beginning to display the wildflowers and blossoming trees for which the region was well known.

Upon reporting to the officer-in-charge at the city gate around mid-day, I was immediately escorted to the official residence of General Avitus for a briefing. After entering the city, the pastoral picture quickly changed to a teeming urban environment. We rode past foul-smelling backstreets where the dilapidated buildings were full of men working leather, shaping iron, or tanning hides. I also saw women who were sweeping garbage, working at looms, or begging for alms.

Furthermore, there were seemingly endless rows of shops with their proprietors selling pottery, salt, fish, bread, cloth, meat, and every other conceivable thing. I encountered men wearing strange clothes and talking in languages which I'd never heard before. Many of the older buildings were of Roman construction, and these edifices were often three and four stories tall, teeming with people and smelling of the noonday dinner. Packs of dogs roamed the streets, and a thick smoke lay over the city like a grey woolen blanket.

The man whom I was going to visit, General Eparchius Avitus, was born in Nemessos, Gaul to a family of Roman nobility. He began his military career as an officer serving under Aëtius in his campaign against the Juthungi and the Norics (from 430 to 431 AD) and later in the fight against the Burgundians. In 439, he was appointed as the Praetorian Prefect of Gaul and began to pursue a close personal association with King Theodoric and the Visigoths.

The following year, Avitus retired to private life at his estate in Southern Gaul where he lived quietly for the next twelve years until he was recalled briefly to military service when Attila invaded the Western Empire. In the autumn of 454, Avitus was once again recalled to military service by Valentinian following Aëtius' execution, and he was elevated to the rank of Field General. Assigned the task to command the XII Legion from Arausio, he was charged with the defense of the Southern Gaul and Northern Hispania.

Coming from the purest of Roman stock, he revealed an aristocratic look about him, and always gave me the impression he was quite certain of his methods and opinions. He was a small yet powerfully-built man with flowing grey hair and a dark complexion. Although I was never very fond of him, one tends to cling to like-minded citizens in a realm surrounded by hostile faces.

About a week after my arrival in Arausio, I was meeting one morning with Avitus and several members of his general staff when we heard a knock on our door. An officer, fresh from Ravenna, entered the room, saluted, and asked if he could meet with us concerning a matter of extreme urgency.

Avitus nodded affirmatively and inquired, "What's on your mind, Legate?"

The officer was still soiled and rumpled from his long ride to Arausio; apparently, he'd been traveling on the road for the last four days. "Sir, I've some tragic news; Emperor Valentinian is dead."

We were initially dumbfounded by his statement. Immediately, Avitus asked, "What do mean, Valentinian is dead? What happened?"

"Sir, I wasn't there but here's what I've been told by my superiors. Valentinian was visiting Rome, riding his horse on the Campus Martius. When he dismounted, he was viciously attacked by two men – allegedly, by two former officers in Master General Aëtius' old command – and knifed to death. The assassination took place on March 16th."

We just stared at the Legate for several moments; dumbfounded, we just shook our heads, not knowing what to say. Finally, Avitus said, "Heavens, that's horrible news. Do you know the names of the conspirators?"

"Sir, I was told they were Legates Optima and Heraclius. However, I'm not certain."

Both men were familiar to Avitus and me; they served for many years on Aëtius' general staff.

I asked, "So, who's in charge now in Ravenna?"

"Sir, the following day, Senator Petronius Maximus proclaimed himself as Emperor."

"Are you certain it's Maximus?"

"Yes, Sir, I'm certain; but there's more news, Sir."

I thought to myself, what more could there be after hearing the news. "Yes, what it is, Legate?"

"Sir, Emperor Maximus apparently 'persuaded' Valentinian's widow, Empress Licinia, to marry him, and also 'coaxed' her daughter, Eudoxia, to marry Maximus' son."

I shook my head – he's consolidating his power by way of these marriages. I asked, "How about the Senate, have they confirmed Maximus' ascension to the throne?"

"Yes, Sir, he's been confirmed by the Senate – but not unanimously."

Suddenly, Avitus stood up and slowly walked around the room, just scratching his chin with his right hand. He stopped for a moment and said, "Is there anything else, Legate?"

"Yes, Sir, apparently Valentinian has been condemned as a traitor to Rome, and thus, there'll be no state funeral or period of mourning for him."

After the officer provided additional information concerning the mood of the people and the absence of any word from Constantinople, he saluted and departed. After that, Avitus and I talked for several hours about the probable consequences of Valentinian's assassination and Maximus' quick ascent to power.

Valentinian ruled as emperor of the Western Empire for almost thirty years, and it was the first time in nearly one-hundred-fifty years that there was no identified male successor to the imperial throne. Despite his shortcoming, Valentinian had been, in my judgment, a good ruler. Others may try to diminish his reign because his intelligence was only of the second rank and because he was a terribly naïve and superstitious man. Overall, I believed he governed well considering the fact he'd inherited many domestic problems of a sort which might've turned any sane man into a monster.

We weren't certain exactly what to make of the news, and Avitus and I spent much of the next couple of days tossing around possible scenarios while at the same time being careful not to say too much which could later incriminate us. We queried at great length whether Emperor Maximus would be able to consolidate his power base and rule successfully in Valentinian's stead; and we also pondered the next moves of Rome's primary adversaries; King Gaiseric and the warrior who'd be the eventual heir to the Hunnic throne.

Furthermore, we worried about the impact of Valentinian's assassination regarding our strongest allies, King Gunderic and King Theodoric. After assessing their various options and opportunities, we concurred that each of these sovereigns would probably soon make a strategic move.

And we wondered, what cards would Maximus play? Considering the infinite number of variables and possibilities, we agreed the unintended consequences arising from the death of Valentinian could potentially be catastrophic for the Western Empire; but the die had been cast.

After shaking his head at the end of my official visit to Arausio, Avitus smiled at me and said, "Now, we'll see if either of us still has a job. We serve at the pleasure of the Emperor; we might be viewed as threats to him and the throne."

I laughed and replied as I climbed into the carriage to begin my long ride back to Lugdunum, "Yes, we'll see. We should have nothing to worry about if we remain loyal and obedient."

But I was worried nevertheless, and I didn't sleep one night through during the next several weeks.

The reign of Emperor Petronius Maximus barely lasted two months. After gaining control of the palace, Maximus consolidated his hold on power by immediately marrying Empress Licinia, the widow of Valentinian III. I was later told she married him reluctantly. When the Eastern Empire refused to recognize his accession, Maximus sent an emissary to Avitus in an attempt to gain the support of King Theodoric and the Visigoths. At the same time, the Emperor asked Ricimer to seek the endorsement with King Gunderic and the Burgundians. Neither King endorsed the legitimacy of Emperor Maximus.

However, it was the marriage of Maximus' son to Valentinian's daughter, Eudoxia, which eventually doomed his short-lived regime. Apparently, Valentinian previously pledged the hand of his daughter to Prince Huneric, the eldest son of King Gaiseric. Eudoxia's forced marriage to Maximus' son infuriated the Vandal King, who only needed an excuse to begin preparations for the invasion of Italia. In quick order, King Gaiseric claimed the marriage arrangement invalidated the peace treaty of 442 AD with Valentinian, and King Gaiseric invaded and conquered Sicily, Corsica, Sardinia, and the Balearic Islands in short order.

Following his success in capturing this territory, Gaiseric and his army landed on Italian soil on May 31, 455, and finding only token Imperial resistance, he quickly marched to gates of Rome. The Emperor, aware Avitus had not arrived with the anticipated pledge of Visigoth aid, decided it was fruitless to mount a defense of the city against the Vandals.

Thus, Maximus decided to escape the upcoming siege and urged the Senate to accompany him. In the panic surrounding the invasion by the Vandals, however, the Emperor was completely abandoned by his bodyguards and left to fend for himself. As Maximus rode out of the city on his own, he was attacked by an angry mob, who stoned him to death.

Remaining in the city, Pope Leo and a few of the influential senators, including my mentor, Senator Gallipolis, met with Gaiseric in an attempt to save the city from obliteration. After agreeing not to murder the citizens or to destroy the ancient monuments, the city gates were opened, and the Vandals were permitted to sack the eternal city for the next fourteen days.

Although there was little bloodshed, the Vandals looted a vast amount of treasure from the city. Wagons were piled high with objects of gold and silver. In the Forum, the statues of many long-honored heroes – such as, the statues of Aeneas, several of the great generals who lead the Carthaginian and Gallic campaigns, and some of the deified emperors such as Marcus Aurelius and Hadrian – were pulled down and shattered. The city which conquered the world had been captured for the second time in fifty years.

The King also took Empress Licinia and her daughter, Princess Eudoxia, hostage, and he reportedly also transported several shiploads of captives back to Carthage who were later sold into slavery. The Princess eventually married Prince Huneric in 456.

But as fortune had it, the Vandals weren't able to enjoy the fruits of the pillage of Rome. On their sail back to Carthage, much of Gaiseric's fleet was wrecked and sunk by a freak summer storm. Some of the greatest treasures of Roman conquests, from places such as Greece, Egypt, Palestine, Babylon, and elsewhere, are lying on the Mediterranean seabed somewhere between Sicily and North Africa.

Emperor Maximus' demise caused another power vacuum in the Western Empire. Upon hearing the news, King Theodoric declared General Avitus as the new emperor. In return for the King's support, the Visigoths were given total control of the provinces of Aquitania and Lugdunensis, and they were allowed to enter Suevi-controlled Hispania. In my judgment, it was a steep price to pay for the King's endorsement.

After nearly three months of consolidating his authority in Arausio, the new emperor marched from Gaul to the city of Rome and secured the Imperial Throne on September 21, 455. Under a threat of gruesome retaliation, the Senate confirmed Avitus as Emperor of the Western Empire on the following day.

Albeit somewhat reluctant at first, Ricimer and I gave Avitus our tacit support. With Avitus' ascension to the throne, however, much of the Western Empire was now effectively lost. Soon after that, King Childeric absorbed Northern Belgica and much of Germania into the new Frankish Kingdom and declared Treverorum as its new capital.

Not to be outdone, King Theodoric formally established the Visigoth Kingdom, which included Western Gaul and much of Northern Hispania. And of course, King Gaiseric was comfortably in control of much of Northern Africa and the islands of Sicily, Corsica, and Sardinia.

All that remained of the Western Empire was the Italian Peninsula, a portion of Dalmatia, and Southern Gaul – however, the remaining land was only a fraction of the vast territory once held by the Western Empire. Forced to abandon Treverorum, Ricimer's VI Legion marched to Arausio and combined his troops with the XII Legion.

With General Aegidius still tasked to defend Northern Italia, and what remained of General Marcellinus' III Legion supporting Southern Italia and the small slice of Roman territory in North Africa, my job as Master of Soldiers suddenly and sadly, became much easier to manage.

But amid the noise and confusion of rising kingdoms and falling empires, Ursula gave birth to a baby boy on April 12, 455 AD. While there was tremendous joy and celebration around our quarters in Lugdunum, I secretly couldn't help but wonder whether the Western Empire would still exist when our young son grew up to become a man.

CHAPTER XV

Nemausus, July 456

With the ascension of Avitus to the Throne, the Visigoths suddenly became the single most powerful political block Western Europe – because they could raise the largest army. No other military force – including the remaining Legions – was capable of resisting the might of the Goths. Moving quickly and decisively following Avitus' decree, King Theodoric forcibly entered Suevicontrolled Hispania. In a fierce battle near Tarragona, the Visigoths overwhelmed and subdued the Suevi nation.

Then in early 456 AD, the Burgundians, sensing a weakness in Southern Gaul, negotiated a favorable power-sharing agreement with Avitus; thus effectively removing the city of Lugdunum and much of the surrounding area out of direct Roman control.

In an attempt to unify his power base, Emperor Avitus began playing one barbarian nation against another nation and by invoking a price – paid to him in gold – for the transfer of the remnants of the Western Empire to a particular barbarian kingdom. It seemed like the remaining portions of the Empire were now for sale to the highest bidder.

Sensing a crisis in Imperial authority, Ricimer and I believed we needed to exert power immediately if the Western Empire would be able to survive. Working together from our joint command headquarters in Arausio, I authorized Ricimer to lead a combined naval/amphibious attack on Corsica and Sardinia in May 456.

Following a masterful plan of attack, Ricimer and his military forces - consisting of the components from the VI Legion, the Imperial Navy, and a few battalions of Frankish mercenaries – routed the Vandals and restored Roman authority to those islands. Later attacking Sicily, Ricimer, along with the III Legion commanded by General Marcellinus, convincingly routed the Vandals at Agrigentum – thus pushing the remaining Vandal forces out of Italia and the surrounding coastal islands.

Meanwhile, General Aegidius took the offensive and attacked remnants of marauding Hun forces along the Danube River; once again pacifying the northern Italian frontier. Each of these offensives was originated, coordinated, and controlled without any meaningful support, input, or acquiescence from Avitus, who was turning out as a nonfactor in the military activities outside the immediate regions surrounding Ravenna and Rome.

It was time for Avitus to go.

Shortly following our son's birth in Lugdunum, I moved the headquarters of the Master General's staff to my home in Nemausus, and Ursula and I successfully united the two families together for the first time. It was one of the happiest times in my life.

One evening in early July, 456, Ricimer and I met at my home to discuss the immediate future of the Western Empire. After sharing a festive family dinner, Ricimer and I retired to the comforts of my tablinium. Cluny brought in a jug of Gallic wine and a plate of white cheese from Tuscany. After some small talk about the weather and the economy, Ricimer and I quickly got down to basics at hand.

I asked, "Tell me what you're thinking."

Ricimer leaned forward in his chair and replied, "Avitus needs to go. He's selling imperial land to the highest bidder, and he's pocketing the sums for his personal use. Julius, our civilization is crumbling before our eyes."

"What do you mean its crumbling?"

"For over five hundred years, Rome has been the glue which has kept the civilized world together. Imperial power has brought the world 'the *Pax Romana*' so commerce, education, and the arts can flourish. Without the Roman umbrella, the Western Empire will soon fall into civil war, and barbarism will slowly extinguish the light of the world. The dream will crumble. Avitus must be stopped now."

It's always been clear to me that Ricimer was the political and military heir to Master General Stilicho. Like the late Master General, Ricimer was a well-connected barbarian who was proud to follow a Roman military career. Also, Ricimer was committed to the idea that a strong national government was necessary so local, tribal groups didn't destroy civilization by attempting to solve their petty grievances by force of arms or expand their power bases.

I replied, "What do you have in mind specifically?"

"Well, we need to gather an army, march on Ravenna. We need to remove Avitus before the entire empire dissolves under its own dead weight."

"You're not serious, are you? What, incite civil war? There must be a better answer than that, isn't there?"

I was shocked. While we'd talk about the idea of removing Avitus for months and months, it was always theoretical. I asked, "So, who would replace Avitus?"

Ricimer looked at me and smiled, "You, my friend, as Emperor Majorian, the first Emperor of the Gallo-Roman Empire."

I was dumbfounded. Ricimer said, "And we'll need to reconfigure the Senate. It'll no longer work in the grand scheme of things. There's a lot of work to be done."

I got out of my chair and walked around. In the background, I could hear the happy voices of my children playing outside in the garden. "Let me get this straight. You plan to gather an army and march on Ravenna. Then you will remove Avitus – kill him, I suspect – and install me on the Imperial throne. After that, you'll want to revamp the Senate. Is there anything else you want to do while we're at it?"

"Yes, my skeptical Roman friend, there's much more to do after that. These are just the first steps. Much more will certainly follow."

"But, why me; why not install yourself on the throne?"

Ricimer arose from his chair, and looking me straight in the eyes, saying, "Well, initially we'll need the support of the current Senate. You're well known there and well liked in most quarters. Current law still precludes a barbarian from becoming emperor; thus, I can't be installed right now, but perhaps later."

"But it sounds like madness to me."

"Believe me – it has to be you. Right now, I'm too tightly aligned with the Franks; the Burgundians, the Goths, and the Senate would never accept me under the current arrangement. You are a war hero, the Master of Soldiers, and a former Senator. There's not a hint of scandal in your past."

He stopped speaking for a moment to gauge my reaction. "If you agree, I'll deliver you the political support and backing from the Franks. I'm confident the Burgundians will gladly accept you; partly because your wife is Burgundian and your youngest son is half Burgundian. Who knows, perhaps, he'll even become the emperor one day?"

I just shook my head in disbelief and asked, "But how about the Visigoths and the Vandals? We certainly don't have their support or allegiance. And what about Aegidius and Marcellinus? Would they support my investiture?"

Ricimer smiled, "I've already talked to Aegidius about my plan – and he strongly supports it – with you as Emperor. Marcellinus is busy in Leptis Magnus fighting the Vandals. Even if he disapproved – which he won't – he's stuck in North Africa and is unable to march all the way to Ravenna in time to help Avitus."

"But how about the Goths; aren't they Avitus' primary power base?"

Ricimer sat down and took a sip of wine. He popped a slice of cheese in his mouth. "Yes, they supported Avitus' rise to power; but three things happened since then. First, the Goths invaded Hispania, and now they're actively battling the Suevi. Second, the Italians hate the Goths – ever since they sacked Rome in 410. Because of the animosity, most of the Goths have already left Rome and Ravenna. They didn't feel welcome there."

"And third?"

"And third, they only backed Avitus in exchange for granting them the additional territory in Gaul and getting his permission to invade Hispania. They don't need Avitus anymore."

"And the Vandals – how about them?"

"Well, Gaiseric is a non-factor in the puzzle. He wouldn't approve of either you or me or even Avitus on the throne. He wants the slot for himself."

I was still unconvinced of the prospects of invading Italia or in me becoming Emperor. "You know if we fail, we'll hang. You know that, right?"

Ricimer stood up again, "Yes, we'll hang from the highest tree on the Appian Way, my friend. We'll hang together side-by-side if that's any consolation."

He stopped talking, smiled, and said, "But what happens to us personally isn't important. It's what happens to our way of life which is a matter of desperate concern. We are already teetering on the abyss."

I continued to shake my head. "And what about the Senate; what kind of re-configuration do you have in mind? It seems to me that you've already figured this out. Have you?"

Ricimer smiled again, took another sip of wine, sat down, and continued, "Only Roman citizens can serve in the Senate, and the geographic configuration of the Senate membership is limited to only Italia, Dalmatia and Southern Gaul. All the rest of the Empire is – and always has been - excluded from participation. That, of course, must change."

"How would the reconfigured Senate look in your mind?"

Once again, Ricimer smiled. "Of course, the Senate will continue to exist as the Empire's legislative body, but its make-up will change substantially. All freemen in all of the provinces and cities of the Empire will have representation, and the membership of the Senate will be redistributed in specific proportions. For example, the Senate would be 40% Roman, 20% Frankish, 20% Burgundian, and 20% Goths; yes, something like that.

"That'll never happen; you can count on it, my friend."

Ricimer frowned, "We'd structure the Empire as a loose confederation of independent states with a strong central government which would control things such as the Army, the Navy, and the bureaucracy. The various independent nations would fall under an imperial umbrella, with all the nations using the same currency, abiding by the same general laws, and each providing representation in the Senate."

"You're right, that constitutes a change. How about the emperor? Where would he come from?"

Ricimer smiled, "We'd follow a course similar to what Diocletian enacted in the Third century."

I couldn't believe what I was hearing and said, "What another change? You've already mentioned at least twenty major changes by my count."

Ricimer grinned, walked a few steps away, and turned to face me "Well, here's another. The incumbent emperor would change every five to ten years, and the position would rotate among the several nations. Each group would have its chance for one of its own as the emperor."

Late into the evening, we talked and talked about his grand scheme to salvage and reinvigorate the Western Empire. Finally, I said, "I need to sleep on it. I'll tell you my decision in the morning."

He nodded and shook my hand. "Sleep well, my friend. I know it's a weighty matter for you to sort out. I'll see you on the morrow."

As I left Ricimer in the tablinium, I told my chief usher not to disturb me until morning. I went into my bedchamber and bolted the door tightly behind me. The shadows were lengthening, and the air was still warm. It would've been a pleasure to close my eyes, but I needed to get my thoughts together.

I didn't sleep much that night. I prayed, I read, and I weighed the uncertainties over and over in my mind. I walked out on my balcony and watched a waning moon going in and out of a cloudy sky. Sometime during the third watch of the night, Ursula knocked on my door, and I let her in and bolted the door behind us once again. Then I told her everything.

Later she asked, "Are you going to do it – you know, what Ricimer suggested?"

"It would constitute high treason."

"I know, but only if you fail. If you triumph, you'd be a hero. And you'd be the emperor."

"But if I fail, I'll not only lose my life; they'll go after you, our family, and all we've worked for all of these years. Is it worth the gamble?"

"It's in God's hands, not ours. God will decide whether you'll be emperor."

I walked around the room and stopped at the window. The sun was just coming up – a bright orange glow far off in the east. The torches were still aglow in the courtyard below. What to do? I needed to make my decision soon.

I asked her, "What do you want me to do?"

"I know one thing; you were born to be emperor. Rome needs you, my love."

"Will you come to Rome and live with me in the palace?"

She smiled sadly and touched my hand. "No, you know I can't go back to Rome with you – or even to Ravenna. Too many people know me and who I was before we married. We've talked about it before, my love. You'll have to go alone. I'll stay here with the children."

She kissed me and left the room. I'd never felt as undecided. Everything seemed ill-timed – the events were pushing me faster than I chose to go. I knew one thing for certain, however – I'd never have this chance again.

Exhausted, I reclined on our bed and quickly fell asleep. As it often happens, I dreamed – and I dreamed Aëtius appeared before me – dressed in his Master General's uniform. His right arm was extended toward me and in his hand was a parchment. After nodding at him, I took it.

Suddenly, I awoke in a cold sweat, and I got out of bed and looked out the window. The sun was high in the late summer sky, and I could barely make out the remnants of a quarter-moon on the western horizon. I'd made up my mind. I was ready to march on Ravenna.

Over the next several months, Ricimer and I (and selected members our general staffs) met regularly at my home to chart the formation of the new government. Secretly, I prayed Avitus would come to see the error of his ways and reassert his commitment to saving the Western Empire. He did not. Furthermore, because so many people were now privy to our insurrection, I feared somehow our plan of treason would be leaked to Avitus. It was not.

These months at home were also a time of great pleasure and happiness my family and me. For the first time, our two families lived together under the same roof. My children with Octavia - Julius, Minerva, Claudius, Caspian, and Cassius - each seemed to love our new baby, and I remember many summer evenings when the eight of us would walk along the quiet streets of Nemausus or gather in the atrium for family activities.

One afternoon in late August, Ricimer and I were planning strategy in the tablinium. As usual, Ricimer brought several of his military advisors with him, including Legate Rudolpho Gustavus, a young officer from Belgica. While looking out my window at the atrium during a break in our discussions, I suddenly saw Ursula and Gustavus engaged in an active conservation. Also, they were holding hands and gazing into each other eyes.

Later on in the evening, I asked Ursula about the occurrence; she laughed and told me they were just talking about their childhood memories in Belgica, and she desired no one except me. During the night, we made love three times with each time being more pleasurable than the one before. Her words of love and sighs of ecstasy made me forget about everything which could go wrong in the task ahead for Ricimer and me. And I was convinced with all of my being that Ursula loved no one but me and our love would last forever. I was wrong.

CHAPTER XVI

In early October, Ricimer and I – along with a small cavalry detachment – left the relative safety of Southern Gaul for our long ride north to Mediolanum. We were riding on the road to sedition, and there was no path of retreat. While we were confident of victory, with these things, there's no certainty. In any event, I reasoned it's better to die at the head of an army than to perish as the result of Avitus' whim to destroy his rivals.

A sense of autumn was clearly in the air and the days were getting much shorter. Although the weather painted a picture of serenity, my thoughts were focused on the terrible task lying before us. The idea of forcibly removing Avitus and placing me on the Imperial throne weighed heavily on my mind. For many obvious reasons, I didn't take treason lightly. During the church services on Sunday before we left, I prayed God would remove this challenge, and if not, God could help us avoid any more bloodshed than was necessary.

Sitting alone in the military coach with Ricimer, we solidified the final plans. I asked, "Is Aegidius ready for us in Mediolanum?"

"Yes, he'll have the XXIII Legion prepared for the tasks facing us. The morning after our arrival, the three of us will lead the army from Mediolanum to Ravenna."

"Good."

"We'll have a show of power and unity of command. I trust Avitus will not be forewarned; even if he should discover our plans, we'll have superior numbers. I suspect he won't be able to put up much of a fight, my friend."

After a few moments, I replied, "In some ways, I feel like Julius Caesar marching toward Rome on his way back from conquering Gaul."

Ricimer grinned, "In some respects, our task is much harder. We ride to Rome at the twilight of our civilization whereas Caesar rode as the Republic was reaching its apex."

Then to my astonishment, Ricimer began humming *'Ecce Caesar nunc triumphat qui subegit Gallias'* – the song which every schoolboy knows commemorating Caesar's triumphal march into Rome from Gaul.

The sun was now above the tree line, and the morning fog had dissipated. Still shaking my head in almost disbelief, I looked out the window of the coach. Wasn't there a better way to accomplish our goals? We'd just passed beneath the long aqueduct which feeds Nemausus.

"You promised me that Avitus wouldn't be executed," I said. "We still agree on the outcome, right?"

Ricimer took a sip of wine. "While I strongly disagree with you, I fully concur with your wishes. Unless he resists to the point where we must kill him, he'll be made the Bishop of Piacenza. And what a holy bishop he'll be, no doubt."

He stopped for a moment again to gather his thoughts. "But Julius, I'm afraid if he buys some time, he'll try to flee Italia to the safety and support of King Theodoric and the Visigoths, and he'll attempt to reconstruct his political coalition one day. As I've explained many times, it would be better just to execute him now than have to do it later. We'll need the Goths on our side when we attack Gaiseric."

"No, he's a former general who has served with distinction in the field. I don't want his blood on my hands. Let's give him the opportunity to go away peacefully."

"But he is a corrupt emperor who stole from the public trough and enriches himself to the detriment of the Empire. He's no friend to Rome; he's a traitor who serves death."

I just shook my head; but in my heart, I knew Ricimer was probably correct. He continued, "Avitus has lost the backing of the Senate. In fact, there's an enormous amount of hostility to his reign. He has few friends left in Rome; they see him as he is – a goddam traitor."

"Yeah, I know."

"Furthermore, Marcian refused to recognize Avitus as the legitimate Western Emperor. Without the acquiescence and approval of Constantinople, there's no legitimate Western Emperor."

He stopped talking once again to collect his thoughts. "By the way, that's something we'll need to do immediately after seizing power; we must gain the approval of Emperor Marcian. We need the legitimacy which Avitus has failed to acquire for himself."

For good or for bad, I was now a part of the devil's bargain. In return for obtaining Ricimer's political and military backing, I'd need to pay a stiff price. His support of my candidacy would make him, in essence, a co-emperor. While I'd assume the official title and entrapments of Imperial authority, Ricimer would clearly be the power behind the throne.

I knew if it could've been arranged for himself in sit as emperor – something impossible under the law – I wouldn't be needed in this treacherous endeavor, and I could remain in Nemausus with Ursula and my family. But with me as emperor, Ricimer would assume my position as Master of Soldiers, and he'd effectively assume the administrative control the four remaining Western Legions. Perhaps, the office of Master of Soldiers was even more powerful than being emperor.

With the support and backing of the Franks and other tribes in Germania and Belgica, Ricimer would establish himself as the most influential man in the Western Empire. I suspected that one day soon, we'd be involved in a fight to the death for ultimate power. I wondered silently to myself if I'd been outwitted?

On October 14, we reached General Aegidius' garrison outside the walls of Mediolanum. The following day, we began our march on Ravenna with our pennants fluttering and our spear points gleaming in the bright morning sunshine. Avitus had somehow become aware of our plans, gathered up what few forces he could scrape together – mostly remnant groups from the field army which he'd brought with him from Gaul – and he made a brief stand in a small open area just north of Ravenna.

The appearance of such an overwhelming force, however, quickly convinced Avitus' troops to change sides, and the emperor was captured with little loss of life. Following brief negotiations, Avitus abdicated the throne and agreed to accept the title of Bishop of Piacenza.

Three days later, I was presented to the Senate in Rome as a candidate for emperor. With only one dissenting vote – coming from my dear friend Gaius Gallus Gallipolis – I was declared the fifth emperor of the Western Empire – and the fourth one in a little more than two years. At almost the same instant of my formal investiture, Emperor Marcian died unexpectedly in Constantinople.

A few weeks after the state funeral, Marcian was replaced on the Eastern Imperial throne by Leo who agreed to bless my ascension in return for me blessing his rise to the Eastern throne. My, it's amazing how politics makes strange bedfellows.

CHAPTER XVII

The City of Rome, December 456

Mine was the first coronation in the city of Rome since Diocletian was crowned in 284 AD. After that, emperors were crowned in either Constantinople or Ravenna, if crowned at all. Maximus did not serve long enough to be crowned, and Avitus was so unpopular a coronation was never even considered for him.

Recovering from the vicious sack of Rome by the Vandals only two years earlier, the citizens of the city were in a celebratory way that afternoon. Hope, optimism and national pride filled the air, and the city fathers left nothing to chance to celebrate my elevation to the throne. The Flavian Amphitheatre was cleaned and refitted, and the traditional games, which had been absent for many years, returned for a two-week gala.

Chariot races were held once more in the Circus Maximus before crowds of over 100,000 enthusiastic fans. Plays, musical performances, and oratory contests returned to the ancient Theatre of Marcellus for the winter season. The glory of Rome was on full display once again. Furthermore, there were "ritual coronation ceremonies" everywhere I went. After almost a thousand years of republic and empire, the Romans knew well how to cling to ancient practices and procedures.

I was graciously received by the Senate, and I listened to their lavish testimonials and unending tributes. I attended the theater, dedicated new public monuments, and appeared at dinners, festivals, and receptions given by the more preeminent citizens and gilded gentry of the Rome.

And I made speeches to prominent business organizations and civic groups, and I officiated at the games. The festivities went on almost endlessly, and it tired me out more than any military campaign or training exercise heretofore. The Senate and people of Rome were in a joyous mood. Unfortunately, it wouldn't last for long.

A significant portion of my time during the early years of my reign involved my participation in the legal tribunals. Under the law, the final appeal for all Roman citizens in either a civil or criminal matter was to the emperor. As usual, there was a multitude of cases pending at my level of adjudication, and the arguments often went on *ad nauseum*.

When the litigants knew the Emperor was sitting in judgement, the arguments predictably became more animated, and the lawyerly antics tended to be craftier and tedious. With the legal combatants each seeking leniency, a higher money award, or a sense of an outcome worthy of King Solomon, I'm afraid that at the conclusion of their trial, many of the litigants felt they ended up with none of the above.

Regarding my official duties, I appointed Ricimer to the position of Master General – the first barbarian to hold the title since the time of Stilicho – and I filled a large number of provincial and ceremonial offices which were vacant due to a death or resignation. I declined to pursue treason trials against the supporters and benefactors of Maximus and Avitus, except in a few compelling and particularly worthy cases.

Although I'd been acting as emperor since October 18, my official coronation took place in the Basilica Nova on December 28. The grand basilica, begun by Emperor Maxentius in 308 AD and completed by Emperor Constantine four years later, was the largest and the newest basilica in the city of Rome.

Rectangular in design, the basilica consisted of a central nave covered by three groin vaults which were suspended over 120 feet above the floor on four massive piers. I must admit it was an excellent example of contemporary architecture. Even I loved it and I was no modernist. From the day of the basilica's completion, nothing as grand had been constructed in all of Italia.

The gold and silver reflections from the sun, shining in through the windows and bouncing off the mosaics, crosses, swords and chalices, danced in the afternoon light. The air was thick with incense and the aroma of the flowers, which were placed in every nook and cranny of the great building.

An orchestra played a delightful assortment of festive and ceremonial music.

There were men playing trumpets (including cornu, buccinas, and lituus), flutes, tibia, harps, askaules, cithara, lutes, and lyres. Other men pounded on drums, banged cymbala, and rattled sistrums. Together, they made such an amazing sound!

The hall was filled with representatives from all over the civilized world. As the ceremony began with a musical flourish, the Grand Chamberlain announced the entrance of the principal guests and notable to the crowd. Upon receiving the polite applause and the appropriate courtship depending on their status and nobility, each one was subsequently escorted to his seat by an honor guard. To witness the event, Constantinople dispatched the eldest son of Emperor Leo, and King Gaiseric sent the ranking ambassador along with multiple official observers from his palace in Carthage.

After the senior members of the Senate were announced and seated in neat rows near the front of the basilica, the Western Empire's three Field Generals – Aegidius, Ricimer, and Marcellinus, each one in full military regalia – were presented to the audience. My sister, Placida, and my three oldest children, Julius, Minerva and Claudius, were seated in the front row dressed in their finest clothes. Sadly, Ursula elected to remain at our home in Nemausus with my two younger children.

Once all of the guests were announced and seated, the trumpets began sounding the traditional "Hail Augustus" fanfare, and the coronation procession started from the rear of the Basilica and walked slowly to the throne. An acolyte, robed in a floor-length white tunic with a long purple sash along his right shoulder, led the procession, carrying the imperial crown on a pillow.

The young man was followed by twelve priests singing "The Triumph of the Angels." I followed the priests in my full military regalia, bareheaded, and I was surrounded by the members of my elite Imperial Guard, elegantly outfitted in their formal military uniforms.

As the rushes and flourishes continued, we slowly walked down the aisle in the central nave of the Basilica Nova to the throne. Ascending the stairs in a slow and deliberate fashion, we took our places on the raised podium at the front of the basilica. The colossal statue of Constantine the Great, sitting in eternal judgment over his Empire, loomed directly behind the rostrum, and an enormous bronze Roman eagle soared above us on the back wall.

When the music stopped, the Pope rose from his chair and began the coronation ceremony with a short prayer. "Hear our prayer, O Lord, and those of your servant Julius Valerius Majorian Augustus, the noble son of Caesar, who comes humbly before you on this day to lead the mighty forces of the Empire against our evil foes and belligerent adversaries. Bless him, O Lord, and grant him a long life and a glorious victory over the forces of darkness . . ."

Following his benediction, a choir stood and sang the traditional Republican hymn, "Grant Our Nation Always Free" which was followed by a prayer given by the Archbishop of Mediolanum.

After gazing up toward heaven, the Archbishop said, "Look, Almighty God, on him, your glorious servant, and upon our proud land which we call Rome. We pray, may the angels rejoice in Christ our Savior and may the enemies of Rome fall vanquished at her boot heel just as St. Michael drove the wicked Beelzebub and his evil tribe to the great pit of fire and eternal damnation . . ."

Several more prayers and supplications were delivered, and the choir rose several times in chant and song. Once the hall went silent again, the Pope stood up and walked over toward me. On his cue, I arose from the throne and walked five paces to a kneeler and knelt down before him.

The Pope took the golden crown from the pillow, and placing it gently on my head as he exclaimed, "By the grace of God the Father and his beloved Son, Jesus Christ, and in the unity of the Holy Spirit through whom all honor and glory are yours, O Lord, through infinite ages of ages, I hereby crown you Lord Emperor Julius Valerius Majorian Augustus, *Pontifex Maximus*, *Dominus Noster*, *Princeps Senatus*, and *Nobilissimus Caesar*. Arise, Augustus."

The Pope took my hand and lifted me from my knees. After the Pope concluded his blessing, the Archbishop of Nemausus arose from his chair, came forward, and presented me with a jewel-encrusted sword.

He said, "O Emperor of Rome, receive this sword which was given to me from the hands of many bishops, who, though unworthy, are consecrated to serve the Church in the place and authority of the Holy Apostles. We deliver the sword to you, Augustus, with our blessing, to serve steadfastly in defense of our Holy and Apostolic Church. Gracious Majesty, remember what the Psalmist prophesied many years ago, 'Gird the sword upon your thigh, O most Powerful One, that with it, you may exercise equity.'"

After he handed me the sword, he kissed me on both cheeks. Concluding the liturgical portion of the installation ceremony, the Bishop of Spalatum stood and chanted the verses of the traditional *Lauds Imperial* (a series of formal acclamations and responses) followed by the concluding prayer.

He said, "Our King, Christ conquers. Our Hope, Christ conquers. Our Glory, Christ conquers. Our Mercy, Christ conquers. Our Help, Christ conquers. Our Strength, Christ conquers. Our Victory, Christ conquers. Our Liberation and Redemption, Christ conquers. Our Armor, Christ conquers. Our Impregnable Wall, Christ conquers. Our Defense and Exaltation, Christ conquers. Our Light, Way and Life, Christ conquers, Christ reigns."

At the end of the prayer, the assembly responded with a triumphant, "Amen."

Finally, the Pope rose again and prayed to the congregation, "To Him alone be given command, glory, and power through immortal ages."

The assembly responded, "Amen."

"To Him alone be given vigor, strength, and victory through all ages of ages."

"Amen."

"To Him alone be granted honor, praise, and jubilation through infinite ages of ages."

"Amen."

Representing the Senate, Senator Gallipolis, arose from his chair, walked over to face me on the podium, and carefully placed a golden necklace around my neck. Suspended from the necklace was a jewel-studded diadem – the emblem of regal power and authority.

He said, "With the immediate favor of God Almighty and all the hosts of heaven, I invest you with the Imperial robe."

After he placed the cloak around my shoulders, he shouted out for the entire world to hear, "I present to you, Emperor Julius Valerius Majorian Augustus. May he live long and rule courageously over the Western Empire under the authority of Christ our Savior and power of the Senate and People of Rome. Long live Emperor Majorian!"

As I raised the sword triumphantly over my head with my right hand, the assembled multitude arose and shouted in seemingly one voice, "Long live Augustus! Long live the Emperor! Long live Rome!"

For better or for worse, I became a part of the long parade of emperors which began with Augustus and whose end seemed to be approaching ominously just below the horizon.

My immediate predecessors on the throne seldom personally addressed the Senate. Valentinian III detested the Senate and believed it was well below his dignity and station in life. On the rare occasions when Valentinian met with the legislative branch, he preferred to summon the leaders of the Senate to the Palace. There, he'd address the Senators from the throne room in his lavish imperial regalia and dictate the terms of the relationship between the sovereign and the leadership of the Senate.

From the onset of his rule, Maximus was an unpopular monarch, and apparently, he was afraid of the reception he'd receive from the Senators themselves. Avitus considered the Senate as a relic of an earlier time with little current legitimacy. I'd been told he'd planned to abolish the institution along with several other institutions which stood in the way of his pursuit of absolute power in the Western Empire.

Having risen through the leadership ranks of Senate, I was comfortable with its deliberative process, and I believed the Senate was my ally. Throughout my reign, I attended the Senate regularly, and I was the first Emperor since Marcus Aurelius to do so. Additionally, I didn't address the body as its lord and ruler; rather, as a participant in the debates and as a means to set forth my positions in their most forceful and demonstrative terms.

Although the seat of government remained in Ravenna, I spent as much time as I could in Rome – a city I loved like none other in the Empire.

On January 11, I gave my first speech to the Senate as Emperor. Although it was several years ago, I still remember it well. After being introduced by the Senate *Pro Tem*, I said: "Honorable members of the Senate, I welcome the opportunity to serve you as your Emperor."

Then I said, "We are unique in the world. Since the people of Rome threw out the last king and established a republic, the transition of power from one leader to the next leader has occurred for almost one thousand years. Although often violent, the fact the governance of Rome switches its leadership and continues governing is nothing less than a miracle."

I talked about how Caesar Augustus had transformed the republic into an empire, and how his successors kept the three primary sources of government – the Senate, the Courts, and the emperor – healthy, separate, and viable as co-equal leaders of our beloved country. I mentioned how each branch of government was endowed with a definite role, authority, and power.

"From the earliest days of the Republic and forward to the reigns of Trajan, Constantine and Theodosius, the miracle of Rome has continued unabated for a millennium. And I didn't assume the oath of office to have it end here. Let me make it clear – our best days are still before us!"

I stopped for a moment, as there was some polite applause. "Today we are faced with many enemies and with an economic circumstance which is worse than any time in our long history. The fertile fields of North Africa, Western Gaul, Belgica, Germania, Hispania, and Britannia have been taken away from us. Our loss of tax revenue has compromised our ability to respond to emergencies, and it threatens to shatter the Empire. We must reconquer those provinces now!"

The applause grew louder. "These woes did not begin during this decade or even during this century, and we won't be able to cure all of the problems immediately. Meaningful changes must be made in our tax collections, our immigration policies, and our military readiness so that real expansion can occur in Rome over the next several decades. It won't be easy – but it will happen!"

Then I talked about our shared goal – to return the Empire to its rightful place in the world and revitalize the Roman dream. "Look back at our long history. From the inception of a little tiny village on this spot over twelve hundred years ago, Rome became the greatest empire the world has ever known. How did we achieve so much? Because of our Legions and our institutions, we fostered growth and stability. The opportunities which we gave to our citizens allowed them to search the corners of their minds and the limits of their imaginations to develop ways to make life better for all Romans."

I stopped again and looked around the floor of the Senate. "Their dreams are our dreams. Their hopes are our hopes. The price of civilization is high, and all citizens must be called upon again and again to renew our commitment to the aims and aspirations of our ancestors. The price may be high; however, our forefathers have never been unwilling to pay the price with their precious blood, their fortunes, and their sweat. We shall do the same!"

Now many of the Senators were standing and applauding; some were whistling. "Let the word go our far and wide that Rome will not cede its role in the world to any other nation or principality. We may negotiate, but we will not surrender our ideals, our principles, or our way of life to any tyrant or invader. No, we won't!"

The cheering grew even louder. "Today, we also remember the great generals who led the way to these great victories – from Scipio Africanis and Pompey to Stilicho and Aëtius. Every schoolchild in the Empire knows their names and recalls their victories over the enemies of Rome. Other leaders, like these brave men, will rise again, and the armies of Rome will prevail on the field of battle."

Once again they stood; this time, even some Senators who didn't support some of my earlier actions. "To accomplish our goals, we must give our best efforts and utilize our best judgments. With God's help, we'll return the Empire to its splendor and greatness. Generations in the future will marvel at our ingenuity and our fortitude. We shall rise again!"

As they were standing and cheering, I shouted over their applause, "Why should we believe this? Because we are Romans!"

Smiling, I said, "May God bless you and may God bless Rome."

The Senate erupted in applause, and exhaling, I looked around the Senate floor. I noticed something peculiar; one man wasn't applauding. It was Ricimer. He looked disappointed and quickly exited the Senate chamber.

The following day, Ricimer rushed into my office in the palace. He seemed irate. "What the hell was that all about?"

I was puzzled and asked, "What specifically?"

"Your goddamn speech."

I responded, "What about it?"

Ricimer kept pacing. "All you talked about was Rome returning to its prior greatness. That's not what we agreed to."

Now I was puzzled. "Meaning what?"

"The reason I allowed you to become emperor . . ."

I interrupted him, "You allowed me to become emperor?"

"Yes, we were going to change our declining civilization into something much more vibrant; something which will last."

I stood up and walked over to him. "Didn't I say that yesterday? If I recall correctly, I talked on and on about revitalization and change. That's what we agreed to, isn't it?"

Ricimer shook his head, "No, we agreed to establish the framework for creating the Gallo-Roman Empire, a new Senate, and new power-sharing agreements with other principalities. I heard none of that yesterday. None at all!"

"All in good time, my friend. My plan hasn't changed, but first I need to consolidate my rule of Italia. Of course, I must reassert our influence over Dalmatia and Southern Gaul. Change takes time, my friend."

For the next several hours, Ricimer and I engaged in a frank and often bitter exchange regarding politics and timetables. However, in the end, I believed we had reconciled once again. We'd first solidify our hold on the Italian peninsula, then put down the unrest in Dalmatia, and after that, turn our sights on Gaul, Belgica, and Hispania. Once each of these provinces was firmly back under Imperial control, we'd take our aim on North Africa and the Vandals.

In the summer of 457 AD, I faced my first military test when a Vandal invading force, consisting of approximately two thousand troops and led by the brother-in-law of King Genseric, sailed from Carthage to Italia. They landed in Campania at the mouth of the Liri River and began a brutal campaign of burning and slashing Southern Italia, causing massive devastation and a sacking of the region. I quickly understood I needed to assume the offense if I wanted to regain the heart of the Empire.

Leading my troops in battle, we scored a convincing victory over the invaders near the village Sinuessa, and we totally destroyed the Vandal forces. It was the first time in nearly a century a sitting Emperor personally led troops to victory against an invading army. Furthermore, it was the first time in several centuries that a victorious Imperial army was permitted to march into the city of Rome to the spectacle of a traditional triumphal parade. With the decisive victory over the Vandals and a vastly improving economy, the spirits of the city continued to rise.

In October, I dispatched General Julius Nepos with a force of fifteen hundred troops from the garrison in Verona to quell the insurgency in Dalmatia. In short order, Nepos restored order, and the province was returned to full Roman control. With the eastern portion of the Western Empire now pacified, I turned my thoughts to reconquering Gaul and Belgica.

From the beginning of my reign, I worked with the Senate to pass legislation to promote growth and to encourage reform and economic stability in the Western Empire. In a period of only one year, we enacted several pieces of relevant legislation which was aimed at stimulating the economy and stabilizing the fabric of the Roman society.

Among other enactments, we issued legislation which forgave a significant portion of a citizen's delinquent taxes if the taxpayer immediately paid his current tax liability. We federalized the provincial military garrisons and provided additional troops and supplies to the depleted Legions. We passed legislation which was aimed at the preservation of the ancient monuments of Rome, and which prohibited their destruction or cannibalization. In order to add needed funds of the imperial coffers, we enacted legislation which provided that abandoned property became the assets of the Empire.

To aid ordinary citizens in defense of their real and personal property, we changed the old law and permitted private citizens to arm themselves and to assist the army in putting down invasions or insurrections. And to help the Church, we passed an enactment whereby citizens could freely transfer portions of their inheritance to the Church, free of taxation. Finally, concerned with the declining birth rate and the increase in the numbers of barbarians within the Roman territory, I proposed and later enacted legislation which exempted all citizens with six or more children from paying any taxes.

With these legislative enactments behind us, Ricimer, Aegidius, Marcellinus and I began planning for the long and challenging task involved in the recovery of the territory which was lost to the Burgundians, Visigoths, and Vandals. We needed to restore the Western Empire militarily and diplomatically. We decided to initiate the invasion during in the winter when an offensive would not be suspected by our enemies.

As time went by, I began to adjust to my new role as Emperor and with the lay-out of the Palace buildings located on Palatine Hill. Soon, I was able to navigate the tightly-packed labyrinth of these extraordinary buildings and temples situated within the palace boundaries, all different, and often interspersed with hidden features and quiet alcoves. Even the brightness and splendor of the interiors became almost commonplace to me, and I could walk down the corridors and through the elegant rooms without always wanting to stop and gaze at a statue, painting, fresco, or tapestry.

After a short while, I could also easily recall the names and titles of my ministers, the public servants, and my military support staff, and I learned how to deal with the seemingly endless number of courtiers and office seekers. I was feeling more comfortable with my title and position, but I dearly missed Ursula and my children who remained in Nemausus.

Ursula would write me almost every week via the *cursus publicus* to tell me about their lives and their circumstances. In the beginning, her letters were always hopeful and poignant. As time went by, however, I began to notice a hint of bitterness and frustration in her correspondence. Her tone was changing.

In the late autumn of 458 AD, I received the following letter which shattered my almost idyllic role as emperor:

Dear Husband,

I am so lonesome for you, as are your children. Even though you promised me that you'd come home to us on a regular basis, we haven't seen you since you and Ricimer left Nemausus over a year ago. I want a husband and not just a portrait of a gallant man hanging on the wall of our home. While you attend to Rome's urgent needs, you also need to be mindful of necessities of your wife and your children. We miss our husband and our father. My love, you must come home soon!

The autumn foliage is now in its full splendor. Southern Gaul is so beautiful this time of the year. The harsh temperatures of summer are now just a memory, and the color of the sky and the angle of the light in early November please me so much. I wish you were here enjoying it with me.

Yesterday, I went shopping in the agora with Legate Rudolpho Gustavus and a few soldiers. Although the summer fruits and vegetable are long gone, several merchants displayed large baskets full of dates, walnuts, prunes and dried figs for sale. I bought plenty of these because the children love them so. I also bought an elongated amphora of garum – it's a fish sauce the people here in Nemausus dearly love. I enjoy shopping in the agora here; it's so much more interesting than the one in Rome.

There was a small incident, however, which I need to tell you about. Almost as soon as we arrived in the agora, I noticed a man watching us. A short while later, he walked up to me, ripped a necklace from my throat and began running. Luckily, he collided with a soldier, and Legate Gustavus tackled him and beat him severely. And he saved the necklace. The man was arrested and is now in prison awaiting his sentence.

I don't know how many people witnessed the event; however, the rumors are spreading even more since the incident in the agora. Thankfully, Ricimer has absolved Legate Gustavus of any wrongdoing, and I've remained hidden in our household since that date except to worship on Sunday. All of this has rekindled my biggest fears.

In my heart, I still worry about my past catching up with us. As big as it is, the Empire may be too small to contain the truth about me. My love, I dread living without you, and now I dread being your wife. Placida has been a constant comfort to me and as sweet to me as any sister could be. I'm not sure what she knows about us, but soon I must tell her everything about my past - as horrible as it may be. I don't know how she will treat me once she knows the whole truth.

Then, my love, what shall I tell our children? Pray tell, what my love?

I'm so sorry to burden you with these trivialities when compared with the troubles and crises of state. I know the Empire needs their Emperor but your children need their father, too.

Your children send their love.

Always your loving wife,

Ursula

Unfortunately, emperors belong to the people and cannot leave the palace on a whim to travel to other places in the Empire — except when commanding an army. For travel beyond the cities of Rome or Ravenna in normal situations, a host of legal and logistical requirements must be fulfilled to satisfy the well-being of the emperor and the obligations and traditions of the Roman state.

The Praetorian Guard must be notified who must plan for the safety and security of the overall operation. Provisions and accommodations must be provided for the emperor and his entourage, and the emperor's principal secretary must carefully coordinate the details of these plans so that proper courtship and civility are strictly followed. Furthermore, these plans must be made long in advance to satisfy conventional protocols and procedures of an Imperial excursion and to meet local needs and traditions.

Often the emperor is accompanied by an enormous retinue of clerks, scribes and slaves, along with the distinguished leaders of the Church, the reigning consuls, the Praetorian Prefects (the Clarissimi), selected members of the Senate.

Furthermore, the entourage often includes the heads of the major governmental departments (called Illustres), prominent ministers (such as the quaestor), and various distinguished dignitaries such as the local governors, the Count of the Sacred Largesse, the Count of the Privy Purse, the Master of Offices, and the Grand Chamberlain of the Sacred Palace, among others. The list could go on *ad nauseum*.

Aside from these considerations, it was also a difficult time for me personally to loosen the entrapments of power. I was only just beginning to solidify my reign, and I was uncertain whether I'd have a throne to return to should I ever venture beyond either the cities of Rome or Ravenna.

Therefore, I wrote Ursula and told her that I'd come home in the spring and I'd make sure everything would be resolved in a positive way for us. I reaffirmed my love and commitment to her, and I told her once I consolidated the power in Italia, I'd build a new palace in Nemausus for our family. In the meantime, I asked Ursula to send my son Julius to Ravenna so he could begin to understand the workings of the Court. At least, part of my family would be living with me.

My son arrived at the palace in early December and immediately became a great pleasure for me. He didn't know any of the hidden things about Ursula, but I planned that once he grew to be a little older, I'd explain our predicament. Certainly, I didn't want him to hear the snarls of gossip which were beginning to arise in Italia about us.

In the meantime, Ursula's letters were less frequent, and her tone seemed more distant. To save our marriage, spring couldn't come quick enough for me. In the end, my decision not to go to Nemausus immediately has been one of the worst mistakes I've made, and to this day, I regret it deeply.

In late December, 457, I was sitting in my office with my mentor, Senator Gallipolis, discussing politics and procedures. "So, my Lord," he asked, "what's it like being Emperor, if I may be so brazen to inquire?"

"It's more depressing than I'd first imagined or even dreamt. Whenever I'm sitting on the throne, I am treated like a god, not a real person. It's the tiresome rituals of court; every detail of courtship must be strictly and minutely followed, and all matter of manners and protocols must be fervently observed."

I stopped for a moment to complete my thought. "Gaius, I often think of myself as an actor in a bad play. Life is better for me in the camps and garrisons where there is no courtship, and of course, in the private portions of the palace, where there is as little courtship as possible. But when I'm out in public eye, it's dreadful."

Gaius smiled as if he already knew my answer before I uttered it. As Emperor,

I went by the official title of 'Augustus' as had all previously sitting emperors assumed since the reign of Diocletian. However, I excluded my family, Gaius, and Generals Ricimer, Aegidius, and Marcellinus from the directive unless we were out in the public eye.

We sat quietly for a while, and then I looked up at him. "I've meant to ask you something for a long time," I said. "Why were you the only Senator to vote against my ascension the throne? It's something that's always bothered me."

"For two reasons, my Lord: First, nobody should ever receive unanimous support for any job that's as meaningful and as powerful as the Emperor. There should always be some, even if token, opposition."

I smiled, "And the second reason?"

He twisted in his chair and then replied, "I've never trusted Count Ricimer, and I don't trust him now. He's a shrewd manipulator who'll turn against you the instant he feels you are no longer serving his sinister purposes."

"You don't trust him?"

"No, and you shouldn't trust him either. Unless you dispose of him quickly, I firmly believe you won't survive ten years as Emperor unless. He'll become your downfall, my Lord."

Gaius' admonition's stayed with me for a long time after that.

One afternoon in early January, Hector Ulysses Asthenias, my principal secretary, handed me a sealed scroll from Ursula. I believed the prior matter had been resolved between us and that things returned to normal. Happily, I sat back in my chair and unsealed the envelope. I was looking forward to another love letter from her.

> *Dear Husband,*
>
> *I know this note will bring you sorrow, and for this reason, my heart is almost breaking.*

I became concerned, and I thought, what could be going wrong now?

> *Before we married, you promised me that you'd take me away from Rome and we'd live the rest of our lives together in Nemausus. Now you are the Emperor, I know well you*

can never make the promise come true for our son and me. I don't want a life with you in Rome and me staying in Nemausus. You left me here over eighteen months ago, and I haven't seen you since that day. Julius, I sincerely believe there's no real prospect for us ever being together as a family again. I'm weak, and I cannot face a lifetime with only my son, your children, and sweet memories of you. I need much more than that.

I started panicking.

As you know, I met Legate Rudolpho Gustavus a few years ago, and he says he loves me. I'm also carrying his child. Like me, Rudolpho is Burgundian, and we speak the language of our people. He's a good man, and I love him very much. He'll make a good father for our son and the new baby. I've shamed you and myself by this affair, and there is no redemption for me now. I have no choice except to leave.

Elmina is joining us on our journey. By the time you receive this, we'll be well on our way. Please don't attempt to find us.

I dropped the parchment to the floor and gazed out the window. After a while, I picked it up and began reading more.

Your other children are staying with Placida, and perhaps you should bring them to Rome. Your sister is upset with me, but she has said she won't stop me.

I'll always love you, and I'll tell our son all about you; but try as I would, I could never fully forgive you for being a Roman. I hope in the years to come, however, you'll find it in your soul to forgive me.

Ursula

I felt a pain in my heart which I'd never known before. I also experienced a strange combination of rage, anger, sorrow, and despair. How could Ursula do this to our son and me? Yes, my beloved son, whose name, to this day, I cannot say aloud.

I quickly dispatched orders to find her and arrest her lover. I'd deal with him harshly. By the time my orders arrived in Nemausus, however, they had disappeared into the territory which was controlled by the Visigoths. I knew I'd get little help from them.

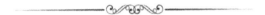

Soon the days became weeks and the weeks became months, and I began to heal. My oldest son was a great consolation to me, and in April, I went home to Nemausus to start making plans for a palace there. I'd received no further communications from Ursula, and my staff told me that she had probably gone to Britannia. They assured me, however, they'd continue to search for her.

In the summer of 458 AD, Avitus surreptitiously abandoned his position as Bishop of Piacenza and secretly returned to Western Gaul – his prior source of political power and influence. After being presented to the Court of King Theodoric, he quickly attempted to reassert his title as Emperor of the Western Empire. However, King Theodoric was unpersuaded by Avitus' petition. Avitus was executed. No charges were made, and apparently, there was no trial. I don't know where he was buried or whether he was even buried at all.

After consolidating our political and military hold in Italia, Ricimer, Aegidius, and I concentrated on the recovery of Gaul and Belgica. To commence our extensive planning, I needed to return to Ravenna, the seat of the Western Empire's military command components.

A few days before leaving the city of Rome, I called Cluny into my office. Upon entering my chambers with his my head bowed, he went down on one knee and said, "Yes Sir?"

After telling him to rise, I asked, "Cluny, if I could give you any gift, what would you want from me?"

"Oh, Sir, you've been good to me. I cannot dare ask for anything, Sir."

"Would you like to be free?"

Cluny looked up at me, almost disbelieving what I'd mentioned. "Free, Sir?"

"Yes, free. Would you like your freedom?"

Head now bowed again, he almost whispered, "Yes, Sir, I'd like my freedom."

"If I gave you your freedom, what would you want to do?"

He looked up at me, "Sir, I'd like to return to my home in Ethiopia."

I smiled. "Cluny, I'll grant both wishes. Tomorrow, Hector will arrange to have you manumitted, and we'll arrange for a ship to take you to Thebes, Egypt. Unfortunately, I'm unable to arrange transportation any further south on the Nile, but I'm sure you'll find a way to make it home from there. I'll also give you a nice stipend to help you begin your new life in Ethiopia."

Tears were running down Cluny's face. His head still bowed, he said, "Thank you, Sir."

I got up from my chair and placed my hand on his shoulder. "Tomorrow I'm leaving Rome, and I may never return here. Cluny, it's a dangerous and unpredictable world out there, and soon, I'll begin a campaign in Belgica and Gaul. While I know you'd gladly follow me, you've performed an excellent service to me over these past five years. I know of no one – slave or free – more loyal or trustworthy than you."

"Thank you, Sir."

"How old are you, Cluny?"

"About thirty, Sir."

"And how long have you been a slave?"

"About twenty years, Sir."

"Yes, it's time for you to be free. May God bless you and walk with you. Thank you for your loyal service to Rome and me."

Cluny looked up to me. "I'll never forget you, Sir. Thank you for my freedom. God bless you too, Sir."

He turned around and, closing the door behind him, walked out of my chambers. While I never saw him again, Hector later told me that Cluny was successfully manumitted and he boarded a ship bound for Egypt.

Later that evening, I took one more walk through the grand monuments of this magnificent city. Concealing my identity to avoid recognition, Hector and I slowly walked the along *Via Sacra* one more time. Leaving the Palatine Palaces, we walked through the Arch of Constantine to the Flavian Amphitheatre. Turning around, we passed the Basilica Nova and the other ancient monuments in the Forum Romanum and up to the top of the Capitoline Hill. Staring out at the magnificent city below us, I had a premonition I'd never see the city again. It seems like I was right.

CHAPTER XVIII

The City of Ravenna, late January 459

For the next several months, Ricimer, Aegidius, and I carefully developed the strategic plan for the re-conquest of our lost territory in Belgica and Gaul. In dividing up the areas of responsibilities, Aegidius was tasked with reconstituting an effective fighting force from the remnants of the once proud Legions.

Traditionally, the Roman army is divided into two clusters: the *limetani,* who are permanently garrisoned at established installations and patrol a particular geographical area or frontier; and the field armies, known as *comitatenses,* which move around the Empire as needed to repel large scale invasions or local uprisings. Borrowing from here and stealing from these groups, Aegidius was able to amass from all parts of the Western Empire, small bits and pieces of combat-ready units – both *limetani* and *comitatenses.* In the end, he assembled a fighting force of almost twenty thousand soldiers.

Ricimer was given the responsibility for establishing a coalition of willing partners. In a similar fashion, Ricimer worked his magic in much the same way as Aëtius had done eight years earlier. By way of promises, threats, and outright intimidation, Ricimer was able to construct a barbarian army, twenty thousand strong, from such diverse groups as the Franks, Ostrogoths, Scythians, and other Germanic tribes.

We spent months putting together a theme of operations – our war plan. In setting up the basic outline of the overall plan of attack, the three of us fully understood, however, that despite our attention to detail and issuance of general orders, war planning is often overrated. It provides the general staff with only a general blueprint of the strategies, lines of advance and avenues of retreat.

Contrary to what many people believe, the conduct of war consists mostly of improvisations. In the heat of battle, the commanders must substitute, tinker, and often make it up as the action proceeds. It's the individual general's skill in adaptation and redeployment of infantry forces and mounted cavalry which often determines the outcome of the overlying plan of attack.

Just before we left Ravenna, I remember Ricimer saying, "It'll be a long and bitterly fought campaign, but I'm confident we will prevail."

Aegidius and I nodded our heads in agreement. But, I wasn't so sure.

In late February, 459 AD, I led the army into Western Gaul with a united force of over forty thousand armed men – crossbowmen, cuirassiers, cavalry and infantry. It was good to be on the move again. As planned, I was easily identified by my troops. Located on top of a small knoll accompanied by my general staff, I sat on my white horse with my purple cloak and my eagle standard. I saluted my men as they cheered me and clattered their shields with their lances.

Our combined imperial/barbarian army quickly defeated the Visigoths at the Battle of Arelate, forcing King Theodoric to abandon Arausio and withdraw his troops to the lands west of Aquitania. The victory was decisive. Under the new treaty, the Visigoths agreed to relinquish their conquests in Hispania and to return to a federate status.

After that, with the help of King Theodoric and the Visigoth army, we entered the Rhone Valley and decisively defeated King Gunderic and the Burgundians. Lugdunum was returned to Imperial control. Despite the fact the Gallo-Roman aristocracy sided with King Gunderic, we offered our adversaries reconciliation and not punishment. Soon all of Gaul, Belgica and most of Hispania were back under Roman control.

Then we turned our attention to the remaining portion of Hispania which was outside our control. In October of 460, the XXII Legion, commanded by General Aegidius, began a campaign against the Suebi in Northwestern Hispania. Following the decisive Battle of Lucas Augusti, he pacified the hostile area in a brutal two-month campaign. It generally is agreed Aegidius' army moved more effectively than the forces of any Roman general since Julius Caesar.

Meanwhile, I gathered up the remaining cohorts of VI Legion, and after adding some of the remaining barbarian forces, we ultimately pushed the Vandals out of Hispania and back across the Straits of Gibraltar into North Africa. Then we turned our attention to North Africa – the former breadbasket of the Western Empire.

When historians write their chronicles about war and the decisive military engagements which changed the course of history, they usually talk of competing armies, shield walls, the use of cavalry, and the ingenious battle plans utilized by the victorious generals. I learned early in my military career, however, war was really about foodstuff, horses, supplies, and sanitation. An army which eats well, that is better supplied, and doesn't fall victim to rampant disease is the armed force which usually carries the day on the battlefield.

Once again, the Imperial supply trains and overall logistical support, along with our subordinate commanders' ability to keep their camps clean, gave our field commanders an advantage which the opposing barbarian forces couldn't match.

Moreover, historians don't mention the fact that occupying forces often do not clean out the pockets of local resistance in the conquered territories or successfully convert the local people to the customs and practices of the invaders. Although the Visigoths, Burgundians, and Vandals had each seized an extensive amount of Imperial territory, they weren't able to solidify their conquests or win the loyalty of the captured people.

Many small fortresses, outlying towns, and remote areas in these subjugated lands remained loyal to their Roman heritage. Frequently the conquerors attempted to put down revolts, subdue minorities, and to control the local populations; but they failed for the most part. It usually takes a considerable period of time to pacify conquered territory, and the barbarian warlords simply ran out of time to erase centuries-long Roman loyalty.

After we had won these decisive battles in Gaul, Belgica, and Hispania, there was often not much left for us to do to re-Romanize the reconquered areas. We were often warmly welcomed by the local people who previously lived peacefully in the Empire for hundreds of years and who despised the imposition of the mandates and authority of the local barbarian warlords.

Consequently, once we defeated the barbarian invaders, life seemed to quickly return to the normal patterns and lifestyles which flourished in these historically Imperial provinces for many centuries. Soon the ravaged fields were plowed and fertile, sheep returned to the higher pastures, and towns were full of commerce and human activity — as if the barbarian invasions had never happened.

Upon hearing about our victories, we learned from our spies that King Gaiseric was worried about the likelihood of an invasion. Fearing the worst, he sent his ambassador to me in an attempt to negotiate a peace treaty. After nearly two months of negotiations, however, we rejected their final proposal.

Apparently believing the legions were ready to cross the straights between Hispania and North Africa and invade the province of Mauretania, King Gaiseric elected to devastate much of the disputed territory. To protect his tenuous hold on the area, he burned the region's fields, vineyards, orchards and villages to the ground, and he annihilated much of the remaining Roman population.

In hindsight, I probably should've either accepted King Gaiseric's last offer of a peace treaty or at the least begun the amphibious invasion of North Africa much sooner. However, our army was exhausted after fourteen months of continuous warfare. Furthermore, our supplies were low, and our fragile confederation with our barbarian partners was beginning to unravel. Ricimer and I jointly decided we needed time to reinvigorate our army, resupply our provisions, and rethink our strategy.

Despite the delay, Ricimer and I also agreed we'd accomplished quite a lot in a relatively short time, and that our dream of forging a Gallo-Roman Empire from the remnants of the Western Empire was still burning brightly.

CHAPTER XIX

The City of Carthago Nova, Hispania - March 461

A prosperous and strongly fortified city, and possessing one of the best harbors in the Western Mediterranean, Carthago Nova was settled by the Carthaginians in 228 BC. Twenty years later, General Scipio Africanus conquered the city. It was selected as the capital of the province of Hispania in 298 AD, and the city remained in Imperial hands until 459 AD when it was taken briefly by the Vandals. Once again, it was back under Roman control.

For the next five weeks, Ricimer, Aegidius and I, along with our barbarian partners, developed and implemented a military and logistical scheme to attack King Gaiseric. Unlike the Suebi, the Vandals would be much harder to subdue. Reaching Africa required a sizeable fleet, and we began the process of gathering a massive flotilla from all over the Empire. Eventually, we settled on a date in late June for the amphibious invasion of North Africa when the seas were generally calmer and the winds were diminished.

By early summer, over six hundred ships were assembled in the local harbors around Carthago Nova. There were ships of war, troop carriers, amphibious assault vessels, and cargo ships which were used for transporting the food, weapons, siege engines, foundries, and other military necessities for a successful attack. Also, hundreds of supply wagon trains and scores of fresh troops were arriving daily. Even with these resources, the three of us agreed the invasion of Africa would be difficult.

Attacking over water always proves to be a bit of a logistical challenge. An amphibious assault requires the coordination of many unusual tactical components, and the standard land-based military infrastructure, equipment, and training are of little use in waterborne operations.

However, Rome's longstanding naval superiority gave us the ability to choose the time and place of the conflicts. With our superior transport capability of troops and cargo, Rome usually had a quantitative advantage when amphibious alternatives were being considered. Over the past five centuries in building and maintaining a powerful Navy, Rome acquired a longer reach, greater speed, better durability, more concentrated firepower, and an extensive knowledge of the ways to pick and probe an enemy target.

At the Academy, and throughout my military career, I learned that the balance of transport ultimately determines success and overall functional security. The Imperial Navy and the extensive Roman road system – enabling the movement of troops and cargo swiftly and decisively – provided the muscle which Rome needed to develop ambitious and multi-faceted schemes of warfare. With these principles in mind, Ricimer, Aegidius and I spent many hours formulating our strategic plan to attack the Vandals.

In an attempt to confuse Gaiseric about the path of the main attack, I ordered General Marcellinus to move elements of the Dalmatian field army to Sicily and feign a crossing of the Sicilian Straits to North Africa. We hoped Gaiseric would take the bait.

In early June, I walked out to a hill overlooking the harbor. For as far as I could see, the square red sails flapped and fluttered from the yardarms in the warm summer breeze. The seas beyond the harbor were relatively calm. We hoped for a good week of weather. In just four days' time, we'd weigh anchor and sail south to Carthage. Soon, I believed, all of North Africa would fall back into Imperial hands.

On the evening of June 6, however, disaster struck. Whether it was lightning, an accident, or a plan manufactured by Gaiseric's spies, much of the fleet, lying at anchor in the harbor in Carthago Nova, was set on fire.

Because the boats were tied closely to each other, the flames darted swiftly from ship to ship until the entire harbor seemed to be on fire. Illuminating the perimeter of the entire southwestern sky, the fleet was completely devastated. The night was bright as the day. Standing in utmost hopelessness at dawn, I realized any hope for reconquering Carthage was lost. I immediately order a formal investigation, and several suspects were arrested and later hanged. But the damage was done

Deprived of the fleet which was necessary for the invasion, I reluctantly canceled the attack on the Vandals. Two days later, I met with Gaiseric's ambassador, and we agreed on a peace treaty. Aside from ceding the cities of Carthage and Hippo to perpetual Vandal control, we recognized the *de facto* occupation of Mauretania by the Vandals.

Ricimer was furious at the terms of the peace treaty.

The next morning, Ricimer stormed into my tent. The air was still thick with the smell of the smoldering fleet. Noticeably agitated, he screamed, "You gave away Carthage and Mauretania? How could you be so stupid? And without consulting me?"

"Damn it, I'm still the emperor, and as a matter of fact, I don't need your acquiescence. Once the fleet was destroyed, there was no way to move our armies into North Africa. Do you agree?"

"Perhaps, but that's no reason to enter into a treaty with the Vandals. They remain our arch-enemy, and they pose little threat to either Hispania or Rome now."

"I disagree. We need to disband our forces, and I couldn't risk another Vandal invasion."

I told him that we couldn't depart Carthago Nova and leave our southern flank exposed. We needed peace in Hispania so its economy could recover after two decades of war and famine. Ricimer kept arguing, however, that we couldn't trust Gaiseric and the treaty gave up too much Roman land.

He said, "Yes, but you have no obligation to conclude this lopsided treaty. You gave away Hippo and Mauretania. It's beyond asinine; it's idiotic and it's criminal. We both know Rome's future depends on reclaiming those territories; it's our breadbasket. Now you've really messed everything up."

I responded, "No, I disagree – the treaty clearly is in the best interests of Rome. Christ, we've already restored much of the Empire, and that's a significant accomplishment in itself. We can go after Carthage again in the future."

"What, are you insane? This matter is over. We can't recreate this scenario on a whim."

"Maybe so, but, I need to go back to Rome; the Senate is ready to commence a 'no confidence' vote. They're fearful of about invasion from the north and they demand we bring Aegidius' XXII Legion back to Mediolanum."

Ricimer was livid. He pointed his finger at me and yelled, "Mark my words;

you'll live to regret this treaty. Without Carthage, there's no goddamn empire."

Then Ricimer stomped around the room, and grabbing a vase, he threw it at the back wall. For some reason, the smashing sound seemed to calm him for a few moments.

Staring me right in the eye, he asked, "So, when are you going to announce our plan for the revamped Empire? Everyone is here – Gunderic, Childeric, and Theodoric – plus other tribal chieftains. Now is the time for us to go forward."

I shook my head and responded, "No, I need to do this process in a piecemeal fashion. We've talked about the matter many times before. First, I need the Senate to accept the fundamental reconstruction idea for the Empire, and I need to approach each of the Kings individually. We still haven't formulated a final plan."

Ricimer was angry again. Now red in the face, he clenched his fists and screamed, "Damn it, we already have a plan. It's a goddamn good one and it's ready to go!"

I shook my head again and said: "All we have is a broad umbrella, but we need to fill in the blanks with substance and details. If I announce something vague and general, it may scare them off. I'm just not ready yet. Like I mentioned, I need to gain the approval of the Senate first."

"You plan to secure the support of the Senate? Are you out of your goddamn mind? It would be the last thing they'd want. What – ask them to surrender the primary source of their power and prestige? Ask them to give up their lifeline to power and riches?"

He stopped for a moment and slammed his fist on the table. "You're already a real threat to these influential Senators, and we'll be taking away the very means used by these bastards to expand their fortunes and influence. You do know they won't join you in their demise, don't you? No, they'll eat you up and spit you out like bad sausage before acquiescing to our plan."

I stood up and walked around. I needed time to calm down. "No, now isn't the time. We need to do it piecemeal and not in some broad and under-thought pronouncement as massive as this one; no, not as long as I'm still the Emperor."

"Nothing lasts forever; you may soon have your wish, my friend." He looked at me with contempt in his eyes, and without another word, he stormed out of my tent.

Later on in the evening, I reconsidered what Ricimer told me. Although he was disrespectful, perhaps the time was right to present a broad plan to our allies. Maybe, I needed to go forward with our overall plan while all of the major players were still camping in Carthago Nova.

I didn't sleep much that night.

During the afternoon of July 1, Hector, my chief of staff, provided me with his last formal briefing from Carthago Nova. Earlier in the day, a courier from the Ravenna arrived with urgent information.

Looking glum and sad, Hector sat down on the chair in front of my desk, and reported, "Sir, I have some news – none of which is good."

"Well, what is it?"

"First, our dear friend, Gaius, died last week in Rome. The courier told me the Senator collapsed on the floor of the Senate. Apparently, they were unable to revive him. He's gone, my lord. He was buried beside his wife at his villa near Palestrina."

I was shocked to the point of disbelief. "Are you certain, Hector? Oh, my God, not him. He's my right arm in the Senate and my best friend in the world. I could lose anyone but him. Christ, I'll miss him!"

"We'll both miss him, Sir."

I stood up and paced my office for five minutes, shaking my head at the terrible news. I couldn't accept it. Gaius was like a father to me. Regaining my composure, I asked, "So, what else do you have for me?"

Hector replied, "Well, Sir, King Gunderic has been unable to find the whereabouts of your wife. She isn't in Atria, and her sister and her family have vanished, too. He's still searching for them, Sir. She may now be in Caledonia."

Disappointed, I shook my head, but in my heart, I never fully believed I'd ever find her and my son again. Hector continued, "Also, the courier reports the Senate is angry over the surging costs of the war. Apparently, the Senate leadership won't appropriate any more funding."

The news wasn't wholly unexpected. Even with Gaius' support, it was an uphill fight. Still, it made me irate. I replied, "What in the hell do they want from me? We've taken back Belgica, Gaul, and Hispania. Did they think I could do all this on a meager budget?"

I shook my head in disbelief, and I thought about all we'd accomplished in such a short period. What the hell more did the Senate want from me? Most of our victories in this campaign were already forgotten; there's nothing so swiftly lost as the Senate's memory of our distant accomplishments. It's always, 'what have you done for me lately' – isn't it?

Hector also reported on several other matters, such as the strength of the Imperial forces, the Empire's economic viability, a new plague rising in Lombardy, and a wide range of information concerning matters such as nomadic threats from other places along the northern borders of the Western Empire.

Yes, Hector was right; the news wasn't good. Gaius' death was a significant loss; Gaius could never be replaced as a friend and as my eyes and ears on the floor of the Senate. It was time for me to go back to Italia and solidify the domestic situation before matters became much worse.

But first, I needed to meet one more meeting with the coalition members and dissolve the expeditionary force.

The following day, I called for a final gathering with the coalition members and my principal generals. Ricimer, however, was not present.

After welcoming them to the Great Hall, we talked about all we'd done together and what was left to be done. I reminded them that for the last eighteen months, our nations worked well together as a fighting force but it was time to break camp and go our separate ways.

I submitted that we'd accomplished much more than most of our critics thought possible. Through strategic alliances and exchanges with the partners, we restored the mainland European boundaries of the Western Empire and brought peace to our people. I hoped peace would last for many decades to come.

Then I said, "Over the past half-century, we've suffered through many wars and invasions, and despite the turmoil, Rome – along with our federates – remains the strongest and most productive nation in the world; but there's much left to do. Although Carthage and Britannia remain still beyond our grasp, I sense a new vision of governance is slowly arising in Hispania, Gaul, Belgica and Germania; one which is both inclusive and expansive."

I mentioned that while wandering around the camps and the cities, I'd seen hope for the future fixed on the faces of the soldiers and the citizens. I said I heard words of optimism spoken in the forums and marketplaces as we passed through the Western Provinces.

Then I talked of the future. "After five-hundred years of imperial rule, our people are seeking a modification of the present order. I hope we, together, can bring about a political revolution peacefully as to avoid any future bloodshed."

I stopped for a moment and looked around the great room. I saw several heads nodding affirmatively. Regrettably, several other heads looked like they were merely nodding off to sleep.

I continued, "There comes a time in every empire, kingdom, and principality for the monarch to reconsider the fundamental mechanisms and structures which have brought him to prominence; and to determine whether the same factors and assumptions remain valid for further growth and prosperity."

I stated that although a vital element in keeping the peace is a powerful military, we can no longer ignore the political realities at hand. "We must now rethink the current model."

I paused. Even now, I was uncertain on whether to announce my plans for a new empire. I took a deep breath and continued, "Over the next couple of years, I'll present each of you a plan about going forward to restructure our ancient model to serve better the needs and challenges of the current age. A stagnant unchanging empire cannot stand forever. As situations change, we must either change with them or die."

Once again I stopped. I was still somewhat uncertain about whether to proceed with this part of my speech. Nothing would be the same after today; it was a pivotal point in Roman history.

After quietly reassuring myself that now was the time to address the problem – the one which Ricimer and I squabbled about – I cleared my throat and continued, "I firmly believe we need to transition from an imperial system of government to a confederation of equal partners. Rome is no longer the sole dominant force in Western Europe. There are new players who need to have a voice in their future."

I suggested all dominions must come to the conference table, and together form a new strategic and political alliance. We must be willing to discuss diverse approaches regarding how to resolve our differences and emphasize our shared values, ideals, and hopes for the future.

I continued, "As one who has personally witnessed the horror and lingering sadness of war, I realize that unless we join in a mutual confederation of national partners, another war could easily destroy our way of life."

Even those who nodded off were fully awake now. It was time for me to come to the main point – my belief Roman civilization must either change or die.

"To all of you gathered here, I pledge my continued dedication to peace and prosperity among our nations. I pray all who yearn for peace and prosperity will understand the need for all of us to remain united and strong."

I told them although I'd soon be leaving Carthago Nova for Ravenna, I'd meet with them again soon, and present my thoughts for a new empire; one which also will last another millennium.

Initially, there was little reaction to my farewell address. Eventually, I saw heads bobbing affirmatively and smiles all around. Over the next couple of hours, we all shook hands and spoke privately about our concerns and plans. How I wished Ricimer had been there to hear my proposals. Perhaps, he wouldn't be as angry.

By late afternoon, the hall was empty and the coalition members began the task of breaking camp and returning to their homelands. For most of them, it was a relief. Armies are expensive to maintain, and more soldiers die due to camp-borne illnesses than in battle. Yes, it was time to go home.

The following morning, I met privately with Aegidius in my quarters. It was a warm and sunny July morning. The region's flowering trees and shrubs filled the air with color and fragrance. In this part of Hispania, the earth was rich and dark in color, and because of the abundance of ground water, the gardens were among the most beautiful in the Empire. On the morrow, I'd begin the long trip back to Italia.

Alone in a quiet garden, we talked about many topics such as the status of the Empire and the remaining capabilities of the Legions. Finally, we turned to the subject of Ricimer's whereabouts. He said, "I don't know where he went. However, General Pulcharius told me that Ricimer left camp a couple of days ago. In his absence, Ricimer left him in charge of the XXIII Legion. However, Pulcharius stated he didn't know where Ricimer went or when he'd rejoin the legion; but he did mention the XXIII Legion will break camp on Thursday and return to Lugdunum."

"That's not like Ricimer, you know, leaving camp without permission or an explanation."

"Well, I know for a fact he's furious with you. I hope he'll calm down once he's away from camp for a while. Keep your eyes open; he was openly talking treason."

"Yes, I heard the same thing from other sources in camp. Although I'll certainly be careful, he'll calm down sooner or later. What other alternatives does he have?"

Aegidius nodded his head and after a few moments responded, "I understand you're going back to Ravenna by land. Wouldn't a sea route be the fastest way?"

"Yes, but the Vandals currently control the lower sea-lanes. With our armada still smoldering, I've elected to go back by the land route. While it's much slower, I think it's safer. I'll see you back in Ravenna, my friend."

He saluted me, and we briefly embraced and parted ways. On his way out the door, Aegidius mentioned he'd remain in Hispania for another month before marching his legion back to Mediolanum. There were things he needed to do. He said, "The Senate be damned."

Accompanied by a contingent of twenty mounted cavalrymen, Hector and I began the long ride back to Italia on the morning of July 5. The weather was delightful, and the countryside was rich in oats and grain which would soon be ready for harvest. Herds of goats and cattle filled the pasturelands and grassy hills, and the fruit trees were ripe and heavy-laden. Further along the way, the green hillsides leveled out, and we rode through rich orchards and lush meadowlands. By day's end, we were well north of Carthago Nova. It was no wonder the Vandals wanted this land.

Our long journey by coach on the Via Augusta took us from Carthago Nova to Valentia, Tarraco, and Barcino, and we turned north and arrived in Southern Gaul near Narbo Martius. Along the way, my thoughts were heavy on my mind.

I thought about my family in Nemausus and how precious they were to me; and I wondered about the whereabouts of Ursula and my son. I also considered the fate of the Empire, the Senate, and the underfunded and overly-stretched Legions, and I contemplated whether my barbarian partners would ever join me in this new political venture. Finally, I questioned how in the hell did Ricimer ever talk me into leaving my job as Master General to become the Emperor of this fragile yet multifaceted empire.

During our long and tedious ride north toward Italia, we stopped from time-to-time in local cities and villages, and we met with the governance of the larger communities. Often, the local people gathered along the main thoroughfares to cheer me. When a proper setting was arranged, I talked directly to them. My message was always positive, and for each of those communities, it had been well over a century since a sitting emperor visited their municipality.

When I first began speaking in public so long ago, I was told I spoke too long and that my tone was too pompous. However, once I became Emperor, all of my speeches were all of a sudden considered as elegant and timely. In my later years, I often chuckled to myself and thought about how one's speaking style often improves with the importance of the office which one occupies!

Twelve days after leaving Carthago Nova, we stopped in Nemausus, and for the next week, we rested in my hometown. Of course, I was given a hero's welcome for their native son, and the town held an impressive victory parade. We began planning in earnest for the new palace – I picked out the precise location and presented the architect with specific outlines for its construction and appearance.

After some gentle persuasion, Placida and her husband agreed to bring the rest of my children to Ravenna for the winter solstice. After spending many years apart from them, I'd have my entire family at last with me in Italia. It was one of the happiest times of my life.

Amid tears, prayers, and promises, we left Nemausus on August 3, and we rode slowly through the cities of Aquae Sextaie and Cemenelum toward Dertona. Just outside the city gates of Dertona, Ricimer's cavalry surrounded us, and Hector and I were arrested. Without either an explanation or a formal charge, I was confined to this prison cell in the late afternoon.

CHAPTER XX

After the noise and confusion of the past several hours, it was remarkably quiet in the prison. Perhaps I may've slept for a brief period – I really don't know. In the dim light, I watched a mouse scurry along the floor of my cell and stop at the plate of food lying at my feet. Taking a few bites, he quickly departed. For a few moments, I envied the mouse.

Suddenly I realized the full measure of my dire predicament. I began to feel immense sorrow and regret. My stomach was tied up in knots and my head was exploding with fear and trepidation. Unable to keep my emotions in check, tears began running down my face. I wept for my children, for they will no longer have a father. I prayed to the saints in heaven that Ricimer's brutal vengeance won't reach them in Nemausus.

I also cried for Ursula and my young son as they traveled to some unknown place of solace and safety. I don't hate her – even now. If by some circumstance, she'd appear before me and beg forgiveness, I'd take her back in an instant and never ask her to explain what drove her away from me. Despite the heartache, I realized I still loved her.

And I wept for Rome and its twelve-hundred-year reign. What will happen to our civilization once the Imperial veil is pierced and shattered? Will the Western Roman world fall into a dark, shadowy abyss as Gaius once predicted, or is this unpleasantness just another bump on the road to redemption and the revitalization of the Empire? Truly, has the golden age ended?

I also wondered who will succeed me as Emperor. Often I thought the history of Rome was just a paean of monotony and dullness. The official record will show that I followed Avitus, who followed Maximus, who followed Valentinian, who followed Honorius, who followed Theodosius, and all the way back to the days of Romulus and Remus. I wondered, are we mere footnotes in the march of history?

Will the history of Rome be written in merely a perpetual parade of sameness – an endless cycle of names, dates, accomplishments, glory, and folly? Aside from historians who are always interested in the mundane and the quirks of power and empire, who will even care about the leadership of Rome a hundred years or a thousand years from now? Who even cares now?

Meanwhile, the barbarians are once again clamoring at the gate – or will be soon should I die. Without the Imperial umbrella and shield, I suspected Gaul, Germania, and Belgica would once again become a place of dark forests, sorcery, and unimagined savagery.

Alone in the darkness of my cell, I thought about the concept of 'fate.' Were my deeds and actions predetermined by God? Looking back, I'd seen a distinct pattern of my life's journey – a continuing circle of sunrise to sundown; of autumn to summer; of year to precious year.

It all began in Nemausus and my journey took me to the city of Rome, to Civitas Turonum, to the Catalaunian Plains, and back to Nemausus again. Once again, destiny took me back to the Eternal City, onto Treverorum, back to Nemausus, and finally back to Rome one more time. Now I am in Dertona; not far from the town where I was born. It's been a full circle.

Once more I wondered whether all of these steps were preordained or whether we are all just raindrops falling from the sky and onto the dry land below, migrating to wherever and however the wind, the river, or the topography of the land may eventually take us.

In despair, I also questioned what Gaius would've thought about my betrayal. He warned me about Ricimer; he predicted Ricimer couldn't be trusted and that one day, he'd become my downfall. Seems like Gaius was right.

Then I thought about my father and pondered how he'd perceive my situation. He was a noble and true Roman who had a lifetime of service with Stilicho and Aëtius. While I'm sure he'd stand firmly by me, he was loyal to the Roman State. Would he have been proud of me or sorely disappointed? I wished I could talk with him just one more time.

And what about my dear Octavia who always believed in me and who always trusted my judgment; what would she think of me now? Alone and chained in my cell; yes, what would she think now?

For thirty minutes or so, I cried bitterly, and finally, the fear was gone and my mind was sharp once again. I remembered my father's teaching that the worst is never as bad as one fears. Knowing there's no escape from the dark, damp prison, I was ready to accept my destiny. Rome often kills its bravest sons, its finest servants. Now it was suddenly my time to die.

In my youth, I remembered reading the great philosopher, Plotinus, and his words always had the power to soothe me. About two centuries ago, he wrote;

"Life here with the things of earth is sinking; a defeat; a failing of the wings."

Yes, death is certain – but as a Christian, I also looked to the promised resurrection of the body, and my fervent wish was to become reunited with my loved ones in Paradise.

I hope. I pray. I hope.

Abandoned and alone, I took a deep breath and looked around me. Almost magically, I felt the presence of Octavia, my father, and Gaius standing beside me in my cell, and I knew that tomorrow, I wouldn't be alone.

My conscience began clear, and although I cursed Ricimer and his lieutenants to the gates of Hell, I realized anger would not serve me well. Instead, I placed my trust in God's great wisdom, and I committed my soul unto His peaceful and omnipotent hands.

Coming out of the darkness, I hoped to find a new sun and a new day dawning brightly.

Less than an hour ago, an officer of the guard escorted Father Claudian to my cell. The priest and I talked for about fifteen minutes until we heard the sound of the jailor coming for me. After asking for his blessing, I knelt down and bowed my head. Making the sign of the cross over me, Father Claudian whispered, "I bless you, Lord Majorian, in the Name of the Father, the Son, and the Holy Spirit. May God have mercy on your soul."

Shortly after that, the jailor opened the door, and along with four heavily armed soldiers, he entered my cell. Forcefully, he tied my hands tightly behind my back and carefully loosened the heavy iron chain from my right ankle.

Then turning around to face me, he ordered, "Come with me now peacefully, and don't give me any resistance – or I'll punish you. I promise you that, Sire."

I exhaled and responded, "There's no need for threats; I'll come quietly."

There was a clank of keys, and the heavy door of my cell opened. Upon leaving my cell, we walked down a dark corridor, stinking of damp mildew. We entered a long antechamber with bare stone walls and a row of cells with barred windows. I looked into each of the cells for Hector but I didn't find him.

After walking through several other chambers with massive doors and up two flights of stairs, we finally reached the courtyard. I guessed it was probably two or three hours after dawn, and after spending the preceding eighteen hours in almost total darkness, I squinted at the bright morning sunlight. Once again, I heard the bells ringing from the tower of the church just beyond the prison walls, calling the faithful to Morning Prayer.

About thirty yards away, a raised platform stood directly in front of me where four men waited patiently for my arrival: Father Claudian, a magistrate, an armed soldier, and the executioner. There was also a large wooden block which was about two feet high and six inches wide where I'd be told to place my head. Squinting, I could readily see blood on the top of the chopping block. Mine wasn't the first execution of the morning.

I looked around the courtyard, and behind a window, about twenty yards away on the second floor of the prison compound, I saw a man whom I assumed to be Ricimer. As I nodded my head in his direction, he quickly turned away.

Slowly we climbed the thirteen stairs to the raised platform. Stopping briefly at the top of the steps, I looked around and noticed several other men in the courtyard quietly going about their business as if it was just another day.

A few moments later, the magistrate unraveled a scroll and began reading from it. Apparently, it was my execution warrant. In the middle of his reading, I stopped him and inquired, "What am I being charged with?"

"High treason, my Lord."

I asked, "Who signed the death warrant?"

"Master General Ricimer, my Lord."

"Will he be attending my execution?"

"No, my Lord; I understand he's in Ravenna."

"I expected as much."

I just shook my head. I knew in my heart Ricimer wouldn't stop my execution. He fully understood that once he went after me, he needed to kill me. There'd be no forgiveness on my part for his act of treason against the office of the emperor. But, it seems Ricimer didn't have the courage to do the task himself.

Then I asked one more question of the official, "My servant, Hector, do you know of his whereabouts?"

The magistrate grinned; only a few teeth remained in his upper mouth. "Why, yes; it's interesting you should make such an inquiry, Sire. Less than ten minutes ago, it seems the poor fellow was here where you're now standing. Yes, right on this spot. Oh, how he begged for his life."

Then he laughed, and reaching into a bag, he pulled out a severed head. "Is this – or should I say was this – your servant, my Lord?"

It was, and by then, Hector's complexion had turned almost entirely ashen. All the blood was drained from his severed head; and his eyes were still open – just gazing at me. Looking at the remains of my servant, I gagged to the point of vomiting and screamed out his name. "Hector! Oh, my God! No, not Hector! He's done nothing wrong but properly attend to his emperor. How could you be so damn cruel?"

The official and the guard began laughing heartily at my reaction. Finally, the magistrate asked, "Well, my Lord, do you happen to have any final words for us?"

Slowly regaining my composer, I said, "Yes, I do."

The magistrate frowned for a moment and stood back from me a couple of paces. Then, I took a deep breath and briefly looked around the courtyard. The person was back in the window, although I couldn't be certain it was Ricimer. I said, "Over the past four years, I've served well the Senate and people of Rome. I am an innocent man. I die today as the last emperor of Rome."

A few moments later, the executioner came forward, and right in front me, he knelt down on one knee, imploring, "Sire, please forgive me for what I'm about to do."

I stared at him – a young man in his early twenties. Looking into his eyes, I wondered whether he even knew who I am and if he'd ever remember this day. Slowly, I nodded my head affirmatively and replied, "Son, I forgive you. Now do your duty well."

The other soldier grabbed me and forced me to my knees. After pushing my head squarely onto the chopping block, he grabbed the collar of my tunic and tore it, exposing my neck. Feeling a massive surge of adrenalin, I closed my eyes and began imagining my children's faces.

Yes, there they are, bright and smiling at me.

Now, I imagine Octavia, also smiling ever so sweetly. Yes, my sweet Octav ...

AFTERWARD

Emperor Majorian's mausoleum is situated on the grounds of the Church of San Matteo in Tortona (formerly Dertona), Italy. When executed, he was barely forty years old. Majorian wasn't the last emperor of the Western Roman Empire; however, he was the last one to exert any real political or military power. In fact, between 461 AD and 476 AD, six other emperors followed him to the throne.

In a surviving literary work entitled *Panegyrics* written in 488 AD, Sidonius Apollinaris wrote of Majorian:

> That he was gentle to his subjects; that he was terrible to his enemies; and that he excelled in every virtue, more than any of his predecessors who had reigned over the Romans.

> The world trembled with alarm while you (Majorian) were loath to permit your victories to benefit you, and because, overly modest, you grieved because you did not deserve the throne and because you would not undertake to rule what you had deemed to be not worth defending.

See Sidonius Apollinaris, *Carmina, V.9–12.*

In 1788, Edward Gibbon wrote the following summary about Majorian:

> The successor of Avitus presents the welcome discovery of a great and heroic character, such as sometimes arise, in a degenerate age, to vindicate the honour of the human species. The emperor Majorian has deserved the praises of his contemporaries and of posterity. . .

> The emperor, who, amidst the ruins of the Roman world, revived the ancient language of law and liberty, which Trajan would not have disclaimed, must have derived those generous sentiments from his own heart, since they were not suggested to his imitation by the customs of his age or the example of his predecessors.

> The private and public actions of Majorian are very imperfectly known: but his laws, remarkable for an original cast of thought and

expression, faithfully represent the character of a sovereign who loved his people, who sympathized in their distress, who had studied the causes of the decline of the empire, and who was capable of applying (as far as such reformation was practicable) judicious and effectual remedies to the public disorders.

See Edward Gibbon, *The Decline and Fall of the Roman Empire*, Chapter 36.

Immediately following the death of Majorian, the impressive coalition of barbarian members quickly collapsed; in the end, most of them owed their loyalty to Majorian and not to Ricimer. Also, Ricimer's murder of Majorian did not sit well with much of the imperial military establishment, most notably Generals Aegidius and Marcellinus. When Ricimer selected Senator Libius Severus as Majorian's replacement, they refused to recognize the new emperor. After that, Aegidius joined forces with King Theodoric and King Childeric against King Gunderic who allied his kingdom with Ricimer, further fraying any hope for a united barbarian front. In May 464, Aegidius died in an ambush – probably set up by forces loyal to Ricimer.

Shortly after Majorian's execution, Ricimer tried to bribe Marcellinus' troops, who were mostly Huns. This transgression caused Marcellinus to leave Sicily and return to Dalmatia where he worked in close collaboration with the Eastern Emperor Leo I. Marcellinus was murdered in Sicily a few years after that; possibly on Ricimer's direct order

For the remainder of his life, Count Ricimer continued his role as the "emperor-maker" by sponsoring Emperor Severus (who ruled from 461 to 465 AD), Emperor Anthemius (who ruled from 467 to 472 AD), and Emperor Olybrius (who ruled in 472 AD). Ricimer died as the result of a probable brain hemorrhage on August 18, 472, six weeks after installing Olybrius as emperor. Because Ricimer was a barbarian and not a Roman by birth, he was never considered as a credible candidate for the throne despite his arguments to the contrary.

As interesting aside, Ricimer's treachery has endured through the ages as he appears as a character in at least six opera libretti composed in the seventeenth and eighteenth centuries.

King Gaiseric's Vandal kingdom was the target of another amphibious attack in 468 AD by the forces of the Eastern Empire. Once again, he was successful in defending his territory in North Africa. In 474 AD, he made peace with the Eastern Empire. Finally, on January 25, 477, he died in Carthage at age 88.

The collapse of the Western Empire occurred slowly over a span of several centuries. Even when the last Western Emperor, Romulus Augustulus, was deposed on September 4, 476 AD by Count Odoacer, a German warlord, the removal of the last emperor caused little impact on the lives of most citizens. Western Europe wouldn't again have an emperor until Charlemagne was crowned by Pope Leo III as *Emperor of the Romans* at Old St. Peter's Basilica in Rome on Christmas Day in 800 AD.

In a scholarly article entitled *Roman Senators and Absent Emperors in Late Antiquity,* Mark Humphries wrote about the role of the Senate during the fourth and fifth centuries:

> Far from being a moribund political anachronism, then, the Senate in Rome continued to act as a major partner in the running of the Empire throughout the last centuries of Roman rule in the West.
>
> Rome's senators maintained a vision of the Empire in which they were still the emperors' partners in government — this in spite of the concentration of effective political power in the hands of the emperor.

After the Western Empire fell, the Senate continued to function. It is interesting to note Count Odoacer, the first King of Italy, established his political power with the cooperation of the Senate, and this body seems to have given him their loyal support throughout the remainder of his reign.

The institution ultimately disappeared at some point around 630 AD when the Curia Julia building (which housed the Senate since 44 BC) was transformed into a church by Pope Honorius I. Curiously, the old Senate building is one of only a handful of Roman structures to survive to the modern day mostly intact. The Eastern Roman Senate endured in Constantinople until the ancient institution was finally abolished in 1391 AD.

Approximately one hundred emperors sat on the throne of the Eastern Empire between Majorian's execution in 461 and May 29, 1453, when Constantinople finally succumbed to the Ottoman Turks. It's ironic the fall of Constantinople occurred exactly one thousand years (to the day) following the death of Attila the Hun.

Less than one hundred years after Majorian's killing, the city of Rome and much of the Mediterranean region of the former Western Empire was reconquered by the Eastern Empire under the rule of Emperor Justinian the Great. By 534 AD, the forces of General Belisarius recaptured all of North Africa and parts of Southern Spain after defeating the Vandals, and by 540 AD, Italy and Southern France were back under Imperial rule. A devastating outbreak of bubonic plague in the early 540's marked the end of the revitalization of the Empire.

Early in his rule, Emperor Heraclius faced a new threat to Roman civilization – the armies of Islam. In 634 AD, the Muslims invaded and conquered Syria and Palestine. Within a short period of time, the Arabs would also conquer Iraq, Egypt, Libya, and Morocco. By the time of Emperor Heraclius' death in 641 AD, the Eastern Empire shrunk to include only present-day Western Turkey, Bulgaria, Greece, and Southern Italy. After that, the Eastern Empire entered a period of territorial decline which wouldn't be reversed until the ninth century.

The city of Rome remained in Imperial hands until 729 AD when the Lombards finally pushed the Eastern Roman government out of Italy. By then, the population of the city of Rome (which was once estimated as well over 1.5 million inhabitants in 210 AD) shrunk to less than 35,000 people. The city would not exceed a population of one million people until the 1930's.

In 1557, German historian, Hieronymus Wolf, coined the term 'Byzantine Empire' as a way of distinguishing the Eastern Empire from the previously unified Empire. The term comes from the word 'Byzantium' which was the name of Constantinople before it became Emperor Constantine's capital in 330 AD.

In fact, the Byzantine Empire never truly existed.

If one could ask any Eastern Roman emperor who sat on the throne in Constantinople between 476 and 1453 AD whether he was a Roman emperor, he'd undoubtedly say 'yes.' And if one would produce a map of the world and ask the emperor to point out the boundaries of the Byzantine Empire, he could not have done so.

If the reader is interested in learning more about the period of history covered by my story, I suggest the following books which I researched in creating my novel: Peter Heather, *The Fall of the Roman Empire*; Giusto Traina, *428 AD, An Ordinary Year at the End of the Roman Empire*; Adrian Goldsworthy, *How Rome Fell*; and of course, Edward Gibbons' masterly work, *The Decline and Fall of the Roman Empire*. Gibbons' opus is probably the greatest work on this particular subject and it remains one of the most renowned works of history ever written.